DOMINIC RANGER is the pseudonym of Christopher Lillicrap, a debut thriller novelist who has worked with numerous police forces over the last twenty five years as a media consultant and been an adviser on several high-profile cases, including the Millie Dowler murder in Surrey. It is his work with the police which inspired MIDAS.

A former teacher, prolific writer and composer, best known as a children's TV presenter in the 70s and 80s. His own shows, *We'll Tell You a Story* and *Flicks*, ran on Thames TV for over ten years. He also presented *Playboard* for the BBC and appeared in several episodes of *Rainbow*. He is still involved in writing for children and his educational series *Numbertime* gained the Royal Television Society award for Best Educational Programme.

Christopher's adaptation with Mike Fields of the J. L. Carr Book, *How Steeple Sinderby Wanderers Won the FA Cup*, co-produced with Bill Kenwright, ran at the Mermaid Theatre for six months. His comedy, *My Wife Whatsername*, written with Jonathan Izard for the Watermill Theatre was produced most recently at the Altmühlsee-Festival in Germany.

He lives in Devon with his actress wife Jeanette Ranger and for part of the year on the Greek island of Symi.

DOMINIC RANGER

MIDAS

Matador
9 Priory Business Park
Kibworth Beauchamp
Leicestershire LE8 0RX, UK
Tel: (+44) 116 279 2299
Fax: (+44) 116 279 2277
Email: books@troubador.co.uk
Web: www.troubador.co.uk/matador

ISBN: SB 978 1780882 482
HB: 978 1783060 467

British Library Cataloguing in Publication Data.
A catalogue record for this book is available from the British Library.

Typeset in Aldine by Troubador Publishing Ltd
Printed and bound in the UK by TJ International, Padstow, Cornwall

Matador is an imprint of Troubador Publishing Ltd

With thanks to:

Roger Williams, my oldest friend, who made me write it.

Jeanette, my long suffering wife, who put up with me while I wrote it.

David Grubb, who persuaded me to publish it after I'd written it and who encouraged me to keep writing.

All those who are in it under different names.
(You will know who you are.)

To my Symi Pal
Crawford Morrow 1954-2013

CHAPTER ONE

The man who was about to become the richest man in the world, put his card into the cash machine outside the First Independent Bank in Farnborough, Hampshire. With very little hope of success, the forty five year old typed in the numbers 5474 and waited. The thin, sallow man pulled at his ponytail as he looked down the shining empty street. "Fifteen years of bloody hard work and I've got a one thousand two hundred and fifty pound overdraft and five quid in my pocket to show for it." He muttered at the cash dispenser as he shifted his weight from one trainered foot to the other. "Come on, tell me I can't have anything, eat the damn card, come on. You've finished my business you stupid bank, come on, stick the knife in."

On that same, wet Sunday evening, thirty five miles away in the Fraud Office of the First Independent Bank in Kings Cross, London, a man, who was about to get the shock of his life, slumped into his chair. The craggy-faced Scot switched on his computer and, while it booted up, sniffed at a plastic cup of black coffee. He hated this shift.

Gary McAllister sipped at the thin black liquid and almost spat it out. "God, that is foul." He span around in his chair. "Bloody Sunday evening," he screamed at the empty building. "I hate this soddin' bank." On his desk, the internal speakerphone rang. He pressed the green button

"Is everything alright Mr McAllister?" A woman's concerned nasal voice issued from the speaker.

"Yes, Sophie," sighed McAllister. "It's just Sunday night and a soddin' bank holiday weekend."

"Yes, sir," the woman replied. "I thought that was it. I've sent you a data batch from ATM control as it just flagged up an unknown alert and they sent it straight over. I hate to tell you this sir but I think you need to look at it urgently so I've linked it to the live feed. Would you like a coffee? A real one?"

"No thanks, I'll survive." The Scot pressed the red button, pulled out the lower drawer of his desk and, from a box file that was lying there, lifted out a half bottle of Glenfiddich. He poured a generous measure into his coffee and, as the screen in front of him burst into life, he typed in his password, 'Whiskey Mac' and waited…

In Farnborough, ten, crisp, twenty pound notes slipped out of the cash dispenser. Alan Marks smiled and reached out his hand. He just had enough time to pick the notes out of the slot before another ten appeared in their place.

In King's Cross, Gary McAllister screwed the top back onto the bottle, placed it back in the box file, and glanced up at the blue screen as the rows of figures scrolled slowly down…page after page…after page after… "Christ this job is boring."

He sipped his coffee and burnt his lip.

"Oh shit!" He spilled the coffee all over the keyboard.

"Oh hellfire..."

He grabbed some tissues from his drawer and pressed the mouse to pause the computer. The scrolling figures stopped as he mopped the coffee, as best he could.

"I need a fag." He snatched at the open packet of Marlboro on the desk and out of the corner of his eye...on the screen...in the rows of figures in front of him…he saw something...or did he?

Yes, he did.

"Oh no!"

He pressed the green button on his phone again "Sophie get me…"

The voice on the other end finished his sentence for him. "John Foley Head of Security? I've already tried his mobile, shall I call his home?"

For the twenty-fifth time, in Farnborough, Alan Marks took ten, crisp, twenty pound notes out of the cash dispenser, which gave a high-pitched single tone as the green screen suddenly displayed the words:

THIS MACHINE IS NO LONGER ABLE TO DISPENSE CASH. ALTERNATIVE MACHINES ARE AVAILABLE AT THE BRANCH IN ALEXANDER ROAD.

The richest man in the world stuffed the final bundle of notes into his leather jacket and zipped it up as far as it would go.

He looked down at his chest.

"God, I look like a Sumo wrestler."

He glanced around at the empty rain-sodden street and walked, awkwardly, to his bright yellow Porsche Boxter.

Having disgorged the money onto the back seat, he took off his jacket and threw it over the scattered notes. He slammed the door shut, stared through the window, and laughed.

"Bloody hell…Jesus…Bloody hell."

He slipped into the front seat, locked the doors, started the engine, took a deep breath and headed for Alexander road…

Gary McAllister was trying very hard to keep his cool as he gripped the phone.

"I don't care what the time is...Tell him it's McAllister and it is urgent OK? … No, McAllister..."

He took a deep breath…

"I don't care what he said...Trust me he will want to be disturbed... Yes he will."

This was unbelievable... "No I'm not going to call back..."

He tried to sound as calm as he could, all too aware that at any moment this au pair or housemaid, or whatever she was, might just hang up.

"Yes I understand Mrs Foley is away and I don't care what Mr Foley is up to or who with quite frankly, what is really important now is that you knock on his door and tell him Gary McAllister, his Chief Fraud Investigator, is on the phone." He sighed. "Chief Fraud…Look, just say a man from the Bank and tell him I said… Midas."

He exploded.

"No you stupid cow not Miras, that's for fucking mortgages...

Jesus I don't believe this…MIDAS...as in gold. You stupid bitch…MIDAS!.. Hello? Hello? Oh shit!"

Alan Marks sat in his car for a long time and gazed, through the water sheeting down his windscreen, at the cash machine in Alexander Road. Maybe it was just that last machine. Perhaps this one would eat his card. After what had happened on Friday, he hadn't expected to get the two hundred pounds he'd requested, let alone the five grand he had on the back seat. Jesus, he'd been told the Company was finished. The bank facility was terminated. All bets were off. All access to funds withdrawn. He assumed that meant his personal account, too.

For Christ's sake, he'd been through hell and back since Friday. Sally didn't even know. She was away at Moira's in Edinburgh. She'd go apeshit. He'd spent most of Saturday trying to work out how to tell her that Lombard Direct wanted the BMW back, for good. Mind you threatening to smash Justin Barnes, his 'Small Business Adviser', in the face and throwing the ripped-up business plan all over his office probably ranked as one of the pettiest things he'd done in a long while. Still, he felt better after it. He relived it for a moment.

"And you can shove this small business plan up your small

business arse you nasty little shit. Got too big too soon did I? Well it was your bloody bank's brilliant idea, and now it's all 'we have to be realistic Alan.' 'There is a need to consolidate our position Alan.' I'll consolidate your position you little pratt, in fact I'd consolidate your face except you bastards would sue me. I hope you bloody sleep nights Justin, because I wouldn't walk down any dark alleys on your own. What, a threat? Me? You bet your damn life it is." The exit was good too, slamming the door and shouting "bollocks" as he passed out through the queue in the bank.

So how come his bank card worked, and then some? Well, there was only one way to find out. He stepped out of the car, almost forgetting to lock it. He glanced around, trying not to look suspicious, but at this time on a Sunday evening there was no one around anyway. He stepped up to the machine. Then a sudden thought hit him. What if it *did* do it again? He went back to the car and opened the boot. He emptied his sports bag with all the sweaty squash gear into the boot, closed it quietly and went back to the machine. As he put the card into the slot, he found his hand was trembling.

PLEASE ENTER YOUR PIN NUMBER.

Alan Marks pressed the keys, 5474, and waited.

The menu flashed up on the green screen. Cash, cash with receipt, balance, other. Amazing, it hadn't rejected his card.

"Right…cash with receipt, no just cash, why? Don't know, but why keep a record? If it was a mistake would I be liable? No receipt, definitely no receipt."

The options appeared just like they had before. £50.00. £100.00. £200.00. £300.00. Other.

"OK a hundred quid, let's not be greedy." He made his choice and the machine kindly informed him that his cash was being counted, if he would like to remove his card and wait for it. The machine whirred and clicked. He took his card. He had the card back anyway. No sooner had he removed it than one hundred pounds in warm twenty pound notes appeared. He took the money and waited… and waited.

"Yes it was a one off, definitely a one-off." He turned to walk back to the car but something stopped him. It was a whirring and clicking and… It was no one-off. "Bloody hell."

The money was coming out again. He took it, but before he could put it in the bag another batch was being dispensed. He stuffed the first hand full into his holdall as more came out, and more, and more. After what seemed like forever and over two thousand pounds, he noticed out of the corner of his eye a blue flashing light. It was a good hundred yards away down the road, but coming up fast. Hell, how could he stop the money? He pressed the cancel button without thinking and was amazed at himself. The money stopped.

"Well, bugger me."

The car was speeding closer, they were in a hurry.

This was it. Oh shit, what would he say? "I was going to report it." Yes that was it. "It's just happened and I'm really worried, thank god you got here..." all that crap. "The five grand in the car?" Oh bollocks, the five grand… the five grand…

He needn't have worried, the police car sped past and screamed around the roundabout just beyond the bank. Somewhere in Farnborough, a taxi driver had rearranged a lamp post, also a black cab and in a minor way the accounts of The Direct Line Assurance Company. That was somebody else's problem, not Alan's.

Alan's problem was that he now apparently had access to unlimited funds. Or did he? A sudden wave of panic hit him. Did he just have an enormous unsecured overdraft? He reinserted the card, but after his pin number, he chose the option to check his balance. PLEASE WAIT stated the machine and, just as he was about to get nervous, it supplied him with the answer. He was still one thousand, two hundred and fifty pounds, sixty pence overdrawn. Exactly the same figure as before he had withdrawn anything. So the money hadn't come from his account. So, where had it come from? Did this mean it was untraceable? He got back in the car, and sat staring forward.

"What the hell do I do now?"

He picked up the mobile phone and dialled.

"Come on Moira, answer… answer. Hello Moira, look, sorry it's so late, but I need to talk to Sally, it's a bit urgent so I'm sorry if… what? No, it's Alan… Alan, Sally's Alan. Well, who the hell else would it be?"

In Room 217, at the Holiday Inn Edinburgh, Sally Marks changed the channel on the television with the remote for the tenth time, sighed, rolled over and took her glass of champagne from the bedside table. She didn't really hear what Justin Barnes said as he came out of the bathroom, naked, but she responded on autopilot.

"What? Oh yeah. It was great, lover… you're a tiger."

"I am?" Justin smiled, walked to the bed and leaned forward.

"And you're bloody wonderful. Oh Sal..."

She stopped him with her right forefinger on his lips. She held up her glass.

"Cheers!"

"Oh, right." Justin turned and got his glass from the other side of the bed. "Cheers." He swung back to touch her glass with his, but she was already drinking. "Oh right." He sipped his own drink as she finished hers and held out the empty glass for him to fill.

"Justin?"

"Yes, my love?" He turned back to his bedside table and picked up the bottle of Laurent Perrier.

"Alan can't find out can he?"

He filled her empty glass.

"Find out? Find out what you sex fiend, that you're bonking his bank manager, oh sorry his ex bank manager?"

He made to suck her left nipple but she pushed his head away.

"Stop it. I'm serious. Alan can't find out about the money can he?"

He sighed again. "Oh, piss off Sal. Look, the Tiger knows what he's doing, OK? Am I the world's greatest bank manager as well as the world's greatest lover, or not?"

She managed a lie, which for her was easy.

"Darling, of course you are...Cheers!"

McAllister poured what was left of the Glenfiddich down his throat and coughed.

"Bloody hell." The phone rang. He grabbed at it. "Yes John, no I'm not taking the piss, its Midas all right...Well yes I'm as confused as you are, I mean so much for our technical boffins telling us to forget it and it couldn't be done and...Where? Both Farnborough branches and Camberley, but that's only the ones I've found so far...No, it's the full works; the card has disabled the cameras in the machines as soon as it's put in so there are no visuals, that's what flagged the alert. Yes...Sophie has put in calls to the key holders in Fleet, Frimley, Guildford and Woking and so far Guildford have said their ATM is empty, although it's not registered here and... but that could be normal traffic in which case I wouldn't get it yet but...hang on..." He stared at the screen and thumped his desk. "Bollocks, Frimley's gone. Sorry John, another one."

Sophie popped her head around the door. "Mr McAllister, Frimley have just checked their machine and..."

"I know, I know, I've just seen it." He waved her away. "Sorry that was Sophie, you see I'm waiting to hear on the others in case... Well because there can be as much as a thirty minute download delay if the server is sending batches at this time of night and...Well no, only about twenty five grand at the moment as far as I can tell, but if I'm right that's only the beginning and...The police? Well no I assumed you would want to do that yourself as Head of Security...Or not, quite, but don't you think they should...No I won't...Half an hour? Of course."

He stared at the phone as he put it down. "Half an hour? That must mean he's already on his way." McAllister glanced at the screen again. "Oh bollocks!" He pressed the button on his intercom. "Sophie? Forget the others, get someone to Fleet... Now!"

Thirty minutes later, true to his word, John Foley, Head of Security arrived. The balding, bespectacled man in his late fifties, dressed in jeans and an ill-fitting thin cotton sweater, opened the door panting, as if he had just run up three flights of stairs, which he had.

"Is he here yet?"

McAllister was confused. "Is who here?"

"Me!" The booming voice behind Foley made him visibly jump.

Sir Charles Bower, the Chairman of The First Independent Bank was your classic public school old boy, man in the city figure; a stereotype with silver hair. Overbearing, overweight, with an overblown sense of his own importance. Gary McAllister thought he looked strangely vulnerable in a crumpled shirt and trousers he had obviously slung on in haste that Sunday evening. He pushed open the door a little wider and then just as he was about to speak again he turned, looked outside the room, both ways up the corridor, and closed the door. He glowered at Gary McAllister. "Who knows?"

McAllister was a little taken aback. "Er, you sir obviously, Mr Foley, me, Sophie of course and, well, the on call staff at the banks who she called when I spotted it."

Sir Charles raised his voice. "What? Surely she hasn't told them about…"

McAllister jumped in "No, sorry sir Charles, no I didn't mean that. No, they have been told to check the machines as they appear to be empty from our computer. They don't know anything about Midas. No, just as agreed in the security alerts protocol sir and…"

"Good." Sir Charles lowered his voice. "Whatever you find now, stop all calls for the moment. "Your girlie there," he pointed towards the wall and the next office, "how reliable is she?"

Gary McAllister was a little thrown by the question and not at all sure where this was going. "She's hardly a girl sir, bless her, but she is solid as a rock. One of the best. She's been in this bank forever. You presented her with her thirty year certificate last year sir, at the annual dinner?"

There was no hint of recognition from the old man. McAllister continued. "I'd trust her with anything."

Sir Charles sighed. "Good. Send her home."

Gary McAllister was now really puzzled. "But if we…"

"Send her home." Sir Charles Bower had spoken with that kind of authority that comes from a complete confidence in one's apparent position in any situation.

Gary stood up and was about to exit to the next office when his door opened and a woman in her late fifties with tied back hair and thin spectacles entered. Sophie Thompson was the kind of spinster who appeared in children's books; everybody's maiden aunt, nobody's wife or lover. She was brisk, efficient, married to her job and just a little sad. You just knew looking at her that sometime early in her twenties there had been a man, probably married, and it had all ended in tears, but she still carried a torch. Sophie had chosen to marry her job, and the bank could not have asked for a better wife. As she walked through that door on that Sunday morning however, she could not have realised how quickly that marriage was about to end.

"Sophie?" McAllister said. "You know Mr Foley and Sir Charles?"

"Good morning sir." Sophie was the ultimate in politeness, in fact, for a fleeting moment McAllister thought she was about to curtsy. Sir Charles merely nodded. She was the best PA a man like McAllister could ever have wanted. She was his diary, his phone book and his memory all rolled into one. Sometimes she knew what he was about to do before he did, which was why the next, very brief, conversation took her by surprise.

"Er, Sophie I'm sending you home. Sir Charles, Mr Foley and I have a little number crunching to do and I won't be needing you for the rest of the day." McAllister saw she was about to say "but" and he forestalled her interruption. "I know it's your on call weekend and I wouldn't have got you in if I'd known you wouldn't be needed, but just for now you can pop off home ok? I'll give you a call later."

Sophie was confused but like all efficient office servants she managed to completely mask her feelings with, "Well if you're absolutely sure Mr McAllister, I'll be off. See you tomorrow."

As she closed the door behind her Sir Charles turned to his Head of Security. "Right Foley it seems that's everything secured here then, I suggest you nip off to control and make sure the lid is kept on it there. Tell them it's a software problem with the cameras and you've got people working on it. It's just us in the know at the moment so let's keep it that way. Anyway, who knows; it could be a false alarm."

John Foley looked a little unsure as he responded. "Yes of course Sir Charles, but as Head of Security I have to say what about…" He got no further.

"What about this Midas thing if it is there? Don't worry, I think our man McAllister here can more than handle that. Off you go." He dismissed Foley with a wave of his hand and McAllister couldn't help smiling as his immediate boss exited, like a less than worthy servant. McAllister's smile was short lived as Sir Charles turned to him.

"Right McAllister, what's to be done?"

For the second time that day Gary McAllister was taken aback by the big man's directness.

"I'm not exactly sure sir. The police should be…"

"No!" Sir Charles calmly sat down on McAllister's desk. "I don't want any police involvement. This is the sort of nonsense that puts a run on a bank. Any sort of suggestion that we cannot assure our customers of security where their money is concerned could sink us. And, not to put too fine a point on it, it could completely screw up any merger plans."

McAllister was now really confused and it obviously showed in his face. Sir Charles responded accordingly.

"Right, well you weren't to know, only three people do and

Foley isn't one of them. We have been having talks with Banco de Silva of Portugal, for some time now. Long and short of it is, multi billion pound deal, at a delicate stage. We can make a big killing or the whole thing can go down the pan and I'm not about to let something like this muck it up. Now, either someone, or some other organisation, has discovered Midas and we need to find out who it is and stop them."

"You did say you thought it might be a false alarm sir?" McAllister queried.

Sir Charles Bower looked McAllister straight in the eyes. "Do you think it is a false alarm?"

"Well, no …"

"No. Neither do I," responded the chairman.

McAllister took a deep breath. This was quite a lot to take in on a Sunday evening on one cup of filthy coffee and a dram of scotch.

"Right sir. Well this is going to take a bit of thinking about."

Sir Charles was up on his feet. "Good, but don't think too long." He picked up a pen from McAllister's desk and scribbled on the pad by the phone. "My secure mobile number. On this one you answer to me and me only, got it?"

He headed towards the door and turned before exiting. "I'll tell you now there were people here who didn't want you. I know you thought we hired you despite that spot of trouble you had with your former employer, the Metropolitan Police, but you were wrong. I hired you, and I hired you because of it." McAllister was about to protest his innocence but he never got the chance, Sir Charles was on a roll.

"I don't care whether you were corrupt or not, all I know is there is no smoke without at least a little spark in the kindling. You were a bloody good detective, my people told me, and you didn't care how you got results. That's fine by me. Every company like this needs someone like you. You know how the criminal mind works. Spend what you need, do what you have to do. If there is shit make sure it doesn't stick to this bank and catch the bastards who are doing this. You've had it pretty easy up to now, sitting in this office with Miss Moneypenny out there doing all the graft and your bottle of Glenfiddich in the drawer keeping you steady. Now go earn what I've been paying you for."

Before Sir Charles was completely out of the door McAllister did manage to get a word in.

"Sir, if I could just ask one thing?"

"What?" The old man snapped.

"Well, is there any chance I could close our ATM machines for tonight and tomorrow until I've formulated a plan?"

Sir Charles was not pleased. "All right, we'll say it's a computer glitch or something. But no longer, it is August bank holiday so no-one can go into the banks to complain."

McAllister was beginning to think. "And the computer story could explain the empty machines, sir, you know if there are any questions?"

Sir Charles managed a very slight smile. "Now you're working McAllister. By the way if this works out well there's a healthy bonus in it. If it goes down the crapper we will completely disown you, you do realise that?" He didn't wait for a response. "Good. Catch the bastards."

The door slammed shut and McAllister slumped back into his chair. "Catch the bastards, go earn what I've been paying you for. Great, easy, piece of piss." He managed a slight smile himself. If he was honest the job had been easy up 'till now, actually to the point of boring. More than once he had considered packing it in, but with his track record and a few unfortunate newspaper headlines involving himself and the Deputy Commissioner of the Metropolitan Police, it wouldn't be easy to get another job on such good money. And it was good money. Now he had to earn that money, but actually he didn't mind a challenge, and it would beat sitting looking at a computer screen for hour after hour. The most fun he'd had in three years was the day he had to visit the Slough branch to expose some errant bank teller who had been internally misdirecting the odd fiver to an unnamed account to the tune of twenty thousand pounds. The boy was sacked, the money retrieved and the press never informed. The poor boy slipped whilst leaving the branch for the last time and broke his ankle. McAllister was standing next to him at the time. But that was eighteen months ago and McAllister had just begun to get bored again. He wasn't going to be bored now however. Reporting directly to the top man, this was more like it. He looked at the screen and scrolled back to the first set of suspicious figures. What to do? Well experience told him that most successful investigations were a result of ninety nine per cent slog and one per cent instinct. His instinct was to print off all the large withdrawals and then visit the scene of the first one. He didn't know why, but it was just instinct, and anyway, he had to start somewhere and fate had dictated that that somewhere would be Farnborough.

Downstairs at the back door of the bank Sophie Thompson said goodbye to George, the security guard.

"You leaving early, Miss Thompson?" he asked.

Sophie switched into professional enigmatic mode. "I've been given the rest of the day off George, and between you and me, I think after thirty years I deserve it."

As George pressed the exit button that allowed her out onto the side alley that ran down the side of the bank, he called after her. "Perhaps you could put a word in for me next time Miss."

"I will," she replied as the door shut behind her.

Of course, what neither she nor George knew was that there would not be a next time.

In his kitchen, Alan Marks stared at the note that had been left for him. How could he have missed it? It must have been have been there all weekend since Sally left on Friday. He had been in and out at least half a dozen times and it was only now when he put his car keys on the hallway table that he had noticed the small yellow envelope. He found he was completely unmoved and unsurprised by the words he was reading. In a strange way, he almost felt relieved. So his wife had left him. So what? And then the comic irony struck him. All the stuff in the note about his lack of ambition and drive, his weakness, for which he read "I thought you were going to be rich and now the business is stuffed so I'm off," was very amusing now. Here he was with apparently access to as much money as he would ever need and Sally had jumped ship because she thought he had none. Why wasn't he upset? He thought about it for a moment as he walked into the kitchen and he put on some coffee. It had never been a partnership of love. Lust yes, love no. It had started in a wave of torrid sex and grown into Alan performing for Sally, in bed, in the business, in practically everything. Alan Marks found himself remarkably relieved. As he took a cup from the cupboard, he found he was smiling and muttering the things his Mum would say when she found out. Things like, "She was never right for you," "Thank god there are no children," "She was always a gold digger, your father never liked her."

As the coffee machine gurgled he turned on the radio and burst into laughter as the Noisettes sang 'Never Forget You.' And he found himself singing along very loudly as they rose to a final crescendo, 'They said we'd never make it, my sweet joy, always remember me.'

He glanced at the note and re-read the final sentence, "Will be back next week to collect some things. I am staying with Moira. Sally."

"Bollocks," thought Alan, "wherever you are it isn't with Moira, but do I give a shit? Actually, no." He screwed up the piece of paper and then burst into laughter once more as ABBA launched into 'The Winner Takes It All'. What was all this? Had Magic FM turned into the Alan Marks personal radio station?

So what now? In a matter of a few hours he had gone from a broke and busted failure to potentially a man with unlimited access to wealth. Should he tell the police? He should. He poured himself a cup of coffee and sat down by the phone in the kitchen. He picked up the receiver and paused; there was a problem. If he had called them when it first happened it could have been a mistake. Five thousand that kept on coming that was a mistake. A car containing nearly twenty five grand was not a mistake. He had been to another four machines since that. Why had he done that? He was angry with the bank, yes. He was curious and potentially amazingly rich. And on top of all that, as far as he could tell, nobody knew anything about this. The police car had not stopped. No-one had called him and his card had never been refused. And to cap it all, he was still apparently overdrawn to the same comparatively pitiful amount on his personal account.

Alan Marks sipped his coffee and put the phone down.

"I am Alan Marks, I am free and rich and the winner takes it all."

What to do next? Now, that would take some pondering. He began to formulate a plan. He could try some other machines, but then what would he do with the money? He would have to work something out. Still, he had time.

Of course, what he didn't know was that time was the one thing he did not have. As Alan Marks considered his immediate future in Farnborough, in Islington Sophie Thompson stepped into the lift of Thornton Mansions and pressed the button for floor five. As the doors closed she wondered what she would do for the rest of the day. She needn't have worried; she would never make it to floor five.

CHAPTER TWO

Konstantina Zouroudi shouted at the cash machine as, for the third time, it rejected her card and displayed the message:

THIS MACHINE IS NO LONGER ABLE TO DISPENSE CASH. ALTERNATIVE MACHINES ARE AVAILABLE AT THE BRANCH IN ALEXANDER ROAD.

"No they bloody aren't, I've been there. Stupid bloody bank."

Alan Marks brought his car to a halt and watched from the opposite side of the road. Having cleaned out the machines in Farnborough, neighbouring Frimley, Fleet, and Hartley Witney last night, he had pondered the situation deep into the early hours until he finally fell asleep. Then, waking up mid-morning he had returned to the first machine. If it was refilled, would the card work again? He still had most of the previous night's money in the boot of the car. On the seat next to him was the sports bag containing his last two withdrawals totalling over seven grand. He had half expected the bank to be swarming with police and forensic teams, dusting the cash machines for his finger prints. As it was, there was one lone girl shouting at the hole in the wall. Then he saw her begin to cry and slump with her back to the wall. Alan left his car and walked across the road towards her. "Excuse me, can I help you? What's the matter?"

The girl composed herself. "No, it's OK, I'm fine Mr Marks." She knew him?

"Sorry," said Alan, "do I know you?"

As she lifted her face, a mixture of recognition and fear ran through his mind. "You were behind the counter, in the bank, last week. You're er..."

"Tina."

"Yes Tina," he continued, "you work here?"

The tears had stopped and her reply was very forthright.

"Did work here, I left on Friday."

"Oh, I'm sorry," responded Alan.

"I'm not." Her anger was obvious. "Except I can't get any money from my account, I expect he's done that on purpose."

"He?" Alan was intrigued.

"Mr Barnes. The man you had the row with on Friday?"

He looked at her and sensed the beginnings of a smile.

"Oh Justin, that little shit. If it's any consolation, I hate the little bastard."

She managed a wry smile. "Well, that makes two of us. We all thought there was going to be a fight on Friday, we nearly called the police."

Alan returned the smile. "I must admit I did come within a couple of seconds of hitting him, but I stopped myself."

Her smile faded. "Pity. Now I suppose I will have to go to another bank or go in here when it opens tomorrow and try and get some money out of my account. At least he won't be there. He's away in Scotland apparently on bank business. Good story, but I know he's off with whoever the married bitch is he's sleeping with now. In fact, I think I'll just close the account and once I've got my money I need never see him again, thank God." She started to cry again. Alan put his arm around her and she immediately pulled away.

"I'm sorry Mr Marks, it's my problem not yours. Did you want to use the machine?" She indicated to the ATM, then thought again. "Oh no point, it's not giving out money. Not to me anyhow."

Alan felt he was in a bit of a trap potentially. Did he use the machine? If he did and it behaved in the way it had before, this girl would know immediately. If he didn't try what was he doing there? Konstantina made up his mind for him.

"Actually, if you do try and it gives you money, then I'll know he's tried to stop me going home."

"Right," said Alan and turned towards the machine. What was he to do? Suddenly he had the answer; it was easy, he would type in the wrong pin number. Then he had a small feeling of foreboding. What if putting in the wrong number broke whatever technical chain had given him unlimited funds? Unfortunately there was little choice. As he inserted the card and typed in the wrong number, something she had said prompted a question. "Going home? What do you mean trying to stop you going home?"

"To Greece," the girl replied. "I am Greek, Konstantina? Tina?"

"Oh I see," Alan had detected an accent but had not really thought about its origin. Then he turned back to her quickly as a light came on in his head. "Greece?" It was said as a question but with some force.

Konstantina was taken aback a little. "Yes, why Mr Marks?"

"Sorry," he saw her slight alarm. "It might be nothing, but you see my company..." Now he was stuck, because to go any further would mean explaining exactly why he was there and everything that had happened in the last twelve or so hours. Or he would have to be really inventive. He decided on the latter and began to make something up. "My company gets some products from Greece and well, this card..." He was getting into trouble. Fortunately he was rescued by the ATM. He need not have worried about the PIN number. His card was returned immediately as a new message filled the screen:

BECAUSE OF TECHNICAL DIFFICULTIES FIRST INDEPENDENT ARE UNABLE TO ISSUE CASH FROM MACHINES TODAY. WE APOLOGISE FOR ANY INCONVENIENCE.

"Oh great." He feigned anger, hiding his relief. "No money, look."

"Oh." Konstantina was surprised. "That's not the message I got a few minutes ago. Something must have happened. I've never seen that before. Oh well, that's it. Soup and a roll for bank holiday lunch. You see, if I was back in Greece now, this wouldn't be a problem, it's not a holiday today."

"Look," before he had really thought it through Alan found himself offering the girl money, "I've got plenty of money on me, I could lend you some, say fifty quid, and you could give it to me tomorrow or whenever."

She objected. "No, no I couldn't do that."

"Of course you could," interrupted Alan, "I'll just get it from the car." As he turned and looked towards the Porsche, he saw them. Two, short , slight figures wearing grey hoodies. The one at the front of the car turned and shouted to the other one who was just pulling the holdall clumsily through the gap between the front seat and the door pillar. "Leave it, the bastard's seen us."

His partner in crime responded, screaming "Tough shit, I've got it."

In his concern for the girl, Alan Marks hadn't locked his car. Now he bounded across the road towards the two young lads. The boy at the front of the car panicked and attempted a less than expert rugby tackle. Mark's endless Wednesday afternoons at the Salesian Grammar School playing fields as a wing back all those years ago awakened a muscle memory as he weaved past the groping boy and grabbed the second youth by the hood. Just as the lad pulled the holdall free, Marks had him. But not for long. Pain seared into the back of his skull as he felt his hair being pulled from behind with great force. Suddenly the trendy ponytail was not such a good idea. The lad who tried to tackle him might be slight, but he was strong. Marks reeled back, letting go of the hooded robber, and found himself spinning onto the bonnet of the car and rolling uncontrollably off the front and onto the floor. He hit the tarmac with his hands in front of him and felt the burning of asphalt against skin on his palms. All at once his ears were ringing, as if some very noisy machine had been turned on right next to him.

He rolled over and looked up, half expecting a further assault of kicks from the young robber. Towering over him was a black leather-clad figure in a black motorcycle helmet. The visor was up revealing a pockmarked face.

"You stay here." The voice was muffled by the helmet and only just audible over the roar of a motorbike engine. But it was strong, rough and unmistakeably Scottish. "I'll have your bag back in a couple of minutes, Mr Marks. As soon as I've caught the little shits."

Alan Marks watched as the man swung his leg onto the Triumph Street Triple R and set off down the street in pursuit of the two hooded villains.

"Mr Marks, are you ok?" Konstantina was by his side.

Alan Marks found he was shaking. "I think so, a bit cut up." He looked at his hands and then at Konstantina's concerned face. "He knew my name."

The girl was confused. "Sorry, who knew your name?"

Alan stared down the street watching as the bike roared around the corner and out of sight. "That bloke on the bike."

Konstantina looked in the same direction at the now empty street. "Who was he?"

Alan Marks should have felt grateful for the stranger's intervention, but instead he was slightly confused and for some reason he had a really bad feeling about what had just happened.

"I don't know who he was," he muttered, "but he knew my name."

McAllister had been sitting astride his Triumph some fifty yards down the street from the bank in Farnborough, watching the girl at the ATM. He had been there for almost three hours and up until now, nothing had happened. As a copper he'd been famous for his hunches, earning him the nick name 'Psychic Mac'. McAllister was the bloke who always knew where to look for the body or where the suspect had hidden the loot, when logic determined the corpse or the money was long gone. He put it down to lateral thinking and an ability to put himself, mentally, in the place of the crook. That and a healthy slice of luck. He would regularly win the Christmas raffle at the nick, especially if it was a bottle of Scotch. In this case, however, he had used intuition born of years of experience. He had reasoned, most villains being lazy, the morning after the first strike, that this was the place to look. All the cash withdrawals had been within a twenty five mile radius, so if the person who had removed the cash from here last night had half a brain cell, they might reasonably assume the machine would be refilled by the morning and so be ready for a second plunder.

Still, after this long wait, he was beginning to think that maybe this was a waste of time. To double check, he had used his Blackberry again, to patch into the bank security programme. No, there had been no activity at this ATM since the Midas withdrawal, and no other Midas activity at any other of the bank's machines.

But now there was this girl, acting in a rather erratic way. She had put the card into the hole in the wall twice now. She was obviously not happy; in fact, she had shouted at the machine. People never liked it when ATMs were empty, but she seemed genuinely upset. She had started to walk away, and then came back to try again. He took a quick snap of her using his Blackberry Curve and instantly blue-toothed it to the miniature computer mounted on the bike's petrol tank. Using the central ball on the Blackberry, he zoomed in on her face. Yes, she was crying. He looked up as he heard the sound of a car. A bright yellow Porsche Boxter pulled up opposite the bank. The girl, having tried the machine a third time, was now shouting at the building. McAllister thought about going over, but instinct told him to wait. He watched as she slumped, back to the wall, and the driver of the car crossed the road and approached the girl. Something about the man's body language was interesting. After years of undercover surveillance and endless courses on interview, not to mention interrogation techniques, McAllister had developed a keen eye for what he called 'dodgy moves.' This man's demeanour was uncomfortable, hesitant. For some reason; he wasn't at ease being there. And the woman's reaction to this stranger, the way her body turned towards him, open, now that was interesting. He wasn't a stranger. She knew him. Now they were deep in conversation. So who was he? Apart from a pension and a less than glowing reference, Psychic Mac had taken one or two other things with him from the Met, as sort of compensation, not that they were aware, of course. So, using the Blackberry keypad, he typed into the bike's computer the registration of the Porsche, 'MKS 01', and using a, not generally available, online database, in seconds had most of Alan Marks' personal details including age, address and, usefully, bank accounts.

He was about to cross check those with the bank records when he saw the two hooded figures come around the corner just ahead of the Porsche and approach the car. He saw them saunter past it and then one stopped the other, dragged him back and pointed into the bright yellow motor. Well, well, there was about to be some fun. He thought he knew exactly what they would do next and he wasn't wrong. As the first lad opened the door of the car and leaned into the back, the other figure ran around to the front. He saw Alan Marks clock what was happening and begin to run across the road. McAllister gunned the bike into life, but by the time he reached the car, Marks was on the floor and the two young thieves were legging it down the road. He stopped next to Alan Marks and propped the bike on its stand. He got off and looked down, just to make sure the man wasn't seriously injured. Alan Marks looked up at him. No, this man was OK.

Things were looking up; this was just so much better than gazing at a computer screen all weekend.

"You stay there, I'll have your bag back in a couple of minutes Mr Marks. As soon as I've caught the little shits."

Back on the bike, he was roaring down the street in an instant. As he rounded the corner, he saw them up ahead crouching over the holdall on the pavement. In seconds he was opposite them. As he stopped the engine and dismounted, both boys stood and faced him. They were both in their early teens, white, with pale spotty faces. The thinnest one on the left had a lip piercing and the boy on the right, who was slightly taller, had a ring through his eyebrow.

McAllister raised the visor. "Oh shit, you're just kids."

"Piss off, fuckin' twat," yelled the smaller lad, "unless you want some of this."

He produced what looked like a serrated fishing knife from behind his back and pointed it at McAllister.

McAllister took off his helmet slowly and held it by his side with his left hand.

"Bollocks," laughed the taller boy, "he's an old git."

McAllister smiled and then spoke in a very controlled and quiet voice, his broad, deep Glaswegian tones adding a slight hint of menace to his voice.

"I think that you will find, boys, that you have made three rather silly mistakes."

"Oh yeah, and what mistakes are them then, you Scots arsehole?" asked the boy with the knife.

"Well let's see, you little dipshit," smiled McAllister. "Mistake one: taking that bag, which I believe doesna' belong to you."

"So?" sneered the taller boy.

McAllister continued; "Mistake two: pointing a knife at me."

"And like, what you doing about it?" said the boy with the knife, waving it in front of him and edging forward.

"We'll come to that in a moment," said McAllister calmly, putting his right hand out in front of him as if to halt the lad. "And your third mistake," he turned to face the other boy with his hand still out to the boy with the knife, "your third mistake," he repeated, gazing the boy straight in the eyes now, "was calling me old."

"So?" said the boy, shifting from one foot to the other.

"So," said McAllister, lowering his voice slightly "I suggest you give me the bag, tell your pathetic little mate here to put his toy knife away, and PISS OFF!"

Both boys jumped.

The youngster with the knife was becoming agitated. "Yeah, like we're giving you this bag, yeah? Why would we do that? You some sort of fuckin' copper or sumink?"

"Unfortunately for you, no," said McAllister still looking at the other boy.

This puzzled the boy. "Why unfortunately?"

McAllister turned his head sideways and looked at him now. "Because if I was a fuckin' copper I wouldn't be allowed to do this."

What followed was swift and brutal.

Without removing his gaze from the boy with the knife, in one swift movement, his hand rose with the helmet and struck the taller boy full on the underside of the chin. Just as the boy was licking his lips, the full force of the helmet hit him, forcing his lower teeth up hard into his tongue. Blood spurted out as he crumpled onto the floor with a yell; holding his mouth. His accomplice was so stunned that he had no time to react as the leather-clad biker chopped the knife from his hand, kicked him in the crotch, pulled him to the ground and before he could breathe was holding his head up by his hair with the knife at his throat.

"Now," said McAllister calmly, "I will give you one chance, you little shit. In a minute I am going to let you go, and when I do, you will help your sorry excuse for a mate up and bugger off to hospital with him before he bleeds to death. Understand?"

The boy whimpered and nodded in acknowledgement.

"Good. Now piss off." He let the boy go and stood up quickly. Both lads scrambled to their feet, the taller one holding his bleeding mouth. McAllister watched as they staggered off. When they were well down the street, McAllister grabbed the holdall. As he picked it up, his curiosity was aroused. Whatever was inside moved, and rustled. He unzipped the bag and smiled. "Well well

Mr Marks, what have we here? And, more to the point, where did we get it?"

McAllister headed back to the bank, but was not that surprised to find, when he got there, that Alan Marks, the girl, and the yellow Porsche had all gone.

Having spent a mere ten minutes scanning details in the banks databases, he looked at the small screen on the front of his Triumph and shook his head. How stupid could some people be? He knew what he had to do as he picked up his Blackberry, but felt vaguely uneasy about the call he was about to make. In fact, something about the whole case was making him uncomfortable.

Sir Charles Bower answered immediately

"Sir Charles," began McAllister. "I know who it is. He's a customer at the North Farnborough Branch called Marks. Runs a small security business called Alan Marks Security. At the moment, I think he's with one of our employees Konstantina Zouroudi, but I don't think she is involved… No, of course I can't be certain but I saw them meet this morning and it wasn't prearranged… No sir, not at the moment, but I think I know where he might be and I'm about to check it out… No I understand we don't want the police sir…sorry, sir? Why the hell has he done it? Well there is something else, which I'm afraid you're not going to like. It's about the small business guy here at Farnborough: a bloke called Justin Barnes. Marks has everything with us; mortgage, insurance, the works. About eighteen months ago, Barnes gave him one of our small business loans but it was a biggie. Now I do not know Marks' numbers but I would be surprised if he qualified for a million, sir… No of course not, it started smaller and extended over about six months… Yes, classic snail trail… You've got it sir, yes it's gone tits up… Security? That's just it sir, I've found one e-file that's been side-lined in Barnes' secure tray relating to a change of ownership on Marks' house to someone called Sally Grant… Yes, it all but screws the cover on the loan, makes it very messy… Why would

Barnes do that? Look, I can't say for certain because I will need time on the main computer, but on first glance at the behaviour files in secure HR, our Justin is a bit of a one for the pussy… Look sir Charles, it smells of a 'spare pot' scam, like the one we had in Ipswich. I'll need time to look into the accounts, 'cause it's been well hidden, but my gut feeling is that our Mr Barnes has got an extra bonus off you, sir. Yes you've got it sir, and by the way, if my instinct is right, he hasn't only screwed you and Alan Marks he's screwed Marks' wife as well. She is called Sally. He's at the Edinburgh small business conference right now… No, obviously I can't, but I've got a lad up there who could… Certainly sir, no don't worry Jamie doesn't do subtle…Marks? Yes, I'm onto him… How did he get Midas? Ah well, that's the bit I don't know yet… Yes right away sir, I'll keep you updated."

As the call ended, and he put Marks' office post code into his satnav, it came to him why he felt uneasy. How did Marks get Midas? He didn't know, but he had a strange feeling that Marks didn't know either.

CHAPTER THREE

A silver Range Rover Evoque with dark smoked windows stopped outside number twenty three Leocharous Street in the Athens Port of Piraeus. A young man in white chinos, blue deck shoes, a cream linen shirt and white Prada sport sunglasses stepped onto the pavement. He was slim, about five ten, had dark olive skin and, as he stepped from the heat of the street into the air conditioned reception area of number twenty three, he lowered his glasses and smiled at the girl behind the desk. It worked, as it always did for Manos, because the girl, who had been deep in conversation with her friend Maria on the phone, suddenly put her hand over the mouthpiece and greeted him, "*Yassas.*"

Manos responded with the more informal "*Yassou*", and eyeing the name on the badge strategically placed just below her ample cleavage. "*Yassou* Mitzy? An interesting name, don't tell me you must be American?"

Mitzy flushed and returned the smile, "Canadian, actually."

"Tell me," said Manos turning up the charm a notch as Mitzy toyed with her long blonde hair, "is there any way I could have your full attention? Just for a moment?"

Mitzy looked confused and then, realising as he nodded at the phone, took her hand from the mouthpiece and spoke into it. "Sorry Maria, I'll call you back something big has just come up."

Manos looked down at his crotch and feigned shock. "Not yet it hasn't, but I'm sure you could make it." His gaze came straight back and into her eyes.

Mizty went instantly red and was considering whether or not

to be offended when Manos slipped into his well-tried routine.

"Oh no, I have offended you, I am so sorry. This is terrible. It is just that I am Greek, you see, and we Greek men, well, when faced with a beautiful woman, sometimes we do not have the sophistication. The polite words. You know, the brain of a Greek man is not always up here." He pointed at his head. "When I see a woman so beautiful, my brain sometimes, how do you say in English, is going south." He grinned. It worked, the girl was doing the coy shake of the head thing that always happened at this point and she was smiling.

Manos was on a roll. "No, I can see you are upset, how can I make this up to you? I know, tonight I will take you out for a dinner. We will go to my brother's restautant, Taverna Loukas, below the Acropolis, the best in Athens, real Greek food like on the islands, yes?"

"Well, I don't know about tonight," the girl pretended to waver.

Manos was straight in. "Good, what time do you finish here? I pick you up, yes?" He glanced out through the glass doors at the Silver Range Rover Evoque, gleaming in the sun. "In my car."

She was hooked. "I finish at seven but…"

"Good," grinned Manos, "seven it is. Now why did I come here? Meeting you has confused me. Do you know why I came here? No, why would you? Oh Mitzy, what have you done to me?"

Mitzy was completely taken in. "Perhaps you came to see someone in one of the companies here?" She indicated the list of companies on the stainless steel plaque on the wall behind her. "We have several offices here and…"

"Stavroulis International Exports," Manos said, pointing at a name on the list. It was said with such force that Mitzy jumped in her seat.

"Oh Stavroulis, OK." Recovering, she picked up the phone.

Manos' hand was on hers immediately, gently but firmly placing the handset back on the receiver. "Nikos. Nikos Stavroulis, he is my uncle. It is his birthday and I want to surprise him."

Mitzy hesitated. "But I am supposed to call up if someone comes and…"

Manos was straight in again. "And on this occasion you will, how you say, make the exception to the rule. Yes?" He grinned again. She melted.

"Well, just this once, but only for you."

"Second floor, yes?" He was already turning away towards the lift. "Oh, and one thing, Mitzy." He turned back. "Tonight, you know, on our, how you say; our date, yes?"

She smiled. "Yes?"

He lowered his voice as he leant towards her ear. "Do not expect I jiggy jiggy with you on first time out. You don't expect that I jiggy jiggy, do you? Because I am not that sort of boy, ok?"

Mizty flushed again. "No, no, I would not want you to er jiggy, no not on the first, well you know, no."

She was lying, and as he headed for the lift, she really hoped he was lying too. He was, but not just about that.

Nikos Stavroulis was a brash Australian Greek. He had left Greece as a young man, like so many in the late eighties, to find work abroad. He had pitched up in Sydney and in the expanding Greek community there, found work in his uncle's printing business. Nikos was a worker and a quick learner, and soon became the blue-eyed boy of his Uncle Yiannis. He watched how Yiannis, who had been no mean businessman in his day, operated, and learned the tricks of the trade while building personal contacts with all the clients. Within a year, everyone knew Nikos by name. Yiannis had no children of his own and was old and tired. Within a couple of years, using his natural gift for charming anyone he did business with, Nikos was pretty much running the business. To Yiannis, he became the son he never had, and so it was no surprise when Yiannis died in 2000, of a heart attack, Nikos inherited the business. He immediately used the rest of the old man's estate to computerise the whole operation and within a year had sold it at a handsome profit.

Nikos had seen the digital future coming and got out of printing just in time. Australia had been good to him, but he missed his homeland and so returned to Greece. By now, he had a good nose for business and he saw that Greece produced very little and so exported hardly anything. He saw this as an advantage. Greek products would be a novelty abroad. Working on the basis of old Yiannis maxim, 'There are people who make things and people who buy them, the trick is matching them up', he began Stavroulis International Exports. It didn't matter what it was, he would buy it and export it. He was the first to export Greek yogurt to British supermarkets. If you saw; 'Genuine Greek Bouzouki' in an English music shop, or 'Greek Delight' (not the Turkish imitation), in a Paris confectioners, the chances were that it got there via Stavroulis International Exports. Nick was a chancer but always with an eye for an opportunity. On this particular morning, the opportunity was his new secretary Loukia. She had come in very upset, having broken up with her boyfriend the night before. She was young and impressionable with beautiful green eyes, long black hair and more than adequate breasts. Nikos judged that she was in need of comfort from an older man, and he was just such a man. It began with him offering his shoulder to cry on whilst he gently muttered words of solace. Pretty soon, the solace was being administered in the form of kisses to the neck and eventually the breasts. Like many Greek men, he was an experienced lover and before Loukia really knew what was happening she was, willingly, bending over the desk as he slowly pulled down her white lace panties, having unzipped her skirt, and began to unzip his trousers, revealing his swollen member.

"So you'll screw just about anything, then?"

Startled, Nikos turned to see Manos standing in the open office doorway.

"Who the hell do you think you are? Get out of my office." His ardour now cooled, Nikos was re-zipping his trousers as Loukia scuttled behind the desk holding her blouse to her naked breasts and trying to zip up her skirt.

Manos sighed and straightened. "Sorry, can't do that, and as for who the hell I am, well..." He shot forward, grabbing Nikos by the throat and pushing him back against the wall. "Who the hell I am is none of your business." Loukia screamed and began to whimper. Manos shot her a glance. "Shut up!" She stopped immediately.

Manos tightened his grip on Nikos' throat as the older man began to gasp for breath.

Manos continued. "Who I am is not the point. The point is who my boss is. Does the name Mrs Manidaki mean anything to you, Nikos?"

Nikos tried to speak but could only gasp.

"Oh, sorry," said Manos releasing his grip. "Can't speak, can you?" He raised his voice. "Mrs Manidaki? Mean anything?"

Nikos spluttered. "Yes," he coughed. "Of course." He took a breath, but before he could take another, Manos had him by the throat again and he was pinned once more to the wall.

"Yes of course," said Manos. "And you had a deal with her, and you have broken that deal haven't you? Haven't you, you stupid Aussie bastard?"

Nikos felt unbearable pain as he crumpled to the floor, clutching his crotch, as a well-aimed kick floored him.

"Please?" Loukia began as she shuffled around the desk.

Manos kept his gaze on Nikos but snapped a reply to her. "I told you to shut up. So shut up. I can kill you, and I will kill you if you don't shut up. Understand?"

"Yes." She stifled a sob and sat behind the desk.

"Now, Mr Stavroulis," Manos removed the gun from the belt of his trousers behind his back, "before I decide whether to finish you off or not, I have been instructed to ask you some questions. Think very carefully before you answer as your life depends on your replies. You get me?"

Nikos managed a weak, "Yes."

Manos bent down and shouted at him, "You get me?" and kicked him in the stomach.

Nikos screamed in pain. "Yes, yes."

Manos rose and cocked the gun. "Now." He pulled a piece of paper from his back pocket, unfolded it and read. "You made a piece of equipment for Mrs Manidaki which you sent to her yesterday, yes?"

Nikos looked up. "Yes?"

Manos smiled "Good, that was the easy one. Now one that is a little more difficult; think hard before you answer. Have you made this piece of equipment for anyone else?"

Nikos looked puzzled. "For anyone else? No, of course not."

"Of course not? Oh dear," Manos smiled again, looking down at his piece of paper, "that means I have to ask you the last question." He looked up. "You know the one that decides whether or not I kill you." He looked back at the paper. "So if you have not made this equipment for anyone else, how come Mrs Manidaki's is not working but someone in England appears to be using one that does?"

Nikos was completely confused. "But that is impossible."

Manos pointed the gun at his head. "That is not an answer. I will ask again. How come someone in England is using it?"

Nikos was trembling and started talking rapidly. "How can somebody in England be using it? I made it for Mrs Manidaki. She has it? Yes?"

"Yes," confirmed Manos.

"There you are," said Nikos. "Nobody in England can be using it."

Manos sighed. "Oh dear, you see Mrs Manidaki was very specific. "*Manos,*" she said, "*Manos, file mou.* If he cannot tell you, even though he is my godson, shoot his balls off." He lowered the gun to Nikos' crotch.

Nikos was beginning to blubber and a large wet patch was spreading across the front of his trousers. "No one can use it in England, don't you see, it can't be done!" The gun was moving closer. "Mrs Manidaki has the only one, unless…" He hesitated as a terrifying thought suddenly occurred to him. Manos saw the realisation dawn on his face and reacted.

"Yes, Nikos? What is it?"

Nikos hardly dare say it for fear of instant execution, but as the barrel of the gun touched his penis, he blurted it out. "Unless somehow there is another one that works properly and…"

Manos laughed, a loud and guttural laugh. "Another one? Right answer you fucking piece of shit. Well, well, well. Another one? Do you know that is just what Mrs Manidaki thought?" He stood up straight and put the gun back in the back of his trouser belt. "Nikos, you are one lucky bastard." He walked over to the desk and Loukia recoiled in fear. He picked up the phone and began dialling. "This means I don't get to shoot you yet, but you get a chance to tell Mrs Manidaki how you are going to sort this out." He pressed the speakerphone button and, as the ringtone stopped, an old woman's voice, thin and rasping, spoke:

"Nikos? Nikos? Can you hear me?"

Nikos pulled himself up into the chair in front of the desk. "Yes, I can hear you."

Mrs Manidaki continued. "Oh Nikos, how could you? I only gave you the job because you are practically family. And you assured me you could do it. I remember your words, 'Godmother, I will do this for you and no-one else will know, trust me, trust me.' And now this. What will your mother say? Isn't it bad enough she has had to put up with your father all these years. Then you and your brother going off to Australia, leaving her on that island with your father and his womanising, though God knows how he managed it. And now you. You come back, appear to make something of yourself, so she's probably thinking she could get you married off so at least she can get grandchildren in her old age. And now you do this. Your funeral would probably kill her. Wouldn't it? I said wouldn't it?"

Nikos was jolted into a response. "Yes, godmother."

The old lady sighed heavily and her voice became stern, much less the voice of a quirky old lady and much more the voice of the head of the biggest crime family in Greece, which she was. Her tone sent a shiver through Nikos as she mimicked him; "Yes, godmother. Yes, godmother." There was a pause. "Exactly. Manos, kill him."

Manos shrugged his shoulders and reached for his gun as Nikos panicked. "No, no godmother, please, I will sort it out, I will. Please give me a chance."

Manos cocked the gun. "Well, Mrs Manidaki?"

There was a silence, and then the old woman spoke in a very matter-of-fact way; "Nikos, you told me that your people were the only ones that knew how to make what I wanted."

Nikos was about to interject, but with a tone that almost sounded as if she could see him, she stopped him with, "Do not speak until I have finished, and only then if you really want to say something that won't upset me. Now, if somebody in your so-called organisation has done the dirty on you, it is only fair that you sort it out. Much against my better judgement, and only because of my love for your mother, I will give you a small amount of time to find the person. You will then do as you will with them and put a stop to this and get the merchandise back. If you do not, then Manos and his brother Loukas will sort it out for you. It will not be pretty as it will mean Loukas closing his taverna for a few days in the height of the season, so he will be angry and people will get hurt. Oh, and you will be dead and I will have to comfort your mother. If you have anything to say, say it now because I am getting tired of this and when I get tired I get bad-tempered."

Nikos stuttered. "How long have I got, godmother? I mean I have to get to the island and…"

He was cut off by the old lady's voice which was loud and angry. "How long? How long? My grandfather had a saying. There is a time for every job and every job has it's time. You will know when you have run out of time, Nikos, believe me, you will know. Now, Manos has a very nice car which I gave him for his name day because unlike you he is a grateful boy. There is a plane to Rhodos in two hours. He will take you to the airport; he already has your ticket. There is a ferry from Kolona Harbour in Rhodos to the island at five thirty. You will be on it and at your mother's house by this evening, and you will take her a present. Something expensive; God knows the woman deserves it. And Nikos? Sort this out… soon!"

The phone line went dead.

Manos walked around the desk behind Loukia and leaned over her to press the speakerphone button. As he stood back up, he fondled her left breast. "Mm nice tits, if I had time I would stay and jiggy jiggy with you but I have to take this piece of shit to the airport. I know, how about I pick you up here at, let's say seven, tonight? We could go to my brother's taverna near the Acropolis. Best food in Greece, just like the islands, and then I jiggy jiggy with you? Oh, and the girl downstairs too, OK? Good. Seven it is."

Later that afternoon, as Nikos fastened his seatbelt on the three thirty Athens to Rhodes flight, and felt in his inside pocket to make sure the gold watch he had purchased for his mother at the airport jewellery store was still there he couldn't help but worry about Manos' parting words:

"See you soon Nikos, see you soon."

CHAPTER FOUR

"This is a strange feeling." Konstantina was concentrating very hard. "I have never driven anything like this before."

A sudden thought came to Alan as he nursed his hands in the front of the Porsche. "You do have a licence?"

Konstantina smiled "Of course I do." There was a pause. "Sort of."

He was about to query this when she suddenly pressed her foot hard on the brake, if Alan hadn't had his seatbelt on, he would have hit the windscreen.

"Sorry," she smiled as the car stalled. "It's very sensitive, isn't it, and not nearly as comfortable as it looks."

Alan winced as he removed his cut and bruised hands from the dashboard. It had been a natural and very painful reflex to put them out in front of himself as Konstantina suddenly stopped the car, but right now he really wished he hadn't.

"Oh, it's cut out." She looked a little puzzled. "Anyway, we're here."

She indicated a small block of flats. "Come on; let's get your hands seen to." She was already getting out of the car as Alan tentatively tried to undo his seatbelt with his fingers. He was struggling. Konstantina had gone around the front of the car and was opening his door.

"I really think you should go to the hospital with those hands I mean, I can put a bandage on, but I'm not a nurse and you should call the police too."

Alan stopped her. "No, I'll be fine honestly, it's been very good of you, but..."

She leaned across him and released his belt. Her long dark hair brushed his cheek and her smell was vaguely musky. For some it reason reminded him of the sea. She briefly caught his eye and paused. It was only a fraction of a second, but it felt longer. Then the moment was gone as she withdrew from the car

"That's a nice perfume." He managed, as he struggled out of the car, trying not to touch anything with the palms of his hands.

"It's Greek," she responded as she walked away.

"Yes, of course." He bumped the door shut with his bum and turned to follow her up the short pathway to the front entrance of Napoleon House. It was one of many newly-built small blocks of flats in the area.

"Ah," said Alan, "you live in one of these? I bet it's pretty small."

She laughed as she reached the door. "Small does not do it justice, Mr Marks. It's tiny, but all I can afford."

She began to type a code into a pad at the front entrance as Alan approached and the door buzzed.

"Hang on," he protested, stopping her as she pushed the door open. "That's it. The door."

She turned, puzzled. "Sorry, what about the door?" She looked at it, confused, and then back at him.

"No not this door, my door, at my office." He wasn't making himself very clear. "Earlier on, when you said you were Greek, I had this strange idea about my bank card."

"Your bank card?"

"Yes, and my door." He could see she was looking at him as if he was talking gibberish. "Look, I know you've done a lot for me this morning already but would you mind doing me one last favour?" She looked puzzled so he tried once more. "Look, I'll explain everything if you just take me to my office. I need to check something."

She didn't move. "What about your hands?"

"My hands?" Oddly enough her mention of them brought back the pain. "Yes they hurt, but there is a first aid box at my office. Please."

She smiled. "Oh, what the hell? It's not every day I get to drive a Porsche. Anyway, I'm not having that much luck with men, am I? I mean, first that prat Justin and now I get a bloke to my front door and he wants to go to his office. That perfume of mine can't be that good, can it? Mind you, I should have known better, you being a married man."

He shrugged. "Hardly." He could see she was confused. "Well yes I am technically married, but she left me."

Konstantina's expression changed. "Oh I'm sorry." Even as she said the words, she was wondering why she felt anything but sorry.

"Look," said Alan. "I wouldn't ask you if it wasn't important."

She stopped him. "Don't worry, Mr Marks."

"Alan," he interjected and looked at her face properly for the first time. He must have seen that face a quite a few times at the bank, but he'd never really seen how attractive she was.

"Oh Alan, right." She flushed slightly and blinked rather too many times. "Right, well anyway, look it's no problem, but I wouldn't mind knowing what's going on." She set off down the pathway to the car. "I mean, I'm sure you have a good reason for not wanting to tell the police you were mugged and for not waiting around to get your bag back, but I can't wait to hear what it is." As she was saying this, she was also thinking to herself, "Why am I doing this for this man?" Although inside she knew. What she didn't predict was what he was about to tell her.

"What do you mean you told him?" Justin Barnes stood in the doorway of the hotel bathroom in Edinburgh, with his face half covered in shaving foam and with only a towel around his waist.

Sally Marks was sat in a thin black slip, carefully applying her eyeliner in the bedroom mirror and was completely unfazed by his outburst. "I told him I was leaving the marriage."

"But what about me?" Justin's blood pressure was rising.

She enjoyed winding him up. "You, darling? What about you?"

"You know very well what I mean about me." He dropped his razor and, as he bent to pick it up, his towel fell to the floor.

She saw his mishap in the mirror. "Oh dear, Mr Stiffy's gone all floppy."

Justin was grappling with his towel. "That's not funny. Did you or did you not tell him about me?"

She stayed cool. "Of course." She left a suitable pause until he was about to explode and then dropped in the word "not." As if it was an afterthought.

His relief was taking the edge off the rage. "Sally?"

She turned and faced him. "I left him a note telling him what a waste of space he was and how I was buggering off. Has Sally been a naughty girl, then?" She was beginning to tease him as she moved forward. "Does Big Tiger want to spank Sally for being a naughty little girl?"

Before Big Tiger got a chance to respond, the bedroom door burst open and the door chain went flying across the room. In the door frame stood a very large and muscular, shaven-headed man in a dark green tartan kilt, complete with full dress shirt, waistcoat and sporran.

"Mr Barnes, I believe?" He spoke with a very cultured Edinburgh accent, strode forward and grabbed Justin's penis as if it was his hand and shook it hard, making Justin squeal. He then turned and shook Sally's hand, using the same hand with which he had shaken Justin's appendage. He then wiped his hand on a handkerchief he pulled from his top pocket.

"Now, folks, I suggest you both sit down while Mr McKay, that's me," he turned to face Justin, "while Mr McKay tells you, Mr Justin Barnes, just how you are going to atone for being a cheeky little tosser. And for Christ's sake cover up that excuse for a prick." He picked up the towel which was still on the floor and chucked it at Justin. He then turned to face Sally and raised his kilt. "That, lady, is what you call a cock." Sally, though terrified was suitably impressed.

“Now then, Mr Barnes,” he continued. “The real question is, after you’ve given the bank back its money how do I dispose of you?”

Justin stuttered. “Dispose of me? And what money, I…” He never finished because the back handed slap that caught him hard on the left cheek sent him crashing to the floor.

Jamie McKay towered over him. “Did I ask you to speak? I don’t recall asking you to speak. So unless I ask you to speak, DO NOT SPEAK!”

He turned to Sally. “I am so sorry for any unpleasantness you may be about to witness.” He stepped forward, treading on Justin’s left hand as he did so, and, turning his foot slowly sideways, he caused Barnes to shriek in agony. “You see, he has had his hand in the till apparently, and we can’t have that.” He swiftly turned and caught Justin Barnes with a sharp kick to the face with his other boot. Justin yelled and rolled over, blood spurting from his nose. McKay walked to the door and kicked it closed. “We wouldna want to disturb the neighbours, would we? Not if we’re having a party. You see. Sally... you don’t mind if I call you Sally, do you? It sounds so much better than ‘whore’, don’t you think?” He slowly put out his right hand and slipped the left strap of her slip off her shoulder, and then repeated the action with the right one. “You see, Sally, after we’ve sorted out the little prick here,” he slowly took her trembling left hand and guided it under his kilt, “we may have to punish you in a much more pleasant way.”

Sally Marks was amazed that, even in her terror, she was beginning to feel a tingling moistness in her crotch and slight tremors in her stomach. What she also felt however was, that what was coming may very well be punishment, but it would be far from pleasant.

In Farnborough, Konstantina was obviously trying hard to take in what Alan Marks had just told her. As she drove the car towards his office in silence, Alan was beginning to wonder just why he had told her all about the card, but the simple truth was, it just felt right.

Suddenly she spoke and her first question came as a big surprise. He had expected something like "But shouldn't you tell the police?" or "What happens if the bank finds out?" Instead what he got was, "Does it work in other banks?"

Alan was really taken aback. "I have absolutely no idea."

"Well," she said, "let's find out." She immediately took a sharp left, causing Alan to put out his right hand to steady himself. He gave a small moan of pain as his hand touched the dashboard.

"Sorry," she was genuinely apologetic, "but there is a Lloyds TSB just down here." She pulled the car up outside the bank in Frimley High Street. "Come on, let's see."

Alan was not at all sure. "I don't know if I should. I mean, what if it works? What if it doesn't?"

"Well then you will know, won't you?"

"Know what?" he queried.

"Whether or not you really have access to any amount of money you want. You will know if you are potentially the richest man in the world."

That thought was so big that for a moment Alan Marks was stunned. "The richest man in the world? Yeah, like that will happen."

"Well, are we going to see or not?" said Konstantina, stopping the engine and giving him a big hint as to what she thought he should do.

"Oh, what the hell?" said Alan, trying to undo the seatbelt with as little discomfort as possible. Konstantina waved his hands away and popped the belt lock. Then she leaned over him and released the door catch. Once more, he smelled the perfume and noticed that this time she made a definite point of not looking him in the eyes.

Just as she opened the door to get out, Alan stopped her. "Wait!"

"Getting cold feet?" she responded.

"Not at all," he replied, "but wait until they have gone."

He nodded forward and she saw through the windscreen a

young couple approaching the cash machine. They eyed the occupants of the Porsche with obvious suspicion as Konstantina clicked the door shut again. The young man put his card in the machine and began to tap in his instructions. After what seemed like an age he retrieved his money, and hastily put it in his pocket. Throughout the whole process the girl kept looking at Alan and Konstantina, then turning back and whispering something to her partner. They briskly walked off down the road, glancing back and muttering to each other. Konstantina began to laugh.

"What's so funny?" asked Alan. "They thought we were very 'dodgy'. And they are right, Tina."

"Yes," she giggled, "but they thought we were after their money. They don't know you've got an endless supply."

He pondered. "Mm... or have I?"

She was already getting out of the car. "Oh come on, let's find out – at least we know this machine is giving cash."

This was true. As he stepped up to the machine, he felt a strange exhilaration. Last night, doing this on his own had been worrying and exciting in equal measure, but somehow with Konstantina there it felt safer, and more of an adventure. He looked from side to side and over his shoulder as he put the card in.

Konstantina stood behind him. "Don't worry, I won't watch your pin number."

"No, that's not what I'm worried about," he reassured her, "it's if someone comes along. Keep an eye out, will you?"

She duly obliged as he typed in 5474. It accepted his number, so he opted for the cash option and three hundred pounds. No sooner had he entered his request than his card was returned and he was instructed to wait for his cash.

"It's working."

Tina turned. "It is?"

"Well," said Alan guardedly, "so far." The money duly appeared. He removed it and waited.

"It looks like that's it," said Tina, disappointed.

"I think," he responded, as the whirring began and another bunch of crisp twenty pound notes appeared, "that it may not be."

"My God," the Greek girl gasped, "some more."

Alan handed her a bunch of notes as even more began coming. He took the latest offering and pressed the cancel button. The whirring and the money stopped.

As they sat side by side in the car, they both found themselves laughing out loud.

She was the first to speak. "That is just unbelievable. And it's not from your account?"

"Apparently not," he confirmed.

"And nobody knows?"

He hesitated before he responded. "I don't think so, but there was something about that bloke who turned up when I was mugged. You know I said he knew my name? I had an odd feeling about him, like there was a reason he was there. That's why I asked you to drive me away."

She remembered. "Oh yes, he came out of nowhere. Hang on." A realisation hit her. "That bag those thugs took, it was full of money, yes?"

"Yes," confirmed Alan, "and if he got it back, he might very well know that."

She nodded her head. "I see. But look, this card of yours, I mean why would it suddenly do this? How does it suddenly get magical powers?"

"Ah well," explained Alan, "that's why I want you to take me to my office. I'm not sure why this has happened, but I've got a funny feeling I might know how."

Jamie McKay stepped out of Room 217. "Hello, Mac? Jamie here, sorry but this phone is shite. Can you hear me now? Good. Yes, all sorted, good as gold. The money, what was left of it, has been transferred back minus my bit, of course. Took bloody ages, seven different accounts, little twat. Clever little bastard but soft as shit.

Yeah, she's taken care of too. What? Now would I, Mac? Yeah, too right I did. Oh come on, you know me. No fun though, I think she enjoyed it. OK mate, any-time, better go before somebody decides to make the beds."

He folded his mobile phone and hung the 'Do Not Disturb' sign on the door handle. It would be the whole of the next day before anyone had realised that Justin Barnes had not put in an appearance at the small business conference. It was when he failed to turn up to give his presentation on 'managing small business loans' that a call was put in to the hotel. The housekeeper who had found him, cowering naked in the bath, was so appalled by his injuries that it became apparent she would be off for some time with post-traumatic stress. Once he was well enough to speak to the police, Justin's explanation of his plight and injuries had police officer Julie Campbell, who sat by his hospital bed, completely confused. As she said when she put in the call to her Inspector, "It's a pile of crap sir, but unless he's going to tell us who did it and lodge a complaint, we're stuffed. If only there had been a witness."

Of course, on the other side of town, the witness there had been was now where she had told Alan Marks she was going to be in the first place, with her friend Moira. Moira was shocked when she saw the state of her oldest friend who suddenly turned up that Monday morning. She took some persuading not to call the police. She did, however, call Alan's mobile, having listened to Sally's story.

"You, Alan Marks, are a sex-crazed, twisted, sadistic and evil monster. Men like you should be locked away and castrated. Don't you ever try to contact Sally again, ever. You'll be hearing from her solicitor...pervert!" As she put the phone down, she felt better but was slightly confused to see the smile on Sally's face. "It will be the stress," she rationalised. "I'll get us both a drink."

"She's been drinking," said Alan, as he stared in confusion at his mobile.

"Who has?" asked Konstantina as she brought the car to a halt outside Alan Marks' office.

"Moira." Alan tried not to sound too amused, but failed. "She's my wife's, sorry ex-wife's, friend and she just called me sadistic, twisted, sex crazed and a pervert."

Konstantina stopped the engine and giggled. "Wow, not only am I in a Porsche with a really wealthy man but he's a sex maniac, too. Perhaps I shouldn't help you with your hands, I mean if you get to use them again who knows what might happen to me?"

They were parked outside the Farnborough Business Centre, a small block of purpose-built offices on a small industrial estate on the edge of Farnborough and as she began to open the door of the car, he stopped her for the second time that day.

"Drive!"

She was taken aback as Alan waved her back into the car frantically. "What's wrong?"

He pointed up the road past several similar office units to where a motorbike had just turned into the estate. "Look, it's him, the bloke from outside the bank quick, drive."

Konstantina shut the door, started the car and pushed down on the accelerator. The Porsche burst into life and like a large cat leapt forward, taking both driver and passenger by surprise. As the wheels screeched, the Greek girl struggled to control the car and it weaved erratically from side to side. Gary McAllister saw the Porsche heading towards him just in time and mounted the pavement as it sped past. By the time he had recovered and turned the bike, the Porsche was gone.

"Jesus Tina," snapped Alan Marks, "I said drive, not kill the bloke on the bike."

"Sorry," she said as she finally got the car under control, "but it's very sensitive. Where to now?"

Alan thought and then looked behind. "He's not following us, I need time to think. I know; the Hog's Back?"

She was puzzled. "The Hog's Back?"

"Yes, the hotel on the Hog's Back, we can park up there and get a cup of coffee in the lounge and I can work out what to do next."

As they travelled down the Blackwater Valley link road towards the Hog's Back, Marks looked at Konstantina and she noticed and shot him a smile. "What is it?" she asked.

"Nothing, just that considering we only really met a couple of hours ago I was thinking, well, it feels like a lot longer."

She was about to reply but Alan's mobile rang. He took it from his pocket tentatively and turned it over. The screen displayed 'Withheld Number'. He carefully and with some pain pressed the green receive button and put the phone to his ear. A broad Scots voice spoke. "Mr Marks, I think you need to know that I know you have Midas."

Alan muttered "Midas?"

The person on the other end obviously didn't hear as he continued.

"Trying to run me down was particularly stupid. I think I might know why you are doing this but you won't get away with it. If it's any consolation, we know about your wife and Justin Barnes and he has been dealt with. I will find you, so why don't we just agree to meet and you can give me Midas before anybody gets really hurt." Alan Marks was stunned and the caller was obviously intrigued by the lack of response.

"I tell you what, Mr Marks, how about I call you in, let's say, about an hour, when you've had chance to think about it, OK? Good."

As the call finished, Alan looked at the phone in mild disbelief. "Jesus Christ!"

Konstantina saw his concern. "What is it? Who was that?"

"The bloke on the bike."

"What did he say?"

"A hell of a lot. I need to work this out. I've got an hour." He glanced behind again. "At least he doesn't know where we are."

Gary McAllister smiled as he looked at the screen on his bike once more.

"Mm, on their way to the Hog's Back, now why would that be?" He slotted the Blackberry into its holder beside the screen and started the bike again. "Let's find out."

CHAPTER FIVE

"He said Midas?" asked Konstantina, as she settled into one of the large, soft sofas in the lounge bar of the Ramada Hotel on the Hog's Back.

"Yes," replied Alan, easing himself down into a large armchair, trying hard not to lay the palms of his hands on the arms of the chair.

"Oh for goodness' sake," said Konstantina, "we need to get some bandages on your hands."

"They're not that bad," Alan Marks protested, but he was too late as the Greek girl was already up on her feet and heading for the reception desk. As she left the lounge area, she passed a waitress coming in with a tray of coffee and cakes and pointed her towards where Alan was sitting.

"That will be eight pounds fifty, sir," announced the waitress as she put the tray down and offered the bill to Alan Marks.

"Oh right." He fumbled in his pocket with his hands, trying not to rub them, and pulled out a ten pound note.

"Thank you sir," said the girl expectantly.

Alan took the hint. "Oh right, yes keep the change."

The waitress headed away, passing Konstantina, who was returning with a roll of bandage, a packet of plasters and a tube of antiseptic cream.

"They gave me this bandage at reception, and these plasters. Go wash those hands; it is pointless me putting antiseptic on dirty wounds."

Alan Marks duly obeyed and headed out towards the gents'.

As he crossed the foyer, had he glanced to the right through the glass entrance doors of the hotel, he would have seen the leather-clad figure on the Triumph Street Triple R entering the car park opposite the front entrance.

By the time he returned to Konstantina, she had poured out the coffee and was unscrewing the top of the tube of Savlon cream. She applied the cream as Alan winced and was about to unroll the bandages when he stopped her.

"No, just a couple of bigger plasters on this graze and that one." He held out his hands. "They're not as bad as they look, it's just grazes really."

"Ok, it's up to you." She conceded and duly put two plasters on the parts of his palms he had indicated. He tried hard to make out that it didn't hurt really, but failed.

"They are not good," she offered.

"They will be fine in a day or too, I've had worse."

"So," said Konstantina, "he was Greek you know?"

"Who was?" He looked puzzled.

"Midas. King Midas. You know the myth; everything he touched turned to gold? You said the man on the phone said Midas."

Alan pondered. "Yes he did, and he said he knew I had it. He knew I had Midas."

"Your bank card?" she suggested.

"It could be, but I'm not so sure."

"Well, it does turn everything to gold, sort of." Konstantina rationalised, "I mean it gives you money."

Alan hesitated. "He also said he knew about my wife Sally and that twat Barnes."

Konstantina put her coffee cup down with a look of outrage. "What? The bastard, the little bastard. I mean I knew he was playing around with some married woman, but I had no idea Alan, I'm sorry."

Alan shook his head. "No, don't be sorry for me. Oddly enough, when he said it, it all sort of made bizarre sense."

"Really? So what else did he say?"

"He said he would call me in an hour and we could meet and I could give him Midas before anyone got hurt."

"Hurt?" She looked worried. "Why would anyone get hurt? Who is he?"

"I don't know, but he might be from the bank." He began to run the call over in his mind. "Yes, he said 'we', he said 'we know about your wife and Justin Barnes and he has been dealt with'."

"Dealt with?" Konstantina sounded concerned. "That doesn't sound good, 'dealt with'. I mean he says you should give him this Midas thing, before somebody gets hurt, and Justin has been dealt with? Doesn't sound like anybody from the bank I've ever met."

Alan considered this. "No, I know what you mean. He did sound threatening. But then if he isn't from the bank, how come he knows about my card, and Sally and the little shit?"

Konstantina thought for a moment. "Perhaps he's the police?"

"Then how come he's not in a police car or a uniform? He would have said so, anyway."

"True," she conceded.

"There is one thing," Konstantina continued and was now suddenly smiling in a strangely false way that puzzled Alan. "Don't look behind you now but our friend has just come into the hotel." She grinned, a widely.

Alan suddenly felt a cold chill. He stayed looking at her. "Really? Where is he?"

She kept smiling. "He has seen us, but I don't think he knows that I saw him."

"Oh?" enquired Alan, still looking at her, "why do you say that?"

"Because," her grin dropped, "he has just gone into the toilets."

Alan shot a look over his shoulder, "Quick, come on." He was up on his feet and heading for the entrance, beckoning Konstantina as he went. She scrambled up from the sofa and followed, knocking the tray, cups and cafetiere to the floor as she went.

Just after they exited through the automatic doors at the front of the hotel, behind them, McAllister, looking towards the lounge, came out of the gents' toilets and walked across the foyer.

Outside a black taxi had just dropped off an elderly couple and the man was just paying the driver.

"You free, mate?" called Alan.

"Yeah, OK," replied the cabby, handing the man his change. "Where to?"

Alan opened the back door and ushered Konstantina into the back of the cab. "Eelmore Road, and quick."

Inside, McAllister strolled into the lounge and was at first baffled. Where were they? Then he saw the mess of coffee, cups and cakes on the floor just in front of where he had spied Konstantina and Marks, and the penny dropped. He spun around and headed at speed for the front entrance. As he got to the front doors an elderly couple were entering and McAllister crashed straight into the gentleman.

"I say," protested the man. "Watch where you're going."

"Sorry," pleaded McAllister as he disentangled himself from the elderly gent. He set off through the doors but felt a hand holding him back by his arm. It was the woman of the couple.

"You want to be a bit more careful you do. You could have knocked Reginald down."

"Yes, I said I'm sorry." McAllister was getting exasperated. He turned to go again. This time it was a hand on his shoulder that stopped him, it was the man. "There's no need to talk to my wife like that." He walked in front of the leather-clad Scot. "I think you should apologise to Pauline."

McAlister was on the verge of losing it, "I am terribly sorry Pauline." He looked down at the small, l grey-haired woman. He then quickly turned to the man. "And as for you, Reginald."

"Yes?" said the thin-lipped gent.

"Get out of the fucking way before I kick your geriatric arse into the middle of next fucking week." He pushed past the man and headed out of the doors just in time to see the back of a black cab exiting out onto the road with two people in the back. He glanced over to the yellow Porsche. "Damn!" He headed towards his bike.

Inside, Pauline was consoling Reginald who was obviously a little shocked. "Never mind dear, he was Scottish after all, and they can be real shitbags when they want to be. Let's have a sherry."

As the cab pulled into the small car park space outside the Farnborough Business Centre in Eelmore Road, Alan spoke through the dividing window. "Would you hang on, mate? We won't be long."

"OK." responded the cabbie, and picked up his radio. "Three seven at Eelmore road, waiting for the fare to go on." He turned back to Alan, who was opening the door. "Where to mate, you know after here?"

"Not sure yet," responded Alan. Konstantina followed him out of the cab, closing the door behind her.

"Right," answered the driver, "I get it. Hey mush. Come back here." Alan was taken aback, but turned back to the cab as the driver carried on. "Not sure, yet? Yeah and that's near 'can't quite decide' and a stone's throw from 'haven't got a bloody clue.' That'll be twenty quid. I wasn't born yesterday mate. I wait here, you bugger off in there and I never see you again, piss off."

Alan handed over a twenty pound note. "We will be back."

"I'm sure you will mate, and David Beckham will become Prime Minister." He took the money. "Do you know without the punters this job would be a piece of piss."

The cab drove away and Alan shook his head. "I don't believe that."

"So why are we here?" enquired Konstantina, getting his attention back.

"What? Oh yes, because I have a sneaky feeling I know how my card got to be so valuable." Alan stopped and put his hand out to halt Tina's progress. "Hang on, that door is open."

The A.M.S. offices were one of several in a row of purpose-built constructions, which where half small warehouse and half small offices. By the front door was a brass plaque with the words 'A.M.S. Security. Security Solutions For The Home And Business.' Alan was right; the front door was slightly ajar.

"Perhaps it's one of your staff?" suggested Tina.

"There were only four and I laid them off on Friday after my run-in with your ex. And it's not the cleaners. It's bank holiday."

"Perhaps it's them." Tina pointed to a small red van parked in front of the next unit. She read out the signage 'Surrey Office Guard'.

"Could be," said Alan, glancing over to the van and noticing that the engine was still running. "They look after all these offices. That would explain why the alarm's not going off. But why has he gone in, in such a hurry?"

"What do you mean?" she queried.

"He left his van running."

"Only one way to find out."

"Suppose so." Alan approached the door with Konstantina behind him and gently pushed it open. "Jesus Christ!"

Konstantina followed him in. "What is it? Oh my God."

The main office area was a shambles. There were papers everywhere and the two desks were overturned and the drawers scattered around the room. Two computer screens were smashed and on the floor and a large filing cabinet in one corner had all its drawers open and the locks had obviously been prised apart.

"I think somebody was looking for something," said Alan.

"Yes, but what?" Konstantina mused.

"I think I might know." Alan felt in his pocket and took out his bank card.

"Your bank card?"

"No," he responded as he went back out of the front door. "This."

Konstantina looked out and saw him looking at a small black plastic box on the wall by the door. The box was thin and flat and about the size of a mobile phone with a slit running down one side of it. On top of it was a small red LED light.

"Have you got your bank card?" he asked.

Konstantina duly produced it from the back pocket of her jeans. "Why?"

Alan smiled "May I?" He took the card and swiped it down the slit of the box. There was a small clicking sound in the door lock and the red light flashed green briefly before returning to red. "There." He handed her back her card.

"What have you done?" she was puzzled.

"I'm not sure," Alan continued, "but I may have made you a very rich woman."

Before she could ask any more, Alan was back inside the office.

"Where are you going?"

"The guard."

She was confused. "What guard?"

"Exactly, where is he? I can't think he did this," he looked at the devastation in the office, "but he must have been in here because the alarm is off. That means he must have used his real swipe card to get in. His van is still outside, so where is he?" Alan picked his way over the wrecked furniture and headed for a door at the far end of the room. "You stay there; I'm going to look in the warehouse."

He pushed the door open carefully. The warehouse was deserted apart from some stacks of boxes neatly arranged on pallets against the far side of the large room. Then he heard it; a dull thumping of something soft on metal. In the far right-hand corner was a large, grey, metal locker secured by a large padlock, and the door was vibrating slowly with a gentle rhythmic pounding. Then he heard the muffled voice. "Let me out you bastard, I'll suffocate you twat, let me out."

Alan walked towards the locker and then saw the trail of blood spatters on the floor in front of him leading to the grey metal door. He stopped. He needed something to prise the door open. He dashed back through the door to the office area. Konstantina was waiting expectantly.

"Well?"

"Whoever did this has trapped the guard in our clothes locker. I need something to open it." He started to scramble over the wreckage. "There is a screwdriver here somewhere, I had it in my desk."

"There." Konstantina retrieved a large black screwdriver from where it was sticking out under a pile of papers. She handed it to Alan.

"Thanks." He took the screwdriver and was turning back towards the doorway into the warehouse when he thought he caught a glimpse of something through the front window. The shock obviously registered on his face as Konstantina spun around and saw the same thing through the window. McAllister was heading down the road towards the building on his black Triumph.

"Shit!" exclaimed Alan Marks. "How the hell does he know where we are?"

"What do we do?" asked Konstantina with a hint of panic.

Alan thought for a fraction of a second and then looked at the screwdriver.

"We get out and fast."

"We can't leave the guard trapped, surely?" she protested.

His response was instant. "We won't have to." As he pushed past her and through the front door, she suddenly heard a deafeningly loud siren wailing all around her. Alan reappeared inside, holding the small card entry box that had been on the wall, the screws still in the rawplugs. He threw the screwdriver down. "We need this and that's set the alarm off." He was shouting over the shrill cacophony of the alarm. Suddenly the phone on the floor in the corner started ringing as well. "And that's the alarm company, come on." He grabbed her by the arm and pulled her through the doorway into the warehouse. "Follow me."

As they passed the locker, Konstantina heard the guard inside.

"What for God's sake is happening now? Let me out, I'm bleeding you bastard."

She stopped, but Alan was quick to grab her, once more giving a yell when he felt the pain in his hand as he tried to pull her.

"He'll be out as soon as the police get here."

"Police?" she was confused.

"Yes, they'll be here as soon as the alarm company doesn't get a response from the phone. Come on, for Christ's sake." As she hesitated, he started shouting even louder. "OK, do you want to stay and meet Scotland's answer to the Hells Angels? Judging by what he did to this guy," he gestured to the locker, "he is not a nice bloke, and we've got what he wants." He held up the small black box. "So let's get the hell out of here." He pulled her towards a door at the back of the warehouse. As he reached for the handle, he realised it was locked. "Jesus! I don't believe this." He kicked at the door to little effect. He was about to barge it when she held him back.

"Wait." She opened her bag and produced a small pair of tweezers. She knelt down and inserted one arm of the tiny implement into the central lock in the handle and started to turn it gently back and forth. "My dad is a locksmith."

From the outer office they suddenly heard a voice shouting over the alarm's wail in an unmistakable Scots accent; "Alan Marks? Alan Marks? I know you're in here and I know you've got Midas so why not be sensible, Marks?"

Alan looked up and saw the figure in black leather coming through the doorway into the warehouse. "Shit!"

"Done it," said Konstantina, pushing the door open, "come on." She pulled Alan through the door backwards as he saw the burly Scot running across the warehouse. As soon as they were outside, Alan looked around. Next to the door was a stack of wooden pallets.

"Quick, push," he shouted to Konstantina, putting the small black box on the floor. They ran around to the back of the stack and pushed at the top pallets. Three tumbled down in front of the doorway with a clatter and a crack of breaking wood.

"Come on," yelled Alan, disappearing around the side of the

building as McAllister appeared in the doorway and began to try to climb over the pile of crooked broken pallets.

Konstantina began to follow Alan, then suddenly turned back and headed towards the doorway. She snatched the small box up from the floor and as she did so caught McAllister's eye. She gave a grin and a small wave, said "Bye", and was gone.

McAllister grabbed the top pallet to heave himself over the pile and felt a splinter enter his left hand as the mangle of wood collapsed towards him against the open doorway. "Bollocks!"

Alan and Konstantina ran up the side of the building to the front. "The van," said Alan. They headed for the small red vehicle. Alan jumped into the driver's seat as Konstantina opened the door to the other side and they both leapt out again as a large barking, snarling German Shepherd flung himself against the black grille which separated his compartment from the front of the van. For an instant, they stood looking at each other. Then they both shrugged and dived back into the van. Alan pressed hard on the accelerator and, trying to use the ends of his fingers, spun the wheel to turn the van around in front of his office unit as McAllister emerged from the side of the building. The Scot stepped back just in time to avoid being run down by the small red van which clipped the handle bars of his Triumph parked on its stand in front of the office building, sending the gleaming black machine crashing to the ground.

"What the fuck?" screamed McAllister after the van which screeched out of the small car park and headed at speed down Eelmore Road.

"I'll get that little shit," he growled as he started to pick up his bike and then saw the broken brake handle. "Oh, for Christ's sake. You bastard."

When they reached the end of Eelmore Road, Alan swung the van hard left at the mini roundabout and headed for the dual carriageway. As they approached a larger roundabout which lead onto the dual carriageway running alongside Farnborough Airfield, the barking from the dog was unbearable in their ears.

"Where are we going?" shouted Konstantina, in an effort to be heard.

"What?" yelled Alan, turning the van onto the dual carriageway.

She tried again. "I said, where are we going?"

"Where are we what?" screamed Alan.

"I said," she tried once more, "where are we… oh forget it."

"Hang on," shouted Alan, slamming the brakes on and screeching to a halt as the car behind swerved to avoid ploughing into them and sped past with the owner's hand firmly on the horn.

"And the same to you," called Alan after the Ford Fiesta as it shot off in front of them. Then he turned and faced the dog who was now barking uncontrollably. He looked it straight in the eyes and bellowed in its face.

"Shut up!"

There was instant silence, followed by a slight whimper.

"Thank you," said Alan and turned to Konstantina. "You were saying?"

She suddenly burst into fits of giggles, but managed, "I said, where are we going?"

"I have a way with animals." smiled Alan. "I'm not sure where we are going yet, but I don't think our biker friend will be following us for a bit." He nodded across to the other side of the dual carriageway where two police cars with flashing lights were heading past at great speed. As they reached the roundabout and headed down to Eelmore Road, their sirens burst into life.

"Oh shit," he suddenly panicked. "What happened to…"

She stopped him with ,"This." She held up the small black box.

"Thank God," said Alan, taking it.

"What's so special about that?" she asked. "Why did you want it so badly?"

"Why?" said Alan. "Because I don't think my card is Midas, I think that this little box is Midas. And there is only one way to find out for sure."

A few minutes before, in Islington, Detective Sergeant Roy

Probert looked at the mobile phone which had started to vibrate on the floor of the lift at Thornton Mansions. He picked it up and read the caller ID: 'Mr Mac' He pressed the green receive button.

"Hello? Miss Thompson's mobile phone, who is this?"

The broad Scots voice on the other end replied. "Hello. Sorry, I was trying to get Sophie Thompson."

"And you have reached her phone. Would you mind telling me who you are, sir?"

"Well I might. Who are you?"

"You are talking to Detective Sergeant Probert of the Metropolitan Police, sir."

There was a brief silence and then a shocked response from the caller. "What? D.S. Pansy Probert?"

The detective was baffled. "And I am talking to?"

"Gary McAllister, you twat."

Probert was as shocked as the caller. "What, McAllister, Psychic Mac? Well bugger me."

"I'd rather not," responded McAllister. "Hang on, why are you answering Sophie's phone?"

"Sorry Mac," said the sergeant, "but I have to ask, why you are calling it? Did you know Miss Thompson?"

"Did I know her? What's happened to her?"

"Sorry Mac, I have to ask you first. How did you know Miss Thompson?"

"She is my soddin' P.A. you prat. What's going on?"

"I'm afraid I have some bad news for you Mac, Sophie Thompson is dead." There was a silence. If Probert had been able to see the caller, he would have watched the burly Scot slump to the ground outside the offices of A.M S. next to his broken bike.

"Hello? Mac?"

"Yeah I'm here, Pansy. Jesus. What the hell has happened?"

"I'm sorry mate but it looks like a mugging that's gone wrong. Whoever it was got her in the lift on her way up to her flat. If it's any consolation, she put up a fight, but it was a stabbing, one strike straight through the heart. If didn't know better I'd say it was a pro hit, but more likely some little druggie who got lucky. And as far as I can tell, she's been here since the early hours."

McAllister was just about able to take it in. "Yeah, well it would be the early hours, I sent her home you see."

"Sorry Mac, but home from where?" asked Probert.

"First Independent Bank HQ in King's Cross, Independent House. Fraud department."

"Oh yeah, I heard you got a cushy number in a bank."

McAllister decided not to rise to the bait. "Yeah, dead cushy Pansy, beats the Met."

Roy Probert heard the sarcasm but was curious. "A funny time to be working, Mac, if you don't mind me saying. I mean, a Sunday night into bank holiday Monday?"

"Don't even go there," responded McAllister. "I'm on a case down in Hampshire at the moment that is turning into a pain in the arse. I was calling Sophie because I need a hire car or bike or, what the hell, I'll sort it, Oh shit." He found he was beginning to feel quite emotional.

"You OK, Mac?" enquired the detective .

"Yeah, it's just a bit of a shock if I'm honest; she was a nice person. What is the bloody world coming to, son? Somebody like her, never done anything to anyone and all for what, a few quid out of her handbag?"

"Oh no," responded Probert. "Her handbag is still here. Not even opened as far as I can tell."

McAllister was confused. "But you said it was a mugging?"

"Yeah, reckon he was disturbed. Hey, one thing Mac, does the word 'mida' mean anything to you?"

McAllister, though stunned by the question, was rather proud of his reaction. "'Mida'? No, can't say as it does, why?" He was amazed he sounded so nonchalant.

"Oh nothing, she obviously didn't die straight away and she's tried to scrawl something in her own blood, it looks like mida or mika or mila. Can't make it out. Probably nothing like that; it's all over the place to be honest. Anyway, look, when you're back, pop into Maida Vale and dash out a statement."

"A statement?" McAllister was a little thrown.

"Yeah, you might be one of the last people to see her. You know what it's like mate, I've got to tie up the paperwork. No rush. When you're back. Poor cow. Oh before you go, I've got to ask you. I mean, I'm saying mugging, but you don't know of anyone who might have wanted to hurt her?"

"Sophie? Jesus, no," said McAllister.

"I mean, do you know of any men friends, or even women if you follow?"

"No, not at all." In that instant, it struck McAllister how little he actually knew about his P.A. And that was sad.

"Any family contacts?"

McAllister was grasping at straws. "She mentioned a sister in Eastbourne, but if you call our HR department in the morning they would know."

"Thanks, Mac. Sorry to be the bearer of bad news. Look when you come in we'll go and sink a few. I want to pick your brains. To be honest with you, I'm getting sick of meaningless crap like this. I could do to get out of this game and be off on all-expenses trips like you obviously get eh?"

"What? Oh yeah, sure." McAllister responded.

"Sorry mate, I can tell it's got to you. No sense in it, is there? Like you said, somebody like her and all for what, eh? Why?"

McAllister ended the call and stood for a moment beside the broken Triumph. "Why? Why indeed?"

His pondering was suddenly broken by the wail of police sirens and he looked up to see two patrol cars heading down Eelmore Road towards him. This was going to be interesting to explain. He reached in his pocket for his cigarettes. He took them out, looked at them and threw the packet away.

CHAPTER SIX

As the Dodecanese Express rounded the headland of the Greek island of Symi, the Port of Yialos began to reveal itself to Nikos Stavroulis. He stood at the front on the top deck of the high-speed catamaran ferry, basking in the warm evening breeze. As the headland retreated, the myriad of white houses like small sugar cubes revealed themselves slowly, layer upon layer, as they spread from the sea and the harbour up the hillside to a blue and white church bathed in the evening light. For those who lived there or visited regularly, whether by day, or night when the scene was transformed into a huge fairyland of lights, this first revelation of one of the most beautiful island sights in the world never failed to amaze. Then the smell hit him as the boat neared the land. That musky, heavy and pungent smell of wild herbs; thyme and rosemary, oregano and wild sage. It was heavy on the warm evening air and just for a moment, as he closed his eyes, Nikos forgot all about his problem. He was a boy again, running with his friends down to the stony beaches and chasing goats and girls through long-neglected olive groves. Hunting tortoise on the craggy headland at Marathunta bay and diving for octopus in the bay of St George. Throwing firecrackers into the church on Easter night and being scolded by the fierce papas and the not so fierce old ladies, who then grabbed you and showered you with Easter biscuits and kisses. For a brief moment he was innocent again. But only for a brief moment, because his mobile rang, causing him to jump with alarm. He flipped it open and looked at the screen. "Oh my God." He answered immediately.

"Yes godmother, its Nikos. No, I'm just getting there now. Yes, it looks as beautiful as ever." He began to walk to the back of the boat as it started to turn, ready to back into the quayside. "I will, godmother, I will as soon as I can. Just one thing, if you don't mind me suggesting it, a thought occurred to me…" He coughed and wondered whether to continue, but as he had begun, he was already committed. "Yes a thought, while I was on the plane. What was it? You know I said my boys could make the piece of equipment for you, and indeed they did and you received it and…, no I am getting to the point godmother. The thing is they only made it to the blueprints you sent to us. I mean, they are clever but they are not… No, what I'm suggesting is, well, whoever invented the thing might well be the one who…" Nikos stopped halfway down the steps to the lower deck as his godmother spoke and he slowly repeated her words. "He's dead. He died five minutes after he finished the design? OK... No I don't need to know how…His what got crushed?…Yes that is a nasty way to go. I agree. No boy should go that way, especially such a talented one…You're right, a terrible waste for such a promising student…Yes I will keep that in mind, godmother." He began to move again. "Of course I will give your regards to my mother… What? Yes, a watch, yes… Very expensive…Very. I will… *Yassou*."

He folded his mobile and sighed. How the hell had he got into this situation?

"She wouldn't really kill me, would she? She just might."

The broad rear gangway of the ferry was dropping to the quayside ready to disgorge its cargo of people and assorted cars and motorbikes. On the quay a varied group of trucks surrounded by a gaggle of people was waiting. As the heavy metal gangway hit the stone, the first people laden with bags were already on their way off. Almost immediately, a mêlée of vehicles and people going both ways ensued. It never failed to amaze Nikos that nobody actually died every time a ferry came in. He pushed his way through the mob to the front. As he stepped off the gangway, a rather smart man in light tan trousers and a blazer, so obviously English, wandered in front of him. The man stopped, transfixed by the sight of cars, vans, people and livestock all jostling to get off and on the boat at the same time. He turned to the equally smart middle-aged woman next to him and said: "Good God this is organised chaos."

Nikos could not help himself as he nudged the couple to one side and lapsed into his broadest Australian. "It may be chaos mate, but it sure as hell ain't organised."

As he broke free of the crowd, he saw the large bearded figure of Kostas sitting at a small table outside Minas Café. There were two glasses of beer on the table. Kostas was in his late forties overweight, and probably Nikos' oldest friend. As Nikos approached the table, Kostas greeted him with: "Your beer, boss, and what the hell is all this about? I've had Loukia on the phone in tears and I can't understand a word she's on about. Something about your godmother, a man with a gun who is going to shag her and somebody in England. She was in a hell of a mess. What is going on?"

Nikos downed the beer in one. "I'll tell you later, right now I need you to get our three technical whiz kids, the little bastards, together and quick. And I mean like immediately. We will need somewhere quiet."

Kostas was thrown by Nikos' attitude. Nikos' default manner was a happy-go-lucky guy, but this was obviously serious. For one thing, he never drank beer down in one.

Nikos put the glass down and suddenly called out to a woman who was passing on a moped. "Jean! Jean! Stop, Jean!" He put his fingers to his lips and whistled loudly. The trim woman of middle years, with blonde bobbed hair and wearing a smart black cocktail dress, turned the moped and approached the table. She stopped the engine and spoke through cherry red lipstick in a broad Birmingham accent.

"Excuse me Mr Stavroulis, but I am not one of your common floozies who come at your beck and call, or in this case your whistle. Bloody cheek. What d'you think I am, some sort of tart? Don't answer that."

Nikos smiled. "Then how come you stopped? Ah must have been shock."

She began to grin. "Shock? Shock? And why would it be shock, you cheeky bleeder?"

"Well," said Nikos, "I mean, it's got to have been a while since any bloke whistled at you."

She feigned effrontery and turned to Kostas. "Kostas, smack him. Go on, there's a free drink at my bar for you if you smack him one."

"One drink?" queried Kostas.

"What else do you want?"

Kostas put his hands behind his neck and leaned back. "Any chance of a blow job?"

Jean was warming to the banter. "Bloody typical Greek men. Brains in pants. From what I've heard, it would be like sucking on a matchstick. Anyway Nikos, what do you want? I've got my bar to open up top, I can't stand around here chatting to you two aging *kamaki*, fascinating though this intellectual banter is."

Nikos beckoned her closer and lowered his voice. "Any chance of using the courtyard in front of your bar for half an hour? I need somewhere for a quiet meeting."

She was puzzled. "Well yeah, but when? I mean, I open at half nine."

"I have to pop in on Mama, but then we'll be up there." He squeezed her hand. "Don't worry, we'll be finished well before nine thirty. It's nothing dodgy."

She started up the moped and laughed. "Nikos Stavroulis, with you it's always something dodgy." She knew him too well, and she also knew that something was very wrong.

"What about the dog?" asked Konstantina as Alan turned the van into the car park of the Ramada Jarvis Hotel on the Hog's Back.

"Good point," he replied. "We can hardly leave the poor sod in the van… I know." He parked the van on the opposite side of the car park to the yellow Porsche. "You still got the car keys?"

"Yes, why?"

"Good." He looked in the storage well in the driver's door and shook his head. "No." Then he opened the glove compartment of the van and pulled out a box of tissues. "Perfect." He began to wipe the steering wheel and the inside door handle. "Here." He offered her the tissues. "Wipe anything you've touched." She looked puzzled. "Finger prints," he explained. "I've seen it on the telly. They always do this, oh and the outside handle." He stepped from the van. Konstantina was smiling and shaking her head, but she obeyed.

He leant back into the van and picked up the small black box from the floor. He handed it to Konstantina. "Take this and put it in the glove box of the Porsche. Start the car and I'll be out in a minute." He was heading for the hotel reception when he turned back "Oh, bang on the roof of the van, would you?"

Stepping out of the van, she looked at him as if he was talking a foreign language. "What?"

"The roof of the van, bang on it."

She shrugged her shoulders and then obliged. Immediately the dog broke into loud barking and howling. It was so forceful that Konstantina jumped back in alarm.

Alan shouted, so as to be heard. "Now start my car." He disappeared inside the hotel as she headed for the Porsche.

The girl at reception looked up as Alan Marks approached. "Can I help you, sir?"

He smiled but tried to look extremely concerned, just as the elderly couple from the taxi exited the lounge and passed behind him. "Look, I don't want to worry you," he said, "but somebody has left a dog in a van out there and it's going mad. It's a warm day and, well, it was there when we left almost an hour ago and it's still there now."

"A dog, left in a van for an hour?" piped up the elderly Pauline, her words ever so slightly slurred, "that's shocking. Did you hear that, Reginald?"

"I did," replied the old man with a grin on his face, slightly the worse for wear. "Dog in a van, shocking."

The receptionist responded with brisk efficiency. "No need to worry Mrs Parker, I'll get it sorted out immediately." She turned to Alan. "Thank you sir, I will get the house manager to look into it." She picked up her phone as Alan turned away and set off for the door.

"I say, young man?" It was the old lady beckoning him back. Alan turned and approached her. She beckoned him even closer and lowered her voice to almost a whisper. "I wouldn't be surprised if it was that nasty Scotsman who was here earlier." Alan could smell the sherry now. "Nasty man, nasty."

Reginald echoed his wife "Nasty."

She glowered at him. "Shush, I said that."

Reginald continued in his own world. "Nasty."

Pauline rolled her eyes and settled on Alan again. "Anyway, young man, if I was you I would get gone and quick, in case he comes back and finds out you've told on him. He's a nasty man, nasty."

"Nasty," echoed Reginald again.

Alan smiled at the elderly lady. "Thanks, I will bear that in mind, and I'll get going. Goodbye." He shook her hand and headed away.

The old lady watched him go, then turned to the receptionist as she put the phone down.

"Nice arse."

The girl was taken aback, then glanced to where Alan was exiting through the doors. She smiled, nodded at the old lady and winked.

"Let's go," said Alan settling into the passenger seat of the Porsche.

"Where to, oh masterful one?" chuckled Konstantina.

"Oh, I'm sorry." Alan was suddenly embarrassed. "I didn't mean to sound…"

"I'm joking," she reassured him. "What's happening with the dog?"

"It is being sorted."

"Good. I tell you what, I don't know about you Mr Marks; but I'm starving, I haven't eaten all day and it's nearly six."

Alan looked at his watch. "So it is, Christ what happened to the day?"

"Quite a lot, what is it you say in England, 'time flies when you're having fun'?"

He laughed. "Yeah, not sure it's all been fun. Look, if you want we can get something to eat?" He was suddenly a little shy. "I mean, you know if you fancy it?"

She smiled and he detected a slight blush. "Yes, why not?"

"Great, but er, if you don't mind, could we go back to the Lloyds cash machine in Frimley first? We know that one works."

"Frimley?" Konstantina backed the Porsche out of its space and then turned it towards the exit. "Frimley first? OK, but why?"

"Because I want to know if I've made you as rich as me," he explained.

"I have no idea what you are talking about Alan Marks,' said the Greek girl, "but I am perfectly willing to find out."

He was just beginning to think how quickly they had become so familiar with each other when, as they turned onto the Hog's Back, she put her foot down and Alan was pressed back into his seat with a sudden jolt. "Wooo!" she exclaimed, "I'm getting the hang of this now."

Alan was less than convinced.

McAllister sat on the kerb in Eelmore Road and spoke into his Blackberry. "I seem to have convinced the local cops that I was here totally coincidently to check on our asset, you know as Marks has gone bust." He had felt the need to update Sir Charles as the local police would no doubt check his story with the bank. "They thought it was odd being a bank holiday but I gave them the old 'well that's the time the clients least expect it' bullshit… No sir, the security guard said it wasn't me that bundled him in at knifepoint. He didn't see who it was but it wasn't a Scotsman…Yeah, well they have checked me out of course and once they knew who I was it turns out there are others out there who think the deputy in the Met is a tosser. So I'm one of the good guys... No, I don't think Marks trashed his own place sir, I think somebody broke in…Why? Who knows? I don't see how anyone else could know about Midas, do you sir?.. No sir, I think Marks has got it. Whether he knows what it is, is another matter… Well yes sir, he might…I'm waiting for a hire car…Yes, total nightmare, but I've found one…Yes I will get him sir, no matter how long it… No I hope it doesn't either. Look, it occurs to me he may try other banks now we have shut down our facility. So I wondered if you wanted to…No that's up to you Sir of course…Yes, we know it will take them weeks, possibly months because it's our card but... Very well sir your call. Oh there is one other thing…" He was about to tell Sir Charles about Sophie but he stopped himself. "But it can wait sir… No, nothing, nothing important to you, sir…Yes I will, as soon as I have anything."

As he finished the call he reflected. Why hadn't he told Sir Charles about Sophie? He wasn't worried that he hadn't mentioned it, just curious. It was something he had discovered about himself, about how he operated. Sometimes he just didn't reveal all his cards, or go with an obvious course of action. Sometimes he had an instinct to hold back and would usually find, sometime later, that there was a very good reason, he just wasn't aware of it at the time. He smiled. "It all adds to the Psychic Mac persona." He didn't know why he hadn't mentioned the death of his P.A., but he hadn't, and he had no doubt that at some point in the not too distant future he would find himself saying "Oh yes Mac that was why."

What worried him far more now was, where was his soddin' car? And looking at the screen he now had in his hands, why was Alan Marks in Frimley High Street?

In Symi, Nikos was struggling as he made his way up to the bar high above the main harbour. As a youngster he would have thought nothing of bounding up the four hundred or so steps of the main *kalistrata* which linked the lower port of Yialos with the higher village of Chorio. Even in the middle of the day he would have hardly have felt it. Now, as he puffed his way past the elegant white buildings with their Romanesque embellishments, a relic of the Italian occupation and wealthier times, he was out of breath. As he passed the large Taverna Georgio just before the village square, several people glanced and nodded at him. A few of the men playing backgammon outside a café by the square exchanged greetings and smiled "*Yassou Niko, ti kaniss?*" (How are you?) Nikos gasped a response "*Kala!*" (Good) which he felt far from. Nikos was well known in Symi. Not always well liked, but well known. Up a narrow winding street beyond the main village square was a small bar. It stood above the stone street and steps rose up to a double wooden doorway. On the whitewashed wall, lit from above by a dim single lamp was a blue painted sign 'Jean & Tonic Bar. The Late Place.'

Nikos mounted the steps and pushed one of the doors open. Inside was a small stone courtyard which led through to the inner bar, a small room decorated with paintings and photographs and signed football shirts of Aston Villa. Nikos poked his head through the door into the inner bar. "Jean?" The bobbed blonde head came up from behind the bar. "Bloody beer pump's playing up again, soddin' thing." She grabbed a hammer that was lying on the bar, disappeared and Nikos heard a loud clanking sound. She re-emerged. "Here, have a beer so I can get it going." She pushed a glass under the beer spout and attempted to pull a pint. The froth sputtered and coughed and then beer began to arrive. "Bingo. Thank Christ for that." As she filled the glass, she eyed Nikos. "So Mr Stavroulis, what's wrong ?"

"Wrong?" He took the beer. "Why would anything be wrong? No nothing's wrong."

She took the top of the ice bucket and popped two cubes into a glass. "Nothing's wrong? Right, and I'm Naomi bloody Campbell. Don't kid a kidder, what's up?"

As Nikos sipped his beer, she poured herself a scotch. "Well?"

He put the glass down. "Nothing you would want to know about."

She raised her glass "*Yammas*. Hey it's nothing to do with your godmother, is it? It is, I can tell by your face. You're right, I don't want to know, so don't tell me. I don't want a horse's head in my bed, mind you, it would beat what's there now."

"Look," said Nikos, lowering his voice. "I know you've got to set up in here while we're having our little get together out there," he pointed out to the courtyard, "but keep anything you hear to yourself, please."

For the second time that night, she acted affronted. "Nikos Stavroulis, this bar is like a Catholic confessional, what is said in here, stays in here. My God, if I told half the things I've heard in here, nobody on this island would be married for a start. I mean, did I ever tell you about your dear old mum and the baker's son? No. And do you know why I didn't tell you? Cause it never happened." He managed a small grin. "Jesus Christ Nikos, what's happened to your sense of humour? You really are in trouble, aren't you? Well just be careful."

The outer door opened and Kostas came into the courtyard followed by two boys in their mid-teens. Nikos stepped out of the bar to meet them. "Welcome gentlemen. I would offer you a drink but quite frankly until I discover which one of you little twats has tried to be clever with me I'm not feeling that generous. Where's Dimitri, anyway?"

In Frimley High Street, Konstantina turned off the engine. "Right, so you want me to use my card in that cash machine and see what happens?"

"Exactly." Alan explained the theory once more. "Look, like I said, when I went to the office on Friday night it was dark. I swiped my bank card in the security box first, by mistake, saw what I had done and then used the proper entry card."

"And you think that turned your card into a lottery winner?"

Alan shrugged his shoulders. "I don't know, but it's the only thing that makes sense. I've not done anything else with the card and it didn't do this last week."

She began to open the door. "Oh well, what the hell?"

As they approached the machine, she turned to him. "Eh, do I get to keep the money if it does it right?"

Alan laughed. "Well, I might take a commission."

She laughed as well. "Tell you what, if it works I buy dinner, deal?"

"OK," he responded, "deal."

"Put out your hand?" she demanded. "Palm up."

Puzzled, he obeyed and extended his right hand as she spat on her own hand and slapped it, palm down, onto Alan's. He yelped and she grabbed it. "I'm so sorry, I forgot. It's just the way we seal a bargain in Greece."

"Very elegant." Alan smiled. "It's OK, it's not that bad, but for that you get to buy the wine too."

She faced the cash machine. "Here goes." She typed in her pin number when requested.

"How much should I ask for?"

"Doesn't matter; I just want to see if it works."

"OK, two hundred." She finished the request and the card was returned. They both watched the machine as two hundred pounds was dispensed very quickly. There was silence. "Right, well that seems to be it."

"Wait," said Alan. "Listen."

She leaned in to the machine, and she could hear what he heard; a whirring and clicking and then another sheaf of notes appeared. She took them, and immediately more began coming.

"Oh my God, how do we stop it?" She was passing notes to Alan, and dropping some on the floor. "Oh my God," she cried as the machine appeared to go into overdrive.

"Press cancel." He leaned over and pressed the red button. The process stopped. They both stood for a moment in silence looking at the machine and then Konstantina erupted in joyous squeals of delight as she performed a small dance on the spot and then flung herself at Alan.

Alan looked up and down the street. “Hey, calm down, you’ll attract attention.” He indicated, with a nod, a small elderly man with a Jack Russell on a lead walking on the other side of the road. He was glancing over with a bemused expression on his face.

“Oh sorry, but I can’t believe it,” she whispered, stuffing some notes into her pockets and then bent down and picked up others and began to put them into her handbag as Alan knelt to help her.

She was finding it hard to contain her enthusiasm and so as she spoke it was through gritted teeth but with a giggle. “This is just incredible, I mean just incredible.”

“That is just what it is,” said Alan picking up some notes and handing them to her, “incredible.” As he looked up, he met her eyes with his. “Incredible.” There was a pause and then she broke the moment with: “So hang on, that little box did this to my card, and yours. But why?”

“Why?” he said, standing up. “Why? Good question.”

She rose up, pushing the last notes into her bag and struggling with the catch. “Where did you get it?”

“Ah well, that’s just it. It was given to me, as a sort of sample,” he paused, “by a Greek.”

She looked up immediately. “You’re kidding? You’re not kidding. My God, hey you know what they say about us don’t you? Beware of Greeks…”

He finished it with her. “Bearing gifts. Yes I know.”

She laughed. “Whoever it was can’t have been Greek.”

“Why not?”

“Look, I’m Greek, trust me no Greek would willingly give you all that money…Unless,” she waivered.

He was intrigued, “Unless?”

“Unless there was something in it for him.”

"Oh I see," said Alan, "that's how you Greeks are, is it? And I suppose now you're only going to buy me dinner if there is something in it for you?"

She gave him a knowing smile as they walked back to the Porsche.

"You English are not very good at this, are you?"

He opened the door and got in and she sat down bedside him in the driver's seat.

"What do you mean?" he asked.

"There was already something in it for me." She shifted in her seat and pulled the bank card from her pocket. "I agreed to buy you dinner if the card worked, right?"

"Right, so?"

"So it worked. You get dinner, but I get…" she held up her card and kissed it, "…a never ending supply of money. Now who do you think got the best deal?"

Alan Marks laughed out loud. He took the small black security card reader from the glove compartment. "OK, you win, but I can't see what the bloke who gave me this got out of it."

"True." She started the engine. "Who was he anyway?"

Nikos Stavroulis was wondering how the hell he had ever got into this. Standing now in the small courtyard of the Jean and Tonic Bar, looking at two very confused young boys, he was wishing he never had got into it.

"So you two are trying to tell me that you can think of no way that a copy of the special card copier we made could have ended up in England?"

The response was silence and blank faces. "If one of you two little twats has shafted me I will have your balls." There was still no response… "Jesus this is a nightmare." And like all nightmare notions, it had seemed a good one at the time. The Hellas I.T. Greek government funded-scheme paid out money to companies who encouraged computer development for young people on the

Greek islands. Lots of money. The more remote, small and deserving the island, the more money was available. Nikos came from Symi. Symi was small. It was reasonably remote, well, a ferry ride from Rhodes. Deserving? By the time Nikos had finished wining, dining , and generally showing the rather prim young lady from Hellas I.T. in Athens a good time , it was deserving. Adrianna Savvastopolou left on the ferry back to Rhodes without her virginity but with a smile on her face, and Nikos had secured a very healthy grant. Stavroulis Computing was born. All he had to do then was find the young people he told Adrianna he already had: The youngsters desperate to develop a career in megabytes as opposed to fishing, goats or having sex with tourist girls. He found three at the school. Petros, sixteen, spotty, shy, thin and pale, and into a Nintendo DS his uncle had sent him from Athens last Easter. Yiannis, seventeen and a mathematical obsessive. Yiannis could calculate the variable density of a body travelling at three times the speed of light given that the variable was x and the relative power was three to the seventh cubed. He consequently had no girlfriends, in fact no friends at all. The last candidate was Dimitri who was nineteen and disabled. In the final throes of ecstasy, whilst being taken from behind, bent doggy fashion on the beach at Aya Marina, Miss Savvastopolou had revealed that, in the true European spirit of inclusivity and diversity, if a disabled youngster was included in the scheme the grant tripled. Nikos did check this with her, and had it confirmed by the climaxing Adrianna who shouted "*Neh*," the Greek for yes, several times, very loudly. Dimitri was therefore recruited.

Nikos could see, however, looking at Petros and Yiannis, that when it came to who had copied Midas, they hadn't a clue what he was talking about. That left Dimitri and that was unthinkable. He could operate a computer in terms of basic word processing and send e-mail but that was about it. He was born twisted and distorted and it was thought he would not survive. He did, but at the age of nineteen he was confined to a wheelchair most of the time, being unable to walk, just about able to talk, and after numerous operations in Athens he was still severely disabled.

"He's gone fishing?" questioned Nikos, looking at the blank faces in front of him.

Kostas looked at Nikos with a puzzled expression. "But you said he could go with his father for the week."

"I did?" Nikos stopped himself. "I did."

When it came to Dimitri, he got special treatment in terms of time off because Dimitri was essential to the operation of Stavroulis Computing as his grant made Nikos a healthy profit, even if none of the supposed software development products the boys were apparently working on brought in a euro. None of them did of course, except for the special job he had the boys do for his godmother. And that was the nub of the problem.

If only he hadn't had too much to drink at his cousin Georgo's wedding and got into conversation with his very sober godmother. "Oh yes, I have my own computing business and it's doing very well," he could hear the words coming back to haunt him. "Of course the secret is employing experts, young people who know all about this cyber stuff." And then the fatal piece of boasting. "Make a piece of kit from blueprints? Well there aren't many outfits in Greece who could do it, but we can, oh yes." Oh yes, what a fool he had been. Of course he would have to see the blueprints. They were produced in a matter of minutes. Straight away Nikos found himself in the back room of the *taverna* in Thessaloniki where the wedding was being held, surveying them, and pretending to know what he was talking about. Then, with another glass of *retsina* inside him, he went one step too far. "Ah well I didn't realise it was so complex. In fact, there is no other company in Greece or Europe for that matter who could do this." Why the hell did he say it? When Mrs Manidaki told him what she was prepared to pay, it wasn't the time to say "I was only joking."

Accompanied by one of his godmother's gorillas, Paco, he had sweated for twenty four hours before he got to Symi and showed the boys the plans. He was so beyond relieved when Yiannis said: "Yeah, that's easy, we'll need to adapt a small motherboard and create the software package but otherwise no problem." When the boys asked what it was for, he explained he had been told it was to copy bank and credit cards. They were of course sworn to secrecy because it was top secret government business and a very important contract. They made the small rectangular card reader, complete with its own small keyboard, adapted from a palmtop, in two weeks. The device was delivered by hand and Nikos was several hundred thousand euros better off. Now he was staring into the abyss. He called inside to the bar. "Jean, get me another drink."

Kostas could see he was getting desperate. He took him away from the boys, up towards the doorway into the bar. "Look Niko, these boys wouldn't do you over, even if they knew how, and I don't think they do. And as for Dimitri, he doesn't even do any of the software stuff, he couldn't, and he didn't have anything to do with the making of that special card thing."

"I know," Nikos was resigned, "but Kostas, I am in the shit. We are all in the shit. Somehow that thing, or a copy of it, has turned up in England."

"But we haven't got any connections in England," protested Kostas.

"Your beer, Mr Stavroulis." It was Jean. She sidled through the door with a large glass of pale amber beer. "And I hope I'm getting paid for this, your tab is getting to be longer than 'War and Peace'." She saw Kostas' puzzled expression. "It's a book, a very long book... Oh never mind. Beer, Kostas?'" Kostas nodded his head. "On his tab?" Kostas nodded again. "I thought so. Cheeky bleeder, I'm running a charity for Greek alcoholics here." She turned to go back into the bar and then turned her head back. "And I am not listening to your business as you know, but you do have a connection in England." She was disappearing into the bar but Nikos stopped her.

"What do you mean?"

She turned back again. "You have a connection in England."

Both men looked at her blankly. "Nikos, I distinctly remember you telling me about some bloke you met at the Euro Trade Fair in Paris. You asked me where Hampshire was 'cause that's where he came from. Sparks, Larks, something like that."

"Marks!" The realisation dawned on Nikos. "Ian Marks, no Adam, Alan, that was it Alan Marks. He sells house alarms in England to protect people from burglars. He couldn't get his head around the fact that there would be no market for them here."

"There you are then, that's your connection."

Kostas chipped in. "But hang on. We haven't sent him the thing we made for Mrs Manidaki. We sent that to her people, and she got it, I checked."

Nikos was puzzled. What he was thinking made no sense, but he said it anyway. "We didn't send him the card copier, but I sent him something else. Perhaps that's it. I can't see how, but it's the only thing that makes any sense."

Kostas was now totally confused. "Niko, what are you talking about?"

"I met this Marks at the trade fair and I told him about the cheap Chinese swipe entry boxes we had. I said they were Greek, of course, and that we could do a deal. Let's face it, we needed to do a deal we haven't shifted any. He was interested, and pissed at the time, so I sent him a sample with a couple of cards. He wasn't sure if it would work on the English electrical system even though I told him it ran on batteries and you just put it on the door with its own lock. I even sent the lock. He wanted to see if it could operate with his alarms. I haven't heard from him. Very odd people, the English."

"Thank you," said Jean. "Well there you are, that's your English connection."

"But that entry box isn't the thing we made for your godmother Niko," protested Kostas.

"Same casing," muttered Petros.

Both men looked at him instantly and spoke together. "What?"

Petros felt obliged to continue, stuttering as he went. "We used the case from one of the entry things to put it in." He started talking as if he was defending himself and his lower lip trembled. "It was the right size and had the slot in the right place and you said it would be cheaper 'cause nobody was buying the Chinese shit, and..."

"What?" screamed Nikos.

"And it's the only thing we have sent to England?"

As he said this the outer door from the courtyard to the street creaked open.

"Well if it's the only thing you have sent, then that must be it."

Framed in the doorway was the slender figure of Manos who was texting on his mobile as he spoke. "Surprised to see me? I said it would be soon, Stavroulis." He folded the phone shut. "Nice easy flight, wasn't it? That blonde hostess had great tits."

Inside the bar, the phone rang. Almost instantly Jean emerged holding a cordless handset. "Nikos, it's for you, I think it's…" she saw Manos. "Who the hell are you? I'm not open yet." She looked him up and down. "Mind you, for you I could make an exception."

Manos smiled, a less than warm smile. "I am Manos and you are perfectly safe, English lady, I only like the taste of fresh meat."

As she passed the handset to Nikos, she advanced towards Manos totally un-phased and with an equally cold smile spoke to him in perfect Greek. "I'd eat you for breakfast, you arrogant little twat. Anyway, I gave up teaching a long time ago, now I prefer mature, real men not skinny boys from, let me see, Athens I believe by that accent." She could tell by his puzzled reaction she had hit the mark. She put her hands on his shoulders, turned him around and then in her native tongue said, "so piss off." She pushed him out of the door and slammed it shut behind him. The boys sitting in the courtyard were amazed. As she turned, the door opened again and Manos tried to step in. "I am here to see Nikos Stavroulis."

"There he is," indicated Jean, "so now you've seen him." In one swift movement, he was out of the door again and she had slammed it shut and turned the key.

Then she opened one of the top shutter sections of the door which looked out onto the street, and smiling, spoke. "Come back when you've grown up, or nine thirty whichever is the sooner. "Til then," she dropped the smile, "fuck off." She shut the wooden opening and walked back inside the bar.

Nikos could hear a voice on the end of the phone. "Nikos? Nikos?" He recognised it and his heart sank. He put the phone to his ear. "Yes, godmother?"

The thin voice was very matter-of-fact. "I knew this Marks person had the device, I just didn't know for sure how he got it. Now I do. You have two choices. Get it back, Nikos, or I will instruct Manos to help you get it back, understand?"

Nikos realised there was only one choice in reality. "Yes, godmother."

"Good." Nikos heard a television in the background. The voice yawned. "So get on with it. I have to go, 'Who Wants To Be A Millionaire' is starting, don't make me miss it. Goodbye."

The line went dead. Nikos sighed. Jean appeared in the doorway and took the phone from him. "Use your mobile not my phone bill, and it's double zero double four."

"What is?" asked Nikos. She smiled at him. "The dialling code for England."

Gary McAllister didn't like cars, and he particularly didn't like automatics.

"I said I wanted a manual, not an automatic."

The young lady in the smart red Hertz uniform smiled the well-practised customer care smile. "I am aware of that, sir, but unfortunately at short notice this is all I could locate. However, I can tell you that you will be getting it at the reduced rate for corporate clients and a special offer if you rebook within two weeks. Here are the keys and the discount vouchers and if you would like me to show you…"

"Stop." McAllister stopped short of shouting and tried to stay calm. "I have waited for over two hours for this heap of Toyota shit and I am not about to go through all this crap, thank you." He took the keys, opened the door, threw his bag, phone and small computer screen into the passenger seat, got into the car, started it and pulled away at speed, leaving the girl open-mouthed on the pavement.

He glanced at the screen on the seat beside him and picked up his mobile phone.

"Now Mr Marks, where are you?"

"You didn't have to have the most expensive thing on the specials board just because I was paying." Konstantina smiled as Alan took a mouthful of his steak and looked up at the large blackboard on the wall of the Dolce Italia Restaurant in Farnborough.

"True, but I like steak, and the rib eye just happened to be the most expensive. Anyway, you are a woman of substance now, you can afford it. So about the wine." He sipped the rich red. "I am very impressed. You ordered that as if you know about wine. I mean not that a woman, well, a Greek woman shouldn't know about wine but."

She interrupted him "They have a special board for that, too." She pointed to the opposite wall.

"So they have, you cheated. Why didn't I spot that?" He looked at the four chalked-up wines on the blackboard. "Hey, this must be the special reserve Chianti." He drank some more. "You are driving, yes?" He was having fun, and also realised, as she did, that he was flirting too. "You see, with my expensive steak I am working on the Greek principle of getting something out of the deal. That is what you said, isn't it?"

She laughed quietly, but before she could respond, his mobile phone rang. Alan picked it up and looked at the small blue screen. "Unknown number. Now then, who can this be I wonder? Our mystery Scotsman, do you think?" He put it to his ear.

"Hello. Hello. Jesus, Nikos. Am I glad you rang, I was going to call you…sorry, what? This is a dreadful line...The swipe card box? Funny you should say that…Calm down, I can't understand you… Yes I do know what it can do… Bring it to you? What in Greece? You're having a laugh aren't you? Nikos why would I want to… hello? Nikos? Hello…sorry who is this?"

Konstantina watched Alan and his expression as it changed from puzzled to deep concern and then to fear.

"Yes, I understand, forty eight hours…In person. I get it… I do understand that yes…Hello? Hello?" He stared at the phone. "He's gone."

"What is it, Alan? Who was that?"

"I don't know, but I'm going to Greece." He gulped down the rest of the glass of wine and refilled the glass.

Konstantina placed her hand on his. "What is it? What was all that about?"

He drank another mouthful of red wine. "It was Nikos, the Greek bloke I told you about, the one who gave me the box. But then there was someone else." He took another drink. His hand was shaking.

"Who? Alan, what did they say?"

"I don't know who it was, but if I don't get this box to Nikos Stavroulis in forty eight hours, in person, he said he will kill him."

Outside the restaurant in the blue Toyota Yaris, Gary McAllister put his phone down and looked across the road to the couple in the window of the restaurant. "Well well Mister Marks, this is getting interesting." He picked up his phone and was about to call Sir Charles, then had second thoughts. "No. It can wait. There is obviously a bit more to this Midas scam than we thought. I could get the device off Marks right now, but what's all this Greek thing, and who was that on the phone to him? I wonder." He picked up the Blackberry and pressed a few buttons. "OK, international number." He pressed a few more buttons on the tiny keypad. "A mobile? Begins with 69?" He pressed a single button and then put the phone to his ear. "Unobtainable? Oh of course it's Greek. Hang on what's the code?" He started pressing more buttons to access the internet.

In her bar, Jean faced up to the menacing figure of Manos. "OK, so you can smack a Greek." She glanced down at Nikos who was holding his nose. It was bleeding profusely. "I am quite sure you could lay me out too. But think on this, pretty boy." She held her manicured hand with its bright red nails in front of his face. "It will come at a price. You have a choice. You can leave my bar with your handsome features still intact or you can tangle with me, smack me about, and leave scarred for life." Manos stared at her but her eyes did not leave his.

"One day lady, one day."

Her stare did not waiver. "In your dreams sunshine, in your dreams."

Manos turned and looked down at Nikos. "Forty eight hours, Stavroulis." He kicked Nikos hard on the legs and left the bar. As he exited through the outer doors, he picked a piece of wood off the splintered surround of the handle. "By the way lady, your lock is broken."

Jean walked over to Nikos. "Nikos Stavroulis, you are one dumb fucking Greek." She was about to pick him up when his mobile phone rang on the bar where Manos had left it. She turned to Kostas. "Well pick him up, thickness." Then she picked up the phone.

"Hello, Nickos Stavroulis' phone. No, this is not the Marriott in Athens it's a mobile phone in the Jean and Tonic bar in Symi, you've got the wrong number." She put the phone down. "Scottish prick!"

McAllister stared at the phone. "Stavroulis? Who the hell is he? And Symi? Where the hell is that?"

CHAPTER SEVEN

"Oh great!" Alan Marks looked down Napoleon Avenue and brought the Porsche to a sudden halt. "A police car."

Konstantina looked at him. "That's your house, is it? The one with the police car outside?"

"You've got it," he confirmed. "Now what the hell do they want?" He drummed his fingers on the steering wheel.

"We won't find out sitting here," Konstantina shifted in her seat. "And you can't go to Greece without your passport. So give me the door keys and I'll go and get it."

He turned off the engine, pulled out the keys and handed them to Konstantina. "What will you say to them?"

She thought for a moment. "Well, if they ask about you, I'll say I'm a friend checking up on the house while you are away in Greece. How's that?"

"But what if they know about this Midas thing?"

She smiled. "I'll think of something." She stepped out of the car. "Where is the passport anyway?"

"In the first top drawer on the left as you go into the kitchen. Oh, and when you open the door the alarm code is five four seven four." He looked down the road and saw a female police officer get out of the car and start to walk into the driveway of his house.

Konstantina walked briskly down the broad avenue of large fifties houses. As she turned into the gravel driveway of Alan's house, the small police officer in her stab vest was just turning away from the door and talking into her radio.

"No sir, nobody in at all and no car in the driveway, oh hang on here comes someone now, I'll call back sir. Excuse me Miss but do you know the owner of this house?"

Konstantina smiled, "Mr Marks? Yes, is there something wrong?" She was surprised at her lack of nerves, but then the police officer was smiling too.

"If you don't mind me asking, how well do you know him?"

Konstantina kept the smile up although inside she was beginning to tremble a little. "Oh, I'm more of a friend of the family. I'm just checking up on things while Mr Marks is away in Greece. Is there a problem with the house?"

"Just a moment, Miss." The short blonde officer put the radio up to her mouth. "Delta one, delta one, ah yes sir. Bit of a snag, apparently he is in Greece. I don't know sir, I'll ask." She looked up to Konstantina. "No, the house is fine Miss, but do you have a contact number for Mr Marks?"

Konstantina now had to think on her feet. "I have his mobile number, but it's at home. Is there something wrong?"

The girl lifted the radio up once more. "Just a moment. Sir? Yes we have a contact, but the lady I am talking to has it at her house. Yes sir, I'll go and get it with her." She turned back to Konstantina. "I'm sorry Miss, but if you don't mind I'll come to your home with you and get the number."

Konstantina was stuck now. She needed time to think this out. "Fine, but I just need to check the house and water the plants." She stepped up to the door. "I won't be more than a few minutes."

The police woman nodded "I'll just let my sergeant know." She turned the radio on again.

As she opened the door, Konstantina heard the alarm system begin to beep and she saw the key pad just inside the door. She hurriedly typed in five four seven four and the sound stopped. Once she had got the passport, which was exactly where Alan had said it would be, she slipped it into the back pocket of her jeans and headed for the front door. She still had no idea what she was going to do next, but she realised the last thing she needed to do was make this young police girl suspicious in any way. As she opened the door, the police woman was talking on her radio.

"No, I don't sir but I will ask her now." She turned to Konstantina. "Your name Miss, if you don't mind?"

Konstantina was about to lie but thought better of it. "Konstantina Zouroudi." She turned back and locked the door as the officer continued on the radio.

"Did you get that sir? Not sure, might be Polish, I'll ask."

"Greek." Konstantina said it loudly, straight at the radio. The officer smiled a big smile.

"Apparently, sir," said the police woman into the radio, "it is… That's right sir, Greek." She grinned at Konstantina. "I'm sure you did hear it, sir. Yes I will sir." She turned off the radio and looked up at Konstantina. "Sorry about all this Miss, but there has been a break-in at Mr Marks' offices and we can't seem to get hold of him."

"Oh, that's dreadful." As she said it Konstantina heard herself sounding a little too concerned and hoped she wasn't going over the top.

As they walked towards the police car, the young officer stopped. "The alarm Miss, you didn't put the alarm on?"

Konstantina was furious with herself as the girl went on to explain. "I noticed when you went in you turned an alarm off, but I didn't hear any sounds when you came out?" She was looking at Konstantina's blank expression. "I don't think you put the alarm back on."

"Right." This was all she needed; a budding Miss Marple. "Yes, you are right I didn't. Because…" Her mind was racing, "I'm coming back." The officer looked puzzled. "To water the plants… Yes…After I've got you the phone number. I didn't water them just now, you know when I went in." She was aware she was beginning to talk too much, but somehow couldn't stop. "So I will come back, you know in a bit, and water them then."

"Fine." The blonde officer was beginning to look at her with curiosity as they reached the police car. "So, where are we heading to, are you a neighbour?"

Now Konstantina had a dilemma. Did she give her right address? She had to. But what about when they got there? Why had she said she had Alan's phone number?

"Miss?" said the girl. "Where do you live?"

Konstantina began "I live in…" But she got no further as the police radio crackled into life with: "Delta one, delta one." The girl switched it on immediately.

"Delta one, what?.. Queen Elizabeth Park? About two minutes. But I'm taking this woman to…Right, OK, straight away. Shit!" She turned back to Konstantina. "Sorry about this Miss Zouroudi but some little toe rags have set light to some bushes in the park, little sods. Would you mind waiting here for a bit while I sort the little darlings out? You could go back in and water the plants?" Konstantina felt the last bit was said with a slight edge that implied "I don't quite believe you." There was a pause as if the officer was waiting for a response but before either of them could speak the radio burst into life again: "Delta one, delta one."

"Yes, I'm coming." The police officer opened the car, got in and started it. She wound down the window. "See you in a short while Miss Zouroudi, get watering."

As she drove off, blue lights flashing, Konstantina made as if to go back into the house. She waited for a moment and then went to the front of the driveway again and looked down the road just in time to see the back of the police car turning left at the junction which was the end of Napoleon Avenue. She ran immediately up the road to the yellow Porsche. As she got in she tossed the keys to Alan.

"Quick, drive to my flat."

Alan started the car. She was obviously worried. "Why, what's up?"

Konstantina sighed, smiled and handed him his passport. "Here's your passport, I need mine."

“Oh right,” said Alan. He was about to drive off. “You need your passport? Why?”

“Because I’m coming to Greece with you.”

Gary McAllister sat in his car just outside the entrance to Queen Elizabeth Park and muttered to himself as he scanned the information on his small computer screen. It was beginning to get dark outside and this made the screen easier to read.

“Symi Island…part of Dodecanese, north of Rhodes… nearest airport Rhodes… short ferry trip… most beautiful harbour in Greece, interesting… A hundred years ago Greece’s most prosperous island…no modern concrete construction…fine old houses…the spirit of the island remains intact…” “What does that mean I wonder? Have they got an ATM? That would be more to the point. Nice pictures, Greek paradise, but how the hell does Midas have anything to do with this place? Well I’m about to find out. But first, where are you now, Mr Marks?” He touched the screen and it changed to a map of Farnborough with a small red dot moving along Napoleon Avenue. “Right, so if I’m not mistaken, you have your passport Alan my boy, and you will be off to the airport. Now following you closely might not be a good idea. Don’t want to spook you. If I play this right you just might lead me to Mr Big, which would give me lots of brownie points with the silly old bastard who employs me. I know where you’re going, but how do I get to Rhodes?” He touched the small keypad on the screen and began a search. “Flights to Rhodes… Gatwick? Gatwick it is.” He checked his wallet. “Driving licence, cards, and passport.” He always carried it when on a case. Until now he had never needed it on a job but he felt very pleased with himself that his diligence had at last paid off. He was about to call Sophie to get his tickets sorted when he remembered. “Sod it.” He sat for a moment and was surprised that the realisation that she had gone had such an effect on him. It was only then that he began to ponder on her attempt to write Midas in her own blood. Yes, Sophie had known about Midas, but why try to write it? Or did it have something to do with whoever killed her? That seemed unlikely. He was stressed but didn't want a cigarette. And he'd thrown them away. That was her. "They'll kill you Mr Mac, you have to give up." He smiled at the recollection. He would always respond with "What are you the smoke police?" Now she was gone. His smile faded and his deliberations were cut short by a real police officer knocking on the car window. Outside was the face of a very pretty uniformed blonde girl.

"Would you mind moving your car, sir? There will be a rather large fire engine coming in here any minute and you're blocking the entrance to the park."

McAllister started the Toyota and opened the window. "Sorry, no problem Miss, can't stop anyway, I'm off to Greece. Oh, you wouldna happen to know the way would you? Is it left or right at the bottom of the road?"

The girl was astonished by the question. "Would I know the way to Greece?"

"No, course not, probably a bit off your beat. It's OK," he grinned at her. "I'll get it on the satnav."

As the blue Toyota pulled away PC Beth Pantlin wondered to herself. "Why do I always get the weirdo?"

As Konstantina got back into the Porsche outside her flat, she tossed a small bag into the tiny back seat and saw Alan's questioning look. "Change of underwear," she said, "and girlie stuff. And this…" She held up her passport, but she could see Alan was worried.

"Look," Konstantina protested, "if I stay here, the police will find out where I live and then want to know why I didn't hang about. Then they will want your mobile number, which actually I don't have, and that police woman was beginning to look at me a bid oddly."

"I don't know," protested Alan, "it might be dangerous."

She laughed. "Like what's already happened today hasn't been?

Being chased by some strange biker and sharing a van with a rabid dog. I tell you what Mr Marks, it beats working in a bank any day."

Alan couldn't help but smile. "But look, I shouldn't have got you mixed up in this."

Konstantina faked a concerned look. "True, it was very bad of you. In fact, you had better get me un-mixed up right now."

He laughed. "Un-mixed up? I'm not sure that is even English."

"Probably not, but I bet my English is better than your Greek."

He readily conceded. "True, I don't speak any Greek at all."

"Exactly!" She said in triumph. "So you'll need me when you get there."

She had a point. "Oh all right, if you're sure I mean, you don't have to come. This is my problem and..."

She stopped him with "Alan, I want to come. It's my home country. Now where in Greece are we going?"

"Oh my God," said Alan. "Where in Greece? How big is it, I mean is there more than one town?"

She frowned at him and he smiled.

"Somewhere called Piraeus." He said. "Leocharous Street."

"Piraeus? That's the port for Athens." She replied. "Hey, how do you know where to go? Did he tell you on the phone?"

Alan held up the small card reader. "He didn't have to." He turned it over and pointed to a small label on the base of the device. "Stavroulis Computers," he read. "Stavroulis International Exports. Fifteen Leocharous street, Piraeus, Athens Greece and load of numbers."

"Olympic." Konstantina replied.

"Sorry?" asked Alan.

"Olympic Airways, to Athens," she explained. "We need Olympic to Athens from Heathrow."

"Right," responded Alan. "We could probably go British Airways of course as well."

Konstantina gave him a rather smug smile. "Trust me, we need Olympic."

As they were talking, neither of them was aware of a small blue car which had pulled up just behind them without its lights on.

Alan picked up his phone and Konstantina took it from him. "Let me, I know the number." She quickly dialled and then began to press a series of buttons. "I hate this stuff, press one for reservations, press two for flight times blah blah blah, Oh hello, *Yassas*..." Alan sat fascinated as she suddenly went into rapid and fluent Greek. After about a minute, she broke off from the Greek conversation and spoke to Alan. "Two thirty in the morning, Heathrow Athens, two hundred quid each standby, yeah?"

"Well yes I suppose so," said Alan and before he could say more, she was back into Greek on the phone, then she suddenly broke, again. "Aisle or window seat?"

"Er window please," he responded.

She looked at him. "Mm, OK we'll argue about that when we get on." She spoke into the phone again. "*Neh*, Alan Marks, *neh, neh*, Konstantina Zouroudi..." Suddenly she was off in Greek again, this time laughing and very animated. "*Neh Zouroudi, ah Ochi Tsavari, Zoe, Neh Thessaloniki...Yiannis? Neh...*"

Alan had no idea what she was saying, but he got the feeling that booking the tickets was now not the main thing in the conversation. Suddenly she turned to him again. "Card?" she whispered. "Can we pay with a card? Will it work?"

Alan was nonplussed and whispered back, "I have no idea."

She shrugged her shoulders, produced her card and said, "Well here goes." She was back on the phone, and although he could not understand the language he could see that she was reciting the numbers on the card, giving the security code as she turned it over and confirmed her name and address. Then she went silent, looked at him and dropped the corners of her mouth in a comic will-it-work expression. It made him smile. Suddenly she was all animation again and grinning at him as she spoke into the phone. Obviously it had worked. What neither she nor Alan saw was the door of the blue car behind them opening. Very slowly, a dark figure got out, carrying a long barrelled hand gun.

Konstantina put her hand over the mouthpiece of the phone and turned to Alan. “Sorry but it turns out the girl on bookings went to school with my brother.” She whispered again, “I think it was his first, if you follow. I’m about to find out.” Alan looked at her, slightly disbelieving. Here they were on a mission to save some Greek bloke’s life whilst being pursued by some mad Scotsman and she was chatting on the phone about her brother’s sexual awakening. This girl was full of surprises. It was frustrating, but he actually quite liked it.

She saw his look and put her hand over the phone. “Well, come on, we have to be checked in by half past midnight.”

“No problem,” he said, starting the car, “it’s about forty five minutes at this time of night.” He glanced in the mirror and saw the small blue car behind them. Where had that come from? Looking in the mirror, he continued: “We will have to park though, but we’ve got loads of time, barring any mishaps.”

“Oh, great,” she replied. “Mishaps? Don’t be so pessimistic, I mean what else could happen?”

There was an almighty crash and a shower of glass shards flew across in front of both of them as an elbow came through the window of the car by Konstantina’s head. She yelled as a hand grabbed the phone from her and flung it back through the window. As she turned towards the shattered window, she came nose to barrel with a gun.

“Midas please Mr Marks,” said a deep-throated cockney voice outside the car, “or the Greek tart dies.”

Alan was shaking “OK, OK don’t shoot her, it’s yours.” He leant across to the glove compartment in front of Konstantina and as he pressed the release she suddenly spoke.

“No. Alan, don’t give it to him.”

Alan stopped. “What? Don’t be crazy, he will kill you.”

“He will anyway.” Her voice was trembling. “Isn’t that right, whoever you are?”

The voice gave a short laugh. "Clever girl, of course I will, so hand the thing over." There was a click as if some sort of safety catch had been released.

"See," said Konstantina. "Of course Alan, there is one thing our friend out there hasn't thought of." Her voice was strained now and breathy as nerves began to kick in.

"What haven't I thought of?" said the voice, intrigued.

"This," said Konstantina, and in one quick movement her hands were round the barrel of the gun pushing it upwards "Drive!" she screamed, and bit into the wrist of the gun holder. There was an agonising yell and Alan, almost as a reflex action to Konstantina's command, put his foot hard down on the accelerator pedal and the Boxter shot forward in a cloud of smoke and burning rubber, dragging the gunman alongside. As the gun went off with a deafening bang and the windscreen exploded in a cascade of glass, they sped away, Konstantina still holding the gun and dragging the gunman along with them for about twenty-five yards. Then speed, increasing the drag, forced her to let go and the man rolled onto the pavement. Howling in pain, he crashed into a lamp post.

"Bloody hell," Alan was still shaking as he sped down the Farnborough Road. "How did you do that?" He was shouting as the full force of the air with no windscreen as a barrier hit his face.

"I'm not sure," she struggled to respond.

He was going at speed now as they jumped the red lights at the junction of Farnborough Road and Highgate Lane and a black cab sounded its horn whilst trying to turn onto the main road.

"Jesus, Tina you were amazing," he turned to her.

"Alan!" she screamed, pointing forward. He faced forward just in time to see a huge fire engine turning in front of him across the road into Queen Elizabeth Park. He pressed hard on the brakes and spun the wheel, shooting into the centre of the road and just clipping the back of the fire engine with his wing mirror. It flew off and bounced on the road, into the air and straight through the back window of PC Beth Pantlin's Vauxhall Astra police car which was parked in the entrance to the park. Beth slumped forward onto the steering wheel, activating the horn, as the wing mirror caught her on the back of the head and knocked her clean out. At the same time, Alan pushed down on the accelerator and spun the wheel again to straighten the Porsche, now on the wrong side of the road, and saw the two motorbikes coming head-on towards him. He pressed down hard on the brakes with no hope of turning to avoid them and they fanned out either side of him at speed. One, to his right mounted the pavement, jumped into the air and crashed down. Spilling its rider onto the floor. He rolled over and over, as the bike slid on its side, spinning round and round into the ironwork fence bordering the grounds of Farnborough Hill Girls School. The other motorbike squeezed miraculously between the back of the Porsche and the fire engine but clipped the back of the huge vehicle with its right hand handle bar. This immediately sent the rider and bike into a wobble as the rider desperately tried to hold on, finally lost control and the rider and bike parted company. The rider tumbled onto the road as his bike slid gracefully on its side in a hail of sparks towards the traffic lights. By the time it hit the pole of the lights, it had almost stopped. There was a gentle clang as the metal of the bike's petrol tank slowly bounced off the pole and stopped. There was a slight pause and then an almighty thud and whoosh as the entire bike exploded in a plume of smoke and flame.

Alan brought the Porsche to a halt well down the road and looked back. "Bloody hell!"

"I think we should go," said Konstantina, "or we won't be leaving the country."

Alan was torn. "But what about all that?" He was still looking back in horror.

"Are you a paramedic?" the girl asked.

He was surprised by her frankness. "Well no, but…"

"Then there is not much you can do."

She had a point, and his mind was made up for him as he suddenly saw the small blue car bursting through the cloud of smoke, swerving past the now stationary fire appliance and heading for them.

"Jesus Christ," he shouted and pressed down hard on the accelerator. Once more, the Boxter leapt forward and Alan headed for the M3. "That wasn't the Scotsman was it?"

"No," said Konstantina, "but perhaps he isn't alone."

"Oh great," he muttered as he swerved around the roundabout at the end of the road and headed for the motorway slip. "But how do they know where we are?"

As he reached the roundabout before the M3, Gary McAllister glanced down at the computer screen and pondered out loud. "Why hasn't Marks left her flat? He should be on his way." The red dot on the map had not moved for some time. McAllister went around the roundabout and was about to doubled back, when he saw a bright yellow Porsche Boxter approach the roundabout and head for the M3. He swung his wheel and followed the Porsche which was heading away from him at speed. "So you've lost your phone Mr Marks but…What the hell?" He swerved to avoid being hit by a small blue car as it cut in front of him and accelerated up the slip road towards the M3.

"Twat!" yelled McAllister. He put his foot down and shouted at his car. "For Christ's sake move you pile of crap."

On the M3, Alan was struggling to keep up speed with the wind hitting his face at force. Konstantina was looking behind. "Alan!" she shouted into the wind, "he's on us." The small blue car was closing on them as they approached road works just before junction three. He opted for the outside lane which was separated from the inner lanes by bollards and went across the carriageway into a contraflow. Someone had once told him that average speed cameras didn't cover the outside lane, and as the sign said "a fifty limit with average speed cameras", it seemed an obvious option. As he swerved to the outside lane, he heard a ping and a piece of the frame of the windshield in front of him flew off. "Christ Tina we're being shot at."

"Jesus," shouted McAllister, "that pillock is after Marks. He pressed down hard on the accelerator and was up behind the small blue car as they approached the road works. The car in front of McAllister swerved into the outside lane, following the Porsche. McAllister duly followed. "Christ this thing has balls after all." He was on the tail of the small blue car and the driver realised. As they entered the contraflow he turned to fire at McAllister, swerved and hit one of the plastic bollards to his left sending it high in the air, he spun the wheel to compensate, over cooked it and went into the concrete barrier which shielded the contra flow lane from the opposite carriageway. The car hit the barrier and bounced off, spinning over several times and ending up on its roof, slowly turning in the middle of the contraflow lane. McAllister slammed on the breaks and the Yaris screeched to a halt inches from the Nissan.

McAllister jumped out and rushed over to the blue car, which had just stopped revolving. The driver was hanging upside down and was not in a good way. Blood streamed from his battered face and the remnants of an airbag were on the roof below his head. McAllister looked up and could see his legs were bent back under the seat. Miraculously, he was still holding the gun in his right hand. As McAllister looked in, the driver spluttered, and a spray of blood droplets filled the air.

"You're that Scottish twat from the bank, aren't you?"

"You could say that," replied the Scot. "Just hang on and I'll get an ambulance."

"Piss off," coughed the driver, sending a spray of red across the car dashboard. "I'm done. Listen, you Celtic bastard, if you're after Midas, leave it alone or you'll get yourself killed. Leave it to the Greeks."

McAllister was shaken, and intrigued. "What Greeks?"

"Leave it out," responded the driver and then suddenly yelled in pain. "Shit, I am in fucking agony. This bloody hurts." He looked up at his mangled legs, and coughed a bizarre laugh. "Well I'm not going to play for Chelsea now, am I? What Greeks, you wanker? You know what Greeks, Manidaki's Greeks you tosser. Oh shit, this hurts."

McAllister was genuinely confused. "Manidaki's Greeks? Manidaki? Who is that? And who are you?"

"Who am I?" He looked straight at McAllister with a stare the Scot would never forget. "I was Andreas Kaladoukas, and Mrs Manidaki is my boss's boss."

McAllister looked at the man who was obviously fading fast. "So this Mrs Manidaki is your boss's boss and..."

"That's right, you dumb fucking haggis shagger." The driver groaned in pain, "And I was Andy Kaladoukas." His voice faded suddenly to almost a whisper. "Andy Kaladoukas."

"Was?" queried McAllister.

"Was!" confirmed the driver and, putting the gun into his own bleeding mouth, fired a single shot.

"Jesus!" yelled McAllister, and ran back to his car. As he reached it, a lorry pulled up behind him. "Sorry mate, there's been an accident." He called up to the driver of the lorry. "I've got to get a plane, can you call it in?" He jumped into the Yaris and drove through the plastic cones sending them flying as he rounded the crashed Nissan and headed for the M25 and Gatwick.

CHAPTER EIGHT

Alan Marks drew the Porsche to a halt in a space between two other cars in the long term car park at Heathrow Airport. Since Konstantina had described the scene behind them on the M3, they had continued around the M25, off onto the M4 and into Heathrow in silence. They sat in the parking space for several minutes until Alan broke the silence. "Christ Tina, this is serious crap. I don't know what to do. I mean, people are getting hurt, and Nikos says he will die unless I get the box to him. I think I should just go to the police."

For the second time that day, he was taken aback by her response. "And tell them what?"

"Well…" he was struggling, "all about the card and that that is why I could take all the money and if they don't act soon …"

She finished it for him, "some man on a Greek island who sent you a box that makes it all possible will die. Oh and by the way, that's why we didn't stop at the scene of two serious accidents."

He looked at her. "Put like that it sounds shit."

She smiled at him, "Alan, it is shit. But we are in it now. I mean, if you go to the police I will have to too. I've used my card as well, and I've been with you all day."

"Oh bollocks," he replied. "I shouldn't have got you into this."

She smiled again. "Well I didn't exactly take much persuading, did I?" She kissed him on the forehead. It was merely a peck but he felt himself begin to blush. He was about to speak but she stopped him. "Look, I've got an idea." She took the card reader from the glove compartment. "Why don't we just get this box to your friend Nikos, hopefully save his life, and then we can think about what to do. If you want to hand yourself in then, I'll do it with you."

This girl was amazing and her logic was astounding. This seemed a simple way out for the moment, and it would give him time to think about what was best. "You would hand yourself in with me?" She nodded.

"Tina," he began, "I don't know what to say except…"

She interrupted. "Say 'yes Tina'. Now come on, we've a flight to catch."

Alan was about to get out of the car when a thought occurred to him. "Money?"

"What about it?" asked Konstantina.

"How much cash should we take?" he responded. "There's a load in the boot but then again too much might look suspicious to customs."

"I see what you mean." she replied. "Well, there is the money I got out of the machine, we can take that between us and change it into euros, and we've got the cards."

"True," said Alan, "but will they work in Greece?"

She thought for a moment. "Good point." She started to take notes out of her bag. "There must be about six hundred or so pounds here. If we split it between us and hope for the best. I mean this card thing came from Greece, so I wouldn't be surprised if it worked there."

There seemed logic in her thinking. Alan took some of the notes from her and stuffed them into the pocket of his leather jacket as they headed for the shuttle bus.

Alan glanced back at his car. "Christ that car is a mess. I wouldn't be surprised if they tow it."

She smiled. "Don't worry about the car, you can always get another one."

He laughed. "So I can. So I can. I don't know about you Tina, but I am shattered." He yawned as he spoke.

"Well, it's a three and a half hour flight so we might get some sleep." She yawned too.

"Great," he mumbled, "so we get in at nearly seven."

"Nearly nine," she corrected him. "Greece is two hours ahead."

They boarded the bus and headed for terminal three.

At Gatwick South Terminal, Gary McAllister was getting extremely angry.

"But I must be able to get there by tomorrow."

The girl at the information desk was struggling to maintain her professional calm.

"Yes sir, as I am trying to explain to you, for the third time; if you go to Heathrow you can get a scheduled flight to Athens, then change to an internal flight to Rhodes. However, by the time you get there tomorrow afternoon there will be no ferry to the island of Symi. You will have to stay overnight in Rhodes."

"Oh for Christ's sake…" McAllister was seething.

"On the other hand," she continued, "if you get the first easyJet flight tomorrow evening, which still has seats on it, from here direct to Rhodes, you will arrive in the early hours of Wednesday morning but be able to get a ferry at eight thirty, local time, to the island of Symi. That is all according to the schedules I have been able to find." Still trying to stay cool, she turned the computer screen in front of her towards McAllister. "I am sorry sir, but I have looked at every other option and that is the situation. Now do you want the seat or not?" She pointed at the screen. Her smile had gone and McAllister realised he had to make a decision. "Oh sod it, alright."

The girl suddenly smiled again, but a too big smile. "Good, now if you would like to make your way over to the easyJet kiosk just over there sir," she indicated across the departures concourse, "I am sure they will be delighted to sell you a ticket for two hundred and fifty fucking quid. Thank you." As she turned away, McAllister found himself laughing out loud.

"Good for you girlie, good for you. I will do that, and thank you for your help." He was beginning to work out a plan. He would buy his ticket, check in to the Holiday Inn and get some sleep, after looking up the name Manidaki on the internet. As he bought the ticket, he considered how he should update Sir Charles. He had to tell him where he was going, but why did he feel uneasy about saying anymore?

He glanced around. He hadn't seen Marks or the girl, but then they had probably found out the same thing as him. What if they were on the same flight? That needed checking. He took the ticket and as he did he thanked the young man behind the desk. "Oh by the way, a mate of mine and his girlfriend are flying out tomorrow night, anyway they said they would meet me here but I've waited and they haven't shown. Unless they booked before I got here. The man's name is Marks and..."

The young man stopped him with, "I'm sorry sir, we are not allowed to give out passenger names."

"No, of course not," responded McAllister, "but I just wanted to know…"

The young man interrupted him again. "But I can tell you that no-one has booked this flight except you since I have been on this shift." He tapped the keys on his terminal and looked at the screen. "Probably because it's been full for over a week except for one seat, and you got that. But don't worry."

"Worry?" McAllister was puzzled for a moment.

The young man tapped the keyboard again. "They will still get on a flight if they turn up." He peered at his screen. "Yes, there is a Thompson charter and a Thomas Cook with plenty of room. More expensive than us, you see." He grinned. "I hope they have some extra cash."

McAllister grinned back. "Oh they've got plenty of cash alright."

At Heathrow Airport, at a currency exchange, Alan changed five hundred pounds into euros and kept a hundred and fifty pounds in sterling.

"Is that going to be enough?" he muttered.

"Well it's all we have at the moment," Konstantina sighed. "Come on, we're early but we may as well go through to departures and get something to eat, as we didn't finish our meal in the Italian."

Alan took out his wallet from his back pocket and removed his bank card. He put it flat on the counter. "Shall I try to get some on this?"

"I don't know," she responded.

"There will be a commission charge of two per cent," the girl behind the glass grille explained. "Where are you going?"

"Athens," Alan replied.

"We can change the money back free of charge if you return from within the EU within four weeks. By the way, have you used the card today, sir?"

Before he had time to think Alan said, "Well yes but…"

"In that case," the girl continued, "we will have to try and get authorisation from your bank depending on your daily limit."

"Thanks." Alan smiled. "I think I'll leave it."

He turned away. "I don't think we want people getting authorisations do we?"

Konstantina gave a small chuckle. "Probably not a good idea."

"No, and anyway," said Alan, "you think the card will work in machines in Greece?"

"Yes, bound to," she said.

Alan couldn't tell whether she was saying this with confidence or bravado. He was about to ask her, as they queued to show their passports at the departures entrance, when she quietly said to him "Good luck."

Alan was slightly thrown. "Good luck? What do you mean?"

"Well," she whispered as the person in front of Alan stepped forward to the passport checking desk, "if the police are onto you this is where we find out."

"Oh great," he responded. He was about to say more when the

woman at the desk, in a border control uniform, beckoned him forward. She took his passport and opened it, looked at him, and gazed then at a screen in front of her, for what seemed like forever. Then she ran the open passport under a light beam next to the screen. As she looked at the screen again, a small red light flashed on the telephone mounting next to her. She picked up the phone. Alan by now was beginning to feel the start of trembling in the pit of his stomach.

"Yes?" said the woman into the mouthpiece. "Alan Marks? I have him right here. Has he really? Yes that is very bad of him, and he looks quite sensible." She turned to Alan. "Mr Marks, we've been a bit naughty with our bank card haven't we?"

Alan was completely unable to put a coherent sentence together and began to babble, "No, I didn't mean, that is, if I had any idea…"

The woman smiled. "Don't worry, this won't take a moment."

Alan jumped, as if hit by an electric shock, when he received a very firm tap on his shoulder. He turned, and standing there, towering over him, was a very large, middle-aged, police officer.

"Mr Marks? Mr Alan Marks?"

"Yes." Alan just about got the word out.

"He is," said the passport woman, holding up his passport.

"And is this your bank card, sir?" The police officer held up Alan's bank card in front of him.

Alan was now shaking inside violently whilst trying not to show anything. "I suppose it must be, yes..." Oh what the hell, he would have to just come clean. "You see officer it might sound stupid to you but I didn't actually mean to..." He never finished the sentence because the policeman did it for him.

"Leave it on the counter?"

"Yes. Sorry?" said Alan

"You didn't mean to leave it on the counter of the currency exchange?" The police officer handed him the card. "You are a lucky man. I mean, they don't give a very good rate of exchange over there," he indicated behind him, "but they are honest. Lucky for you sir, you could have found yourself really stuck wherever you're going. Have a good trip, sir."

Before Alan could thank him, he had turned and gone.

"Good job there are still some honest people about," said the woman at the passport desk.

"Yes," said Alan and started to leave. She stopped him with:

"Mr Marks." She held up his passport. "I think you might want this too."

He took it, and found his hand was shaking.

"Take care love," said the woman, "you look as if you need a rest." She turned away towards the queue, and Konstantina. "Next."

In his room at the Holiday Inn Gatwick, Gary McAllister raided the min-bar for a miniature Scotch, poured it out, swigged it down and then dialled on his Blackberry.

"Yes Sir Charles, McAllister… No, not yet. Yes I know what I said but can I just explain a moment? Look, I know where it is and where Marks is taking it… Why haven't I? Well because there may be bigger fish to fry sir... Yes, I think Marks is not the main man, in fact I'm beginning to think he may be caught up in this by mistake… Yes sir I know he used the card, yes, and several times too, but I think it was as big a surprise to him as anyone… Why did he keep using it? To be fair sir, we hadn't done him any favours had we? The thing is I think he is taking Midas back to whoever gave it to him… Yes, so we could nail the brains behind this. Look sir I think this could be quite big, an Interpol thing so perhaps we should inform…no, fine whatever you say sir... Where? Greece, sir… Yes, I said Greece. A small island called Symi… Yes sir, I'll be there by Wednesday morning… Well I might be able to if I catch him on a ferry or whatever but then if I did get Midas we wouldn't know who…. Sorry sir... Yes of course Sir Charles." He repeated Sir Charles Bowers' words. "Get it before any ruddy Greek gets their hands on it." He drained the last of the Scotch. "I will do my utmost, sir… Yes, I will call you when I get to Rhodes…Yes sir."

He ended the call and picked up the room phone. “Hello, reception? Can you send up a bottle of decent single malt and some ice? Thank you.” He put the phone down. Without his boss, this would be quite a good job. He muttered to himself, mimicking Sir Charles. “Get your hands on it before any ruddy Greek does, call me when you get to Rhodes. Bloody hell, it was like having a wife nagging.” He lay back on the bed and sighed. Something was bothering him, but what was it?

Alan sat back in his seat as the Olympic Airway 737 climbed high over Heathrow Airport. “You know, apart from my bank card that was easy.”

Konstantina looked at him. “I couldn’t believe it when that woman answered that phone and said your name. I thought that was it.”

“But they didn’t even pick up on the card reader in your bag when they scanned it,” he replied.

“I know,” she answered, “but I suppose it looks like a radio or iPod or something. Anyway, we are on our way now.”

“Yes,” he sighed, “I’ll have bit of a nap I think after a gin and tonic.”

“Gin and tonic?” Konstantina sounded affronted. “This is Olympic Airways and you are going to Athens.” She pressed the button above her head and a stewardess headed down the gangway towards her. “*Yassas*,” said Konstantina. “*Theo Ouza parakalo*.”

The stewardess headed back towards the galley at the front of the plane.

“What are we having?” asked Alan.

“We are going to Greece Mr Marks. We are having Ouzo.”

CHAPTER NINE

"Ouzo, Jones!" screamed Marina Manidaki as she waited for the phone to connect. "And with ice you cretin." The grey-haired man shuffled away in his dark blue, rather worn, butler's uniform.

As she waited on her land line, holding the phone with one hand, the old lady was preparing a text on a mobile phone with her other hand, her small, seemingly frail thumb darting from one letter to the next.

"Ah, there you are. Answering the phone in English?" she croaked. "Yes, I know you are in England and I do know what time it is, it is even later here in Thessaloniki, but I cannot sleep and so I don't see why you should. Now listen, you and your family have been in England so long you've gone soft. What happened with your boy Kaladoukas? I know he's dead. What do you want I should send flowers? He is better off dead… Yes, yes, very sad. Don't give me that shit. He messed up and now that English man is on his way to Athens with Midas. That was not meant to happen. You were paid to make sure it didn't happen. So why did it happen Pavlo, why? What do you mean Kaladoukas was being chased? Chased by who? A crazy Scotsman? What the hell are you talking about, what crazy Scotsman?" The old lady listened to the answer, took a deep breath and then spoke very slowly. "Are you sure Pavlo? Are you very sure?" She listened once more. "Thank you Pavlo. Thank you for that. I will send money to Maria. You are still with Maria, yes? Good, she will get some money… What do I mean? God you are stupid. You are in your bedroom, yes? Good, go over to the window and pull back the curtain… Why? Just go over to the window. Are you there? Good." The old lady pressed the button to send her text with her thumb.

"Now pull back the curtain." She listened for the ping as the bullet made a perfectly round hole in the glass of the window. Then the thud as Pavlo's lifeless body hit the floor of his bedroom, and as she heard the scream of anguish from the widow, Maria, she put down the phone. "*Yassas Pavlo, Yassas*."

"Your Ouzo, Ma'am." It was Jones.

"Thank you." She smiled, as she looked at him. "What is it about a Greek man speaking English that is so sexy? No wonder they get to lay all the tourist girls from England. I have just spoken to an absolute fool who had no idea what he was dealing with and yet afterwards I feel very sexy, even at my age. Jones, put down the drink and come here." She slowly undid the top three buttons of her nightdress. "I need some help to get to sleep."

Jones put down the drink and sighed. It wasn't in the job description, but after twenty five years it was expected.

Three and a half hours later, Alan Marks woke with a start as the plane touched down in Athens. He had had broken sleep but now, suddenly felt wide awake.

"You snore," said Konstantina from the seat next to him.

"I do not," he retorted.

"You do, and loudly too."

"Oh dear," he replied, "was I embarrassing?"

She smiled at him. "Most of the passengers were asleep too, so I wouldn't worry about it. We are here."

To Alan, the disembarkation and passage through passport and customs seemed remarkably smooth.

"Well we had no bags, so no waiting," said Konstantina as they walked towards the taxi rank outside the arrivals. There was a small queue but some very demonstrative taxi marshals were beckoning cabs forward to the expectant travellers with shouts and whistles. As they approached, three cabs pulled up at once from where they had been waiting and all the people in front piled in. A tall, thin marshal turned to them and spoke something in Greek. Konstantina replied, "Piraeus." The man hailed the next cab with a whistle. They got in and Konstantina spoke to the driver in Greek and he set off.

As the silver Mercedes taxi pulled away with a screech, the helpful marshal spoke into his mobile phone in Greek. "He is here."

After some twenty minutes, the speeding taxi left the broad dual carriageway and headed into the grid-like maze that is Piraeus. The tiny streets and heavy traffic seemed to inspire the driver. He deftly swerved between the numerous cars parked on pavements in the narrow streets, and Alan wasn't quite sure how he avoided hitting those coming in the opposite direction. It was almost as if the taxi shrank to accommodate the space. At one point, they mounted the pavement to avoid a truck backing out of a side street. He turned to Konstantina, who was blissfully unaware of the imminent danger he felt they were in.

"Jesus Tina, how does he do that, and why at this speed?" He let out a yell as they narrowly avoided a head on-collision with a bus. "Christ, he'll kill us."

The taxi driver laughed and stuck a finger up at the bus as it sped past.

"Kill us? Oh, I doubt it." Konstantina smiled. "He is an Athens taxi driver; they are immortal. Well, at least they think they are."

The driver turned. "Eh?"

Konstantina spoke to him in Greek. He laughed again, and crossed himself.

The taxi pulled up outside twenty three Leocharous Street with a screech of brakes.

"We're here," she said. "That must be the offices." She pointed across the street.

"Right," said Alan, still shaken. "OK, I suppose this is it."

"I'll ask the driver to wait," said Konstantina. "You know, in case."

"You mean," replied Alan, "in case we need a quick getaway?"

Konstantina shrugged, "Well yes, I suppose so." She was about to follow him out of the cab when he turned.

"No, you stay here. I have got you into enough trouble as it is."

"But..." she didn't get any further, his mind was made up.

"Look," he said, "it will probably be fine. You've got the box, right? I will just go in, see Nikos and make sure everything is OK and come back out. But on the off-chance that it gets messy, I don't want you involved."

She protested "But I am already involved."

"You know what I mean." He smiled at her. "Just stay here and I will be back in a couple of minutes."

He crossed the road and entered the front of the building as Konstantina opened her bag and looked down at the card reader.

The taxi driver turned around and spoke a few words. She responded and closed the bag. The taxi, with a squeal of rubber on tarmac, pulled away from the kerb.

Inside, in the foyer of number twenty three, Alan walked up to the reception desk and Mitzy, the receptionist, looked up. "*Yassas*"

"Oh, er *yassas*?" said Alan. "Er, do you..."

"Speak English?" replied the girl. "I certainly do, and how can I help you?"

"Oh right, well you see," he was babbling again, "I am Alan Marks and..."

Again the girl finished his sentence for him, "And you have come to see Mr Stavroulis, yes? He has been expecting you. They would like you to go straight up. Second floor." She indicated the lift.

Alan smiled. The girl was very helpful, so why did he feel unsure? "Second floor? Thank you." He walked towards the lift, and as he did he glanced back. The girl was smiling at him but had one hand on the telephone. He stopped. "Excuse me," he called across to her, "but is there a toilet here?"

"Just there, Mr Marks," Mitzy replied and indicated a door to the left of the lift.

"Thanks," said Alan and entered the door. Once inside, he immediately turned and re-opened the door slightly, peering out. The girl was now on the phone and he could just make out what she was saying.

"Yes, he is on his way up now… No, by himself. Thank you."

Suddenly Alan heard a loud "*Signome*," in his right ear and almost fell out through the door as a large man stood looking at him. Alan didn't know what to do and then realised as the man nodded at the door that all he wanted, was to get out.

"Oh, sorry," he responded, and opened the door for the man who bundled him aside muttering something in Greek that sounded offensive and involved the word "*malaka*" which didn't sound good. The door closed.

Now what was he to do? He opened the door to step out and saw the girl was on the phone again. He pulled the door half closed again and listened. He wished she would speak up but he could hardly shout across to her, "I can't hear". So instead he leaned forward as much as he could without opening the door too wide, and listened intently catching most of what the girl was saying.

"Stavroulis International? Yes that is right…No I am afraid not…I don't know…Mr Stavroulis is in Symi I believe and I am not sure when…His secretary isn't in today either…Yes I can take a message but I'm not sure when…"

Alan stepped back. He was confused. His instinct had been right about the girl. She had said Nikos was expecting him but just told someone Nikos wasn't there. What was it she had said; "They would like you to go straight up." "They"? Who were "they"?

At the Holiday Inn, Gatwick, McAllister awoke with a headache and looked at the half-empty bottle of Scotch on the bedside table. That had been a mistake. He had spent a good hour searching the net for the name Manidaki to little effect whilst sipping the Glenmorangie. He was fairly sure a dentist in Perth, Australia was not the brains behind Midas or a homeopathic therapist from

Wisconsin. There was Marina Manidaki, the widow of Greek tycoon Theodoros Manidaki, who was apparently a recluse living somewhere near Thessaloniki. She looked like the nearest thing, as it was impossible to find out where in fact her husband had made his millions, and there were odd tabloid rumours dating back to the seventies about her and several well-known politicians, both in Greece, England and America. Marina had been a bit of a girl in her day, but there was no photograph of her after 1977, where she was pictured in Monte Carlo with Princess Grace and Prince Rainier. She was next to the Prince, holding his arm. It looked like some big public event, like a film premier, or similar, with crowds of people and photographers in the background.

Up to date knowledge of the woman was virtually non-existent.

He got up and headed for the shower and then stopped as he reached the shower room door. He turned back and looked at the small computer screen on the small round table at the foot of the bed. "It wasn't, tell me it wasn't," he muttered to himself, and walked slowly back to the table. He tapped the small keyboard to stop the screensaver. The picture he had been looking at, of Marina Manidaki, Prince Rainier and Princess Grace, was still there. He tapped another key and zoomed in to the crowd of onlookers in the background of the picture. He scanned to the left and then stopped on a small group of people holding champagne glasses and watching the royal couple. In the centre was a smart man in his late twenties. He looked much thinner than he did now, and with a full head of hair. He zoomed in again and pressed another key to focus the picture.

"Oh shit!" He wasn't wrong; there was no mistaking the haughty features and the slightly arrogant smirk of a much younger Sir Charles Bower.

At twenty three Leocharous Street, Alan Marks emerged from the toilets and smiled at Mizty, who looked across at him. He could hardly just leave, but what else could he do? He pressed the button for the lift and the doors opened immediately. He stepped in and turned round to see the lovely Mitzy still smiling across at him with one hand on her telephone. He had a very strong urge to just step back out of the lift and make some sort of excuse to the girl and leave, but before he could, a rather large woman, carrying a stack of box files very precariously, burst into the lift, and shouted at him, "*Ena, ena.*" Alan had no idea what the woman meant. She shouted again. "*Ena, ena*." Alan began to speak. "I'm sorry I don't…" but got no further as the woman nudged him aside and pressed an elbow onto the button for the first floor. She looked at him and suddenly gave a huge grin as the doors began to close. "*Ena*. Number one." She looked at his bemused expression and felt the need to explain more. "The first floor. *Katalaveno*? You understand?"

"Oh I see," said Alan.

"And you?" asked the woman.

"Oh, the second," he replied.

"English?" enquired the woman.

Alan nodded.

"Mm," said the woman in a way that implied "That explains it." She continued. "If you want Nikos, he isn't here you know?" The woman struggled to keep the box files from toppling over as the lift juddered to a halt and the doors opened. "He is in Symi, went yesterday." She pressed the button for the second floor and exited through the doors. Alan swiftly put his foot in the lift doors as they began to come together. There was a loud 'ting' inside the lift and the doors opened again. As Alan stepped out, the woman turned to see him and the pile of box files crashed to the floor.

"I thought I would get out and help you," said Alan, thinking on his feet.

The woman looked down at the array of files on the floor. "This is helping?"

Alan quickly helped the woman gather the files and carried half of them to her office. As he put them down on a desk, the woman spoke; "I think he is in trouble."

"Sorry?" said Alan, looking up.

"Nikos!" said the woman in a way that meant "Don't you understand anything."

"Right," said Alan. "Nikos is in trouble?"

"Yes. He left for Symi with a nasty-looking boy yesterday. Symi, where his mother lives." The woman started to arrange the box files on a shelf and held out a hand, beckoning for Alan to pass them to her. "How do I know this? I see his secretary."

Alan duly obliged and started to pass the files. "His secretary?" he asked.

The woman needed no more prompting as he passed files and she stacked them.

"I say secretary, I don't think he chose her for her office work if you understand me. She might look good but I'm not sure she could write her name. Anyway, she leaves just after him, her clothes are all in a mess. Looked like a stain on the skirt, if you get me? Anyway I said to her in the lift, 'Where has Nikos gone?' And she said 'Symi'. So then I said, 'And who is the nasty-looking boy?' And she started crying and crying and ran out of the lift and into the street. Yes, trouble. That Nikos can't keep it in his trousers. Some boyfriend has caught up with him, or husband or whatever. He should know better at his age. The number of secretaries he has had up in that office, I wouldn't be surprised if he is gay. It's one of the signs you know. Are you gay?"

Alan was taken aback at the directness and almost dropped the last file. "Gay? No!"

"Oh," said the woman calmly as she took the file from him. "I just wondered, you know, with your hair?" She indicated his ponytail.

"My ponytail?" he responded.

"Are you married?" she asked.

Alan was once again flustered by the direct questioning.

"Yes, well no, I mean not any more, really."

"Ah," said the woman with a knowing look, "I see." And she

flicked the back of her hair up and down as if to imitate the pony tail.

"Right, I'll be going then." He felt the flush come to his cheeks as he left the office and headed for the lift. As the doors opened he saw himself in the mirror at the back of the lift. He turned his head sideways, saw his ponytail and muttered. "Gay?"

Having showered, McAllister sat on the bed in the hotel room for a long time staring at the image on the small computer screen. What was he to do? Was it a coincidence? So Sir Charles Bower was in the background of a photograph taken some thirty-odd years ago somewhere in Monaco, or Nice, or somewhere equally posh. It was some function where a woman who might, or might not be, all these years later, the widow of a major international gangster and involved in a huge scheme to defraud the bank, was also present. Looked at like that, it seemed quite plausible that Sir Charles' presence in the photograph was indeed a coincidence. He wasn't even near the woman. So why did McAllister not believe that theory? He didn't know. So what was the alternative? This Manidaki woman had inherited a Greek criminal empire and Sir Charles Bower was now involved, with her, in an attempt to destroy his own bank, having already told McAllister they were on the brink of a major merger, which would doubtless net the old boy a sum running into millions. That was clearly ridiculous. It must be coincidence. Of course there was one simple way to find out; ask Sir Charles.

McAllister picked up his phone, then put it down again.

How could he call his boss and ask: "Are you involved in major crime with a Greek woman to bring down The First Independent bank?" He could imagine the reply. It would involve several expletives and end with: "You're fired." The more he thought about it, the less sense it made. So his boss was in the background of a photograph taken thirty years ago which featured Prince Rainier and the Manidaki woman. In the circles the old boy would have mixed in back then, it wasn't that much of a surprise really. Yes, it was a coincidence, but that's all it was. McAllister got bored sometimes, but he liked his job overall and it suited him after all his time in the police, to have something that gave him some measure of independence. He was, for the most part, his own boss with a lot of leeway to make decisions. For example, here he was about to follow a hot trail to Greece to possibly foil a bigger crime than he had ever worked on in all his police service. Why screw it up with a stupid phone call? What was it the old duffer had said back in his office? "Spend what you need, do what you have to do. If there is shit make sure it doesn't stick to this bank and catch the bastards".

If his boss was involved, he would hardly be sending him to crack the case. He stood up and began to gather his things. "Catch the bastards?" Yes they were bastards, big organised crime bastards. If the man in the wreck on the M3 was anything to go by McAllister was going to have to be careful. Suddenly, the phone rang. McAllister snatched it up. "Yes?"

"Excuse me sir, you asked for an alarm call?"

He sighed with relief. "Thank you. Yes. When does breakfast finish? Nine thirty? Thanks."

He put the phone down and muttered to himself. "Big bastards, big nasty bastards." He picked up his jacket and instantly realised the one thing he really needed wasn't there.

The lift doors closed in front of Alan Marks. Common sense told him to go downstairs and get out of the building, but his curiosity was getting the better of him. If Nikos wasn't up there on the second floor, then who was? He would just creep up the stairs and quietly look around the corner. As he started up the stairs which were next to the lift, it became apparent there was a flaw in this plan at the outset. His trainers made a squeaking sound which echoed on the shiny marble of the stairway. He tried to tiptoe but it was no good. He took off his shoes and held them in his right hand as he slowly mounted the stairs. As he rounded the bend in the stairs, before they rose in a second flight to the next floor, he heard the lift doors opening on the floor above him. Then he heard voices, angry voices. He slowly crept to the top of the stairs, peered around the corner and jumped back in alarm, dropping his shoes which clattered down the stairs tumbling over and over. The two men with guns who had been shouting at each other in front of the empty lift heard the noise and turned to see Alan in front of them. Just for a moment, it was as if time stood still as all three men froze. Then, without even thinking, Alan span around and jumped down the first flight of stairs to the turn and set off down the second flight as something whistled past his right ear and plaster sprayed off the wall beside him.

"Shit, they're shooting at me." He slithered on the shiny marble floor as he reached the first floor, he could hear the men clattering down the stairs right behind him. He was going so fast and slipping so much in his socks that he misjudged the turn to the next flight of stairs and headed on down the corridor. More by instinct than judgement, he suddenly turned and crashed back into the office where the woman was still arranging the box files. He slammed the door shut behind him. The woman turned and let out a gasp as Alan sprang towards her, clapping his hand over her mouth and pinning her up against the wall. Her shoulders caught the shelf with the box files on. It tipped and they all came crashing down around the two of them. There was silence. Alan whispered softly, still with his hand over the woman's mouth. "Be quiet or we are both dead." Again, there was silence. The men must have gone down to the ground floor, assuming that was where he had gone. Alan slowly took his hand away from the woman's mouth and put his finger up to his lips to indicate that she should be quiet. He edged over to the open window which overlooked the street. He slowly looked out and down and saw the two men standing below him looking up and down Leocharous Street. As if he felt Alan's gaze, one of the men suddenly looked up. Alan darted back, but knew he had been seen. He spun around. What was he to do? He suddenly had an idea. He dashed out of the office and headed for the lift. He looked at the indicator above it and saw it was on the ground floor. He pressed the button and an arrow lit up above the doors, indicating that the lift was coming. He glanced to his right and saw one of his trainers on the floor. He grabbed it, looked up the small flight of stairs and saw the other. He bounded up two steps, grabbed the shoe and leapt down again. He heard footsteps beginning to run up the stairs from below.

"Come on, come on." The lift wasn't coming fast enough. The footsteps were coming faster. The woman appeared in the door of the office and shouted after him.

"Hey, you, what the hell are you doing?" Suddenly there was a loud 'ting' and the doors opened. Alan dived into the lift and pressed the ground floor button. As the doors closed, he heard the two men reach the top of the stairs, what sounded like a shot and a woman's scream which faded quickly as the lift descended. He struggled to put his shoes on and just managed it as the lift doors opened again. He ran out on the ground floor, passing a puzzled Mizty, and through the front doors and out onto the street. It was only then that it struck him as he stared across the street. The taxi wasn't there. He looked up and down the street. No taxi. He yelled. "Konstantina?"

People looked at him as they passed. A couple with a small girl crossed over to the other side of the street.

His mind was suddenly in turmoil. She had gone. Konstantina had gone. Then it hit him; Midas had gone too. She had the little black box. A sudden cascade of thoughts and doubts flooded into his mind. Had he been duped? Had this been an almighty con? She was Greek, and suddenly that seemed more than a coincidence. Had their meeting outside the bank really been by chance? She had been very keen to come to Greece with him and not go to the police. Had she been after Midas all the time, and if so who the hell was she?

His mind was racing. "Christ, what do I do now? Where is the bloody taxi?" In fact, he hadn't realised then, but thinking back, it hadn't been there when he looked out of the upstairs window. He looked up only to be greeted by one of the men looking down and pointing a gun at him. Alan froze. There was nowhere to hide, and running would be pointless. He closed his eyes and waited for the shot.

When he got to reception, McAllister handed over the swipe card key and the hire car keys.

"They will pick it up after five apparently," he told the boy on reception. "I'm going for breakfast, can you get me a cab for ten please?"

"Certainly, sir," said the young man in the smart blazer. "Everything all right with your room?"

"Yes, fine." McAllister hated customer care small talk. He handed over his bank debit card. "Need a receipt please."

"I'll just call a cab now, sir." The young man picked up the phone. "Going anywhere nice, sir?"

"Rhodes." McAllister grunted.

"Greece?" said the young man, "I was in Santorini a couple of weeks ago and…" he broke off. "Taxi at Holiday Inn please for ten?" He looked at McAllister. "To go where sir, north or south terminal?"

"Neither," said McAllister.

"Oh," said the young man, a little confused. "Where to then?"

"Not sure," said the Scot with a smirk. "I need a gun shop."

The young man's smile had dropped as he spoke into the phone. "Not sure, but get here for ten please." He put the phone down and picked up the bank card. McAllister had a little smile as he noticed the quiver of the hand. As he took back the card and the receipt, he held the young man's hand and looked straight into his eyes. "Don't worry son. I'm one of the good guys. Have a nice day."

Alan Marks waited, and waited. There was no shot. Slowly, he opened his eyes to see the side of a huge white van in front of him. It pulled away and Alan could see there was no one in the upstairs window.

"Oh Christ," he thought, "they'll be coming down." He turned and began to run down the street. As he did, he heard a car horn blaring behind him and then was aware of a car coming up alongside. Still he kept running.

"Alan? Stop...Alan...get in."

He turned to see Konstantina shouting through the open window of the cab. He stopped, and the cab screeched to a halt about ten feet ahead of him. He glanced behind and saw the two men emerging from the office building. They looked up and down the street and then one spotted him. He raised his gun but his colleague knocked his hand down and began to run down the street towards Alan. Alan dashed forward as Konstantina opened the door of the cab. He hurriedly got into the car and babbled.

"Go, got to go, now!"

"Look, I'm sorry," said Konstantina calmly, "we had to go around the block because apparently they're hot on parking here and the driver said..."

"Go!" yelled Alan, looking at the driver. Then he turned to Konstantina. "Tina, there's two men with guns."

Konstantina looked out of the back window and suddenly swung around and shouted at the driver "*Pame...Pame.... Amessos!*"

The driver saw what Konstantina saw and let out an expletive; put his foot hard down and the cab shot forward at speed, flinging Alan and Konstantina hard into the back of the seat. Just at the same moment, one of the men grabbed the back door handle and was pulled off his feet by the force of the acceleration. Alan turned and looked over the top of the back seat just in time to see the man being helped to his feet by his colleague. He raised his gun in the direction of the cab but obviously decided they were too far away and lowered it. The car sped through the narrow streets, swerving to avoid oncoming traffic and pedestrians. They squealed around one corner and then another, and then suddenly emerged onto the wide road that surrounds the docks at Piraeus. The driver screeched to a halt at a set of traffic lights which were red, at a large interchange just outside the main gates to the docks. The driver turned around and began to harangue Konstantina. She held her hands up. "OK, OK ." She turned to Alan. "We have to get out."

Alan looked out of the back window again. "Get out? Why?"

The driver continued to shout and Konstantina had to shout at Alan to be heard. "Because he thinks you are dangerous."

Suddenly, the lights changed and within seconds the cars behind began pressing their horns.

"Me, dangerous?" said Alan. He turned to the driver. "Me, dangerous? I've just been chased by two thugs with guns, I'm not bloody dangerous, they are."

"He doesn't understand you," said Konstantina. "It's best if we just get out."

The driver was now shouting out of his window at the car behind which was blaring its horn.

"But that's stupid," protested Alan. "What if they come after us?"

"That's what he's worried about," she replied.

By now the driver was getting out of his car.

Konstantina continued. "He thinks they will have taken his number and may come after the cab."

"Christ," said Alan suddenly changing his tone, "we would be better off out of it." He opened the door, stepped onto the pavement and was about to approach the cab driver, who was now having a row with two of the drivers behind him, when Konstantina stopped him. "Leave it, Alan." She had got out of the other side and beckoned him over the roof of the cab.

"I'm just going to pay him," he explained.

"Bad idea," she said, pointing through the open gates of the docks to where a police officer, who was directing traffic with a whistle on the wide dockside area, was looking over at the row which had now developed behind the cab. He took his whistle from his mouth and began to walk out of the gates. As he had stopped mid-direction, all hell broke out behind him as a large articulated lorry, which he had waved on, skidded to avoid a pick-up laden with crates of chickens. The pickup swerved and the crates immediately tumbled onto the floor and several broke open. The chickens flew everywhere. The police officer span around and began whistling frantically as the elderly and rather round driver of the pickup desperately tried to round up the chickens.

Alan ran around to the far side of the cab and followed Konstantina, who to his surprise headed straight for the mayhem inside the dock gates. Cars were screaming to a halt, the lorry driver was shouting at the police officer from his cab and numerous chickens were gradually spreading over the dockside chased by an increasing number of people.

"Come on," she called, "no one will miss us in this mess."

They entered the gates under a large sign with the letter 'E' on it. The entrance was opposite the train station and was part of the traffic light system. Lorries, cars and vans were all driving around the broad dockside where lines of large passenger and car ferries were docked. The interior road was wide, but without any markings, and Alan was struck by its similarity to a fairground dodgem rink. Just inside the gates, to the right, was a large ticket booth with a big blue 'Anek Ferries' sign above it. Next to it was a small car park and beyond, facing the dockside road a long low building with chairs and tables outside and a 'Starbucks Coffee' sign.

"Christ," said Alan, "they're everywhere."

"Lucky for us," said Konstantina.

A large crowd at the tables were sat or stood watching the show developing at the dock gates.

Alan and Konstantina entered the coffee shop, which was empty of customers as they were all outside watching the fun.

"My shout," said the Greek girl. "I'm having a Greek coffee, what do you want?"

"A latte if they have it." Alan suddenly sat down on the nearest chair and took a deep breath. His legs were shaking.

Konstantina turned back to him, having ordered the coffee. "You OK?"

Alan breathed deeply again. "Yeah, I think so. It must be delayed shock."

"What the hell happened in there with Nikos?" she asked.

"That's just it," he answered. "Nikos isn't there. He's in somewhere called Symi?"

"What, the island near Rhodes?" she asked.

"An island? Is it?" said Alan.

"Yes," she responded. "But if he wasn't there, how did you end up being chased by two men with guns?"

Alan relayed the events that had taken place inside the office building as the coffee came. When he ended his story, he picked up his coffee and found his hand was shaking.

"Jesus Tina, I was shot at. Then I came out and you weren't there. For a minute, I thought…" He stopped himself telling her what he had thought as she looked at him expectantly.

"Thought what?" she asked.

"Oh, nothing," he replied.

"Well it must have been something," she pressed him.

"I thought you might have buggered off." He put down his coffee and found he was beginning to feel quite emotional. "I know it was daft, but…"

"Buggered off?" She looked at him and smiled and put her hand on his. "So I would come all the way to Athens with you, having been chased by some lunatic down the M3 and stalked by some weird Scotsman, and then 'bugger off'. Why would I bugger off? I've got your special little black box in my bag."

As he looked at her, his earlier doubts seemed incredibly stupid.

People were beginning to filter back into the café.

"Ah, the show must be over," said Konstantina looking around and suddenly taking her hand away to pick up her coffee.

He realised her cheeks were slightly flushed, and she seemed a little embarrassed.

"Yeah, right," he responded. "Oh Christ, look." He indicated over to the doorway where two young women were helping the driver of the pickup to a seat. The little old, very rotund, man was covered in feathers. People were patting him on the back and laughing as they came in. Several of them had feathers on them too. One of the women went to the counter and ordered him a coffee as the old man entered into jovial banter with several customers. Then the lorry driver entered, with his hands behind his back, and the café went silent.

"Eh?" shouted the big bearded man. "Eh?"

The old man looked up at him with distain. There was an uneasy pause.

Then the lorry driver produced, from behind his back, a large black cockerel and laughing, roared something in Greek. He plonked the bird in the old man's lap. The entire café, including the old man, erupted in laughter.

"What did he say?" asked Alan.

Konstantina was giggling. "I couldn't repeat it, it's too obscene."

"Extraordinary," said Alan. "That old guy has just had an accident and probably lost half of his stock. He could have been seriously hurt. I tell you what, if I was him, I'd be having a real go at that lorry driver bloke, and the police officer. Yes, and I'd be getting witnesses names and, well look at him. He's laughing."

"Mm," she smiled at him again. "There is one difference Alan. He's Greek."

"Oh right," he responded. "So you Greeks aren't bothered by anything then?"

"Oh yes we are," she said calmly. "The important things. Look at it this way. The old man is OK. He's probably got most of his chickens back judging by the feathers on several of the customers, and he has definitely got his prize cockerel back." She gave a small laugh. "Everyone has had a good laugh, and life goes on."

She looked at the bemused Englishman. "Alan. Nobody died."

"No," said Alan, who found emotion welling up inside him, and a tears coming into his eyes. "But I nearly did."

"Hey," said Konstantina, handing him a napkin and putting her hand back on his. "But you didn't, you're here Alan. Look," she glanced down at her bag, "the sooner we get rid of this little black box the better, don't you think?"

Alan dried his eyes. "Too right." He took a deep breath and sighed. Then he found himself smiling.

"OK. I'm still here, you're still here. We're in Piraeus having coffee in a Starbucks surrounded by people covered in feathers, who think traffic accidents are a gas. We are being chased by gangsters with guns because we have a box which gives us endless supplies of money. On top of that, the one person, who apparently needs that box to save his life, and possibly ours, has sodded off to some Greek island. OK fine."

He took a gulp of his coffee and then another and put the cup down.

"Right, I'll get you another. You're beginning to feel OK," said Konstantina. "I can tell."

"I've felt better," said Alan smiling back at her.

She stood and took his cup. "Same again?"

He nodded. "Yeah. Just one thing. What the hell do we do now?"

At the Holiday Inn at Gatwick, having eaten the full English and drunk several extra cups of coffee and scanned the papers, McAllister walked to the doors of the hotel just as a cab pulled up outside. The window dropped and a driver, with receding ginger hair, looked out. His two words, "Where to?" told McAllister he was from Glasgow.

"Thank God. A kindred spirit," he laughed.

The driver smiled. "Glenwood. A wee while ago now though."

"Shit," said McAllister. "That is uncanny, we will know folk I bet." He climbed into the cab. "I'm Gary. Gary McAllister."

"Alex," responded the driver. "Alex Brown."

"Stone me, I had a cousin was a Brown. Look before we go down memory lane, don't freak yourself like the little shit in there did. I'm an ex copper and I need a gun shop, then the south Terminal. Plenty of time, I've got all day."

The driver turned his head and spoke over his shoulder.

"Ex copper?"

"Yes. Oh yes," said McAllister.

"Ex?" the driver repeated.

"Very," McAllister responded.

"Right," said Alex. "This gun, legit or under the counter?"

McAllister smiled. "Doesn't matter, just a bit of self-protection, small. You see, Alex, in my line of work..."

Alex stopped him. "Don't need to know that. You're a McAllister, that's enough. East Grinstead, not too far, I know someone. Proper shop but he has other things under the counter, eastern Europe stuff, cheap, if you follow. Now then," he started to drive away, "did you have a brother with garage in Glentanar Road.?"

"Bugger me," laughed McAllister. "I did too. Rory, the little bastard. Went bust."

"Too right," Alex replied. "So should have, he buggered up my first car, the tosser."

"Sounds like Rory," said McAllister.

Alex continued. "A mark one Cortina. Remember them? Sienna red with black seats. Jesus I shagged some birds in that. It was beautiful. Christ it would be worth a fortune today. The wanker only went and seized the pistons, the twat. I only went in for an oil change."

In Piraeus, Konstantina smiled as she came away from the Anek Ferries ticket booth brandishing two tickets. "We got the last cabin."

"A cabin?" asked Alan.

"It's a long trip overnight to Rhodes," she replied. "Trust me, we want a cabin. Ten or twelve hours on one of those ferries, sleeping in a chair, if you can get one, is no fun."

He looked at the tickets. "It says deluxe."

"I know," she smiled. "that's why they cost a bomb. Cleaned me out of cash."

"You used the cash?" queried Alan.

"Had to," she responded. "Their card machine is down. Anyway I used false names this time so we can't be traced. If those men who were after you are searching, they won't be looking for Mr and Mrs Miller. Now we need some cash."

"Mr and Mrs?" He raised an eyebrow.

"Hey look." She pointed to a small octagonal building in the corner of the car park. It looked like a rather shabby gazebo or summer house, with a central core of cash machines. Several were adorned with paper signs over them stuck on with tape, which seemed to suggest they were out of order. She continued. "On second thoughts." She glanced around. "That might not be a good idea."

Alan looked at the groups of young men hanging around outside the Starbucks coffee shop and the ticket booth and understood what she meant.

"At the end of the day this is Athens, not one of the islands." she said. "Let's find a bank. We don't sail until seven and we will be in Rhodes by seven thirty in the morning, at the latest. We can get the first ferry to Symi."

"We could have flown," Alan muttered.

"And gone back to the airport?" she asked. "We talked about this and you said 'they', whoever 'they' are, would expect you to do that."

"I know," he said in resignation. "Christ I am hot, it's bloody boiling here. These jeans were a bad idea,"

"Yes," she responded, "and it's making you bad-tempered. I know what, we've got hours to kill so let's get some money and then get you some lighter clothes. They will be looking for a man in jeans with a leather jacket anyway, so we'll change your look. In fact we'll change mine while we're at it. Come on, let's find a bank." She suddenly pointed out of the gates to a building across the busy road. "There, National Bank. Can't see an ATM. I bet it's inside the foyer."

"Assuming our cards work over here," he said.

"Alan Marks you are a grumpy sod." She gave him a stern look and he couldn't help but smile.

"I am, aren't I? Let's go see if we are truly internationally rich, or up the proverbial without a paddle."

"Now, that's more like the Alan Marks I met outside the bank yesterday. We'll get some lunch too, I know a great *Souvlatzidika*."

"A what?" he asked.

She laughed. "A *Souvlatzidika*, a place where you get *Souvlaki*."

His reaction told her he was none the wiser. "Come on." She set off towards the dock gates. He followed her and couldn't help thinking that although it was only yesterday, she felt like a very old friend.

They crossed the road as the lights briefly turned red and walked along the street to the bank. When they got to the entrance, there was a set of external double glass doors leading into small foyer and then an identical set of double doors inside. They entered the outer doors of the bank and the air conditioning hit them.

"Ah great," said Alan, "fantastic."

"Yes look, a cash machine." Konstantina pointed to the machine just inside the doors in the side wall of the small foyer.

"Oh yes," he replied, "but I meant the air con. It's great."

"That's why they have the machine inside," she responded. "Don't look up."

"Why?" he asked.

"Camera," she responded, looking at him and rolling her eyes upwards. Then she smiled at the uniformed guard who was looking out from the interior doors. He smiled back. "Not that those pictures are any good," she continued through her grin, "but you never know." The guard turned away and opened a door for an old lady who was exiting.

"So," said Konstantina, "your card or mine?"

"Oh, right." He felt in his back pocket and pulled out his card. "Makes no difference, but here goes."

He put the card in the machine and this time a message came up in Greek on the top half of the screen . The bottom half had the option for four languages. Greek, English, French, German. "Interesting," Alan muttered. "Obviously recognises a foreign card."

He pressed the corresponding button on the side of the screen opposite English.

The next message was a request for his pin number which he typed in and waited. The screen went to blue, as people passed behind them, leaving the bank. Alan was beginning to feel nervous when three more options appeared: Credit card. Savings Account. Checking Account. "This is more complicated than in England." He pressed the button opposite Checking Account. Suddenly the options for euros in amounts of 50, 100, 200, 300, 400, 500, appeared.

"Right what now? It shouldn't make any difference actually."

"Do five hundred," she prompted. "Then if that's all that comes out, it will be the most you can get. So, then I'll do it too."

This girl was speaking sense. He opted for five hundred. A message appeared on the screen immediately. 'Please take your card. Your money is being counted.'

The card popped out and he took it and waited. There was a whirring sound and the notes appeared in the dispenser.

"Right, there's a result. Hey before I take this, which is the cancel button? We can't have money all over the floor here, and this keyboard is different. Is it that?" He pointed to a button on the bottom right hand side with red writing on it. She nodded.

"Good," he said, as a couple pushed past behind them, entering the bank. He took the money and murmured quietly: "Now for the big one, or not." He waited. Nothing seemed to be happening. "Bugger." There was no whirring sound. "Damn!" The guard looked out again. Konstantina smiled her sweetest smile back at him.

"Tell you what. Why don't we try my card in another bank?" she suggested.

"Yeah. Why not?" Alan saw the guard eye him up before he turned away. "Can't stand here any longer it will look fishy." They turned to go. Alan pulled the handle on the left-hand outer door and let Konstantina through. As he followed her, he heard a man's voice loudly, behind him. "*Ella*?" He turned to see the uniformed guard standing in the open interior door facing him. Alan started to feel a sudden panic as the rather large and fierce-looking guard spoke to him in Greek. The man stopped, obviously expecting a response. Alan was speechless.

Konstantina whispered in his ear. "He wants to know if you want your money."

Alan was confused. "Eh?"

The guard looked towards the cash machine as Konstantina came back in, brushing past Alan. "Your money darling, look you left it in the machine."

Alan looked across to see another large wadge of euros poking out of the dispensing slot.

Konstantina pulled the money out with one hand, and he noticed her press the cancel button with her other hand whilst turning and speaking to the guard in Greek. She was obviously thanking him profusely. She held out the money to Alan.

"Ah, yes dear. Thank you," said Alan, with too big a smile. Then he turned to the guard. "Yes, and thanks a lot to you mate." The guard looked at him with mild distain. "*Poustis*!" he muttered and went back inside the bank.

As they exited through the outer doors, Alan asked Konstantina what he had said.

"You don't want to know," she replied. "But don't worry about it. What he doesn't know is, you are once again, the richest man in the world."

"Christ I am," he replied. "It worked, hey it worked, here in Greece."

"Told you it would," she said.

"Yeah but you were worried," he laughed, "admit it, you were worried."

She stopped, turned and poked him in the chest jokingly as she spoke. "I am a Greek woman. We do not do worried. We do supreme confidence." She paused as she held herself in a confident pose. "We do complete over the top nervous breakdown." She pulled at her hair as she said this. "But we don't do worried."

Alan chuckled.

She continued. "One thing is concerning me though, thinking about it. Your ponytail. It will have to go. Let's find a barber." She turned to go.

"Hang on." Alan pulled her back. "My ponytail will have to go? Why?"

"Alan," she pleaded, "they are looking for a bloke in jeans, a leather jacket, and a ponytail. I just realised. Even if we change your trousers and shirt, look around, not a lot of ponytails. It stands out. It's got to go."

"Can't we eat first?" he protested. "You know that Souv, whatsit thing you said."

"*Souvlaki.* We can grab a *giros* on the way instead," she responded. "Changing your look and getting rid of your tail is more important."

As they set off down the street, after a short pause Alan forced himself to ask.

"It's not because it makes me look gay? You know the ponytail?"

Konstantina stopped and burst into fits of giggles.

Alan looked around at people who were staring as they passed. He considered pretending he wasn't with her. "It's not that funny."

"Gay?" she spluttered. "You, gay? What on earth made you think you look gay?"

He considered telling her, but decided against it. It could wait. As they began walking again, she calmed down, and eventually spoke in a more controlled way.

"Alan Marks, I have only known you for a very short time, but let me say I think you are probably one of the least gay men I have ever met. Look, there is a *giros* stall. Come on." She set off across the street to an open shop front where a man was carving slices of meat from a circular pillar of compressed lamb and putting them onto paper plates with salad and tsatsiki.

Alan followed. 'This woman,' he thought to himself. 'Here I am about to get rid of something I have cultivated, carefully, for a very long time, and yet I feel OK about it. It's bloody annoying.'

Having caught another cab outside the port gates, Alan and Konstantina headed back up to Athens. They bought Alan a pair of light chinos in a trendy boutique. At first Alan objected to the price, until Konstantina pointed out to him that he could actually afford anything he wanted. So then he sought out the most expensive T-shirt he could find. He would have bought more but she insisted they find a barber's shop. She dragged him outside and hailed a cab.

"And that leather jacket," she said, pushing his old jeans and shirt into a rubbish bin outside the boutique. "That will have to go, they will be looking for that." She held her hand out.

"Hang on," he said, taking his wallet out and stuffing it in his back pocket. "There." He handed over the jacket. "I liked that."

"And you can always get another, or several. Come on." She pushed him into the cab and asked the driver something in Greek. He replied and they set off.

"He says he knows a very good barber," she informed Alan. "His wife's cousin's son, over by the Acropolis."

It was a short drive, in which Alan once again, much to Konstantina's amusement, grasped the handle above the door of the cab and told her he thought they would probably die at the hands of an Athens taxi driver.

As they got out, having arrived safely, much to Alan's surprise, at the small shop just below the Acropolis, he protested.

"I really don't think this is necessary."

"I do," said Konstantina, pushing him through the door.

"But shouldn't we get some more clothes. Some sandals would be good, these trainers are hot. Also I need a toothbrush and a razor. I haven't brought any of those things."

She patted her bag. "Ah you see, I came prepared, but then I'm a woman. Don't worry you can get those on the ferry," she insisted. "They'll have a shop with all those things, and more clothes too."

"They will?" he said.

Konstantina spoke to the owner of the shop in Greek and he indicated for Alan to sit in the only barber's chair in the place.

"Oh alright," he conceded, "but tell him not to take too much off. Hey where are you going?"

"You'll see," she laughed, as she disappeared out of the door.

CHAPTER TEN

"Thank you very much Alex," said McAllister as he got out of the cab at Gatwick Airport. He held up a carrier bag. "This could be my life saver, you are all right Brown." He handed over a bundle of notes. "Have a dram on me."

"I will do just that, and thank you," responded the cabbie. "Have a good flight and stay safe now."

McAllister entered the terminal. First things first; he had to get a small bag or suitcase. He had his small holdall with him, but he couldn't carry the gun in his hand luggage, it would be scanned. He had to have a bag to put in the hold. He knew that only a small percentage of those were scanned and with the amount of bags at Gatwick he would be plain unlucky if it was his. Then a thought occurred to him. What about customs at the other end? He would cross that bridge if and when it needed crossing. He bought a small flight case with a handle and wheels. The sales assistant was a little confused when he asked her to leave all the paper stuffing that was in it, inside, so he told her he had some gifts to wrap. He then went to the toilets and locked himself in a cubicle. Once inside he took the paper out and wrapped the gun and ammunition carefully and placed it in the case. He took a quantity of toilet roll as well to bulk out the case so that the gun would not rattle around inside. He picked up the case. It seemed very light. That could be suspicious. He looked out of the cubicle; here was no one else around. He turned back inside and, with a smart kick, took the toilet roll holder off the wall. It was one of the larger round ones with the rolls inside so it had a bit of weight. He repacked the case, including the holder, and only just managed to zip it up. But now it felt more realistic. Now he had quite a bit of time to kill. He could get a meal and some decent Scotch in the departures lounge. 'Yes' he thought 'that would be a good idea.' From what he'd heard this easyJet set up was no frills, bring your own or have a sandwich. "I bet they don't do single malt." he muttered. Yes, a meal and a drink, if they would let him check in early. It was worth a try, after all he was on a bit of a roll. Alex Brown had been a real result.

He checked in his case after queuing for almost half an hour at the easyJet mass check in for all their flights. He apologised for being early but there was no problem. He had to stop himself smiling, as the girl checking him in asked if he had packed the bag himself, and if there was anything dangerous in it and could anyone else have put anything in?

As he headed away from the check in desk, towards the passport control and departures, he was relieved that that part had gone smoothly. He stood in line waiting to be called forward and as he did his thoughts went back to Sir Charles and the photograph. It was a coincidence, definitely a coincidence. Then he was reminded that he had to call the old man when he got to Rhodes. He had specifically asked him to. He smiled to himself. The old duffer probably hadn't realised that he would get a call in the very early hours of the morning. He muttered to himself, imitating the old boy, "Get your hands on it before the ruddy Greeks. Call me when you get to Rhodes." Suddenly McAllister was uneasy again. 'Call me when you get to Rhodes.' Had he said he was going to Rhodes? He had said he was going to Greece, but had he said Rhodes? He must have done. How else would the old boy know? "Now Mac," he murmured to himself, "you're getting paranoid."

The man checking the passports beckoned him forward.

"About time," said the Scot as he handed over his passport. "Hurry up man, I need a drink."

The man handed his passport back and McAllister headed into the departure area and through the security arches. He didn't look back. Had he done so he might have seen Alex Brown standing by the easyJet check in desk and talking on a mobile phone. "Yes, Rhodes, easyJet one zero seven three." Alex walked away from the check in towards the exit doors. "He's just gone through now. By the way he's got himself a gun… No, not much I could do about it but you've no need to worry the ammo is fake… Ammo? Bullets… they won't work, my friend switched them… No of course he doesn't know, and he won't until he tries to fire it…That's alright… Oh thank you, that's very generous of you if I may say so. Any time, it was a pleasure." He finished the call and headed for his cab. "Bloody McAllisters. Wankers. I loved that Cortina."

Having been shorn far shorter that he would have liked, Alan Marks paid the barber and wandered out of the shop. Where had she gone? He looked up and down the street but Konstantina was nowhere to be seen.

"Oh Christ not again," he muttered. He passed a girl with short blond hair who was looking in the window and wandered across the road to below the Acropolis where a large crowd of people was beginning the ascent. Where the hell was she?

"Just ignore me then, Alan Marks," said a voice behind him. He turned. It was Konstantina, in a short bobbed blonde wig.

"Bloody hell," was his instant reaction. "It was you, over there, outside the shop?"

"Yes," she said. "I thought as long as you were changing your appearance I should do the same. You know, to be on the safe side. Now we are two different people. This wig was in the shop next door, run by your barber's sister. They had a black one, but I fancied this blonde one. What do you think? Do you like it?" She turned around slowly.

"Well actually..." he began, "it's different."

"Oh?" She seemed disappointed.

"But in a good way," he added hastily. "In fact it's actually, well it's quite er...you know."

"Sexy?" she said, pulling one side of the blonde bob down to her mouth with one hand, lowering her head and looking up with her large brown eyes.

Alan felt his cheeks flush. "Well actually, if I am honest, yes."

"Mr Marks," she smiled, teasing him with a pretence of shock. "You can be quite charming when you want to be. Oh and you don't look at all gay now."

"Oh good," he said. "Hang on, you said I didn't before."

"I lied," she laughed. "Come on, have you seen the Acropolis and the Parthenon?"

"No," he responded.

"We have well over four hours before we need to get down to the boat," she said. "It's the worst time of the day, but you can't come to Athens and not see that." She pointed upwards to the Parthenon. "Come on." she steered him over to the ticket office and then they set off up the hill following the crowd.

High up in the village, above the harbour in Symi, an eighteen year old boy stood on the broad stone terrace in front of his house and looked through his father's telescope which was mounted on the wall. He focused on the ferry that was docking, one of the three or four that came in every day from Rhodes. 'Every day the same.' The boy thought to himself. 'The ferries dock and streams of tourists disembark, in several lines, each following a guide with a card held high on a stick or a brightly coloured umbrella. Danish, German, Italian, English, lines of "Sheep", parading around the harbour, stopping at the monument denoting the spot where the independence of the Greek Islands was signed , pausing at Manolis' sponge shop to see a demonstration, then on to Stavros herb stall, photographs by the old customs house, late lunch at whichever restaurant the tour guide had managed to do a back handed deal with, postcards, T-shirts, cheap souvenirs, then back on the boat and back to Rhodes having 'seen Symi'."

He smiled, the sheep rarely 'saw Symi' at all. The Symi high up the *kalistrata*, in the jumble of whitewashed houses of Chorio, the village up above. The Symi of stone steps and tavernas. The Symi of churches and bakeries, of donkeys and old women in black. A place where old men with worry beads played backgammon outside cafes.

The young boy watched the tourists flocking onto the harbour side. The ritual always intrigued him, but what interested him most was the fact that many of the young girls arrived dressed very differently to the village girls. Some of them would be wearing very brief attire and swim shorts and tops that amounted to, what his mother called 'little more than underwear.' His mother was deeply offended by the 'cheap foreign sluts', as she called them. Strangely, for a 'good Greek boy', as his mother called him, he wasn't offended at all. The telescope was very powerful and had a zoom capability, so he focused in on a particular blonde beauty who was just descending the gangway from the boat onto the road. She turned and he gave a small gasp as he saw the definite outline of nipples through her pink bikini top. He panned down and saw a small lizard tattoo which disappeared into her very brief pink shorts. Even at that distance, he began to feel a stirring in his groin and, as his bent left hand moved into his pocket, a fantasy began to play out in his mind. He shuffled from one foot to the other and, as he did, he knocked the telescope slightly to one side. He cursed and looked back into it. It was no longer focused on the girl. He looked over the top and then back into the eye-piece moving the instrument slowly from side to side, searching for her. Then suddenly he stopped. He hadn't found the girl, but he had found, sitting on a chair outside a café opposite the ferry, Nikos Stavroulis. That was interesting, what was he doing on Symi? Then he noticed someone else. There was another man sitting just behind Nikos, but staring at him. He wasn't Greek, that was for sure. He was dressed very smartly with a white straw hat and a shirt and blazer with a cravat. It struck the boy that he looked like old-fashioned pictures he had seen of Englishmen in far off countries like India, or even a middle-aged James Bond. Yes that was it; he was English definitely, but wealthy English. But why was he staring at Nikos?

The blonde suddenly walked in front of Nikos and the boy was torn, but something kept him focused on the two men.

Down opposite the boat, the last of the tourists had disembarked.

"Damn," muttered Nikos under his breath. "Where is he?"

"Waiting for someone?"

Nikos jumped and turned to see a rather smart man in a blazer.

"Remember me?" said the man in a very crisp upper-class English accent. "Organised chaos?"

Nikos was nonplussed for a moment and then it dawned on him. "Oh, yes mate, yesterday on the boat? You had a lady with you."

"Yes," said the man, "Lucinda, my P.A."

"Oh, P.A. is she?" Nikos smiled. "It's OK mate, your secret's safe with me."

"Yes well," said the man, "it is true, I have been known to take advantage of her, if you follow, but she is actually my P.A."

"I see," chuckled Nikos, "putting the personal into assistant eh mate?"

The man forced a grin. "Mr Stavroulis, would you like a drink?"

"Don't mind if I do," said Nikos. "A small beer mate. Hang on, how do you know my name?"

The man beckoned the waiter and ordered two beers.

"Sorry? How do I know who you are? Well you see, I was told that if I wanted something fixing here on Symi, that Nikos Stavroulis was my man. Australian Greek, they said, and calls everybody 'mate'. So I put two and two together and figured it must be you."

"Too right it is. So what can I do for you?" Nikos didn't know why but he found something about his new acquaintance ever so slightly unnerving.

"Tolis," said the man. "We want to go to the bay of Tolis."

"Boat or truck?" asked Nikos.

"What's the difference?" enquired the Englishman.

"Ah," said Nikos looking out to sea. "If the wind stays like this, and it will, I think it's the Meltemi."

"The what?" asked the Englishman.

Nikos smiled. "The Meltemi. It's a strong wind we get every year, can last for days, even weeks. Bit early this year, but I think this is it. Anyway, if the wind keeps up then over that side of the island would be a rocky ride. Having said that, so will a truck, because the last part is rough track, off-road practically. Still, it's a great bay and a nice taverna. Only been open a year. How do you know about it? It's mostly the Greeks who go there."

"Yes, so I believe," responded the man, "it was a Greek who told me."

"My old friend Kostas has a truck and I would think he would take you there for about thirty euros. It's quite a way."

"Good," said the man. "Tomorrow, about ten thirty? We are staying at the Old Markets Hotel on the *Kalistrata*."

"It's a deal," Nikos held out his hand, "and be sure to ask Helleni for some of her chocolate cake its…" He stopped speaking mid-sentence as he saw Manos approaching. The young man stopped right in front of the table.

"Hello," said the Englishman.

The young Greek totally ignored him and spoke directly to Nikos, in Greek.

"Well?" demanded Manos. "While you've been chatting to this arsehole that other English twat has not arrived. So have you got hold of him? Do you know where he is?"

"Not yet," Nikos responded hastily. "I've tried his mobile but it's not answering. Perhaps he is on a plane or…"

"Trust me," Manos' voice became more menacing, "he is not on a plane. He is in Greece, and he better get here soon, for your sake."

Nikos turned to the Englishman. "Right, I had better get going. My friend here has some business we need to discuss, nice to have met you." He stood and turned nervously to Manos. "Look let's go over to Pacos and I'll buy you a drink and keep trying on the phone."

Manos smiled, the lifeless dead smile that was his speciality. "Yes a drink would be good Nikos, but it doesn't mean I won't just kill you anyway. Yes I might just slit your throat," he drew his hand across his own neck, "and tell your godmother it was an accident."

As they left, the Englishman called after them, in perfect Greek. "Goodbye, thanks for your help Nikos. By the way young man I don't think killing him is a good idea. I'm not sure his godmother would believe you."

Manos stopped and turned back. He looked at the Englishman, who continued, "Well I mean people don't tend to get throats cut by accident, do they?"

The two held each other's gaze for a moment and then the Englishman gave a broad smile. "*Yassas*."

Manos turned away and, as the two men walked off, the Englishman heard: "Who the hell is that?" "I don't bloody know, some stupid tourist wants to go to Tolis."

Just then, Lucinda appeared from the other direction with some carrier bags and sat down next to the Englishman.

"Oh good, there you are," he said. "Drink?"

"Too bloody right," she responded in an equally plummy accent. "I am dripping, this place is too hot. Still I got a sponge, and this." She produced a large loofah from one of the bags.

Her boss responded with some surprise. "I am not even going to ask what you're going to do with that, but I wouldn't mind watching. Now look," as he spoke he waved at the waiter. "I noticed one of the cafés over there has got wi-fi ." He turned to the waiter. "I don't suppose you have Pimms do you? I can tell by your face you have no idea what I am talking about. OK, a small beer and a g and t, sorry gin and tonic." He turned back to Lucinda. "Where was I? Oh yes, wi-fi, can you let London know that there is a goon here babysitting Stavroulis? Nasty looking little shit. Now, that's not a problem, providing he's the only one, but I would quite like to know what we're dealing with. So, anything on one of their boys called Manos would be handy. Oh and you'd better tell them the Scotsman is on his way and he has a gun."

Lucinda stopped him. "Christ Toby, that's a bit of a worry."

"No," he reassured her, "because he hasn't any live bullets." She was about to interrupt when he stopped her. "Don't ask, just trust me on this one. He will be firing blanks, unlike yours truly." He ran a finger over her hand, which was resting on the table.

She feigned an objection. "Sir, this is most inappropriate. What would the chief say, or even the Minister? I may have to complain about sexual harassment."

He laughed. "I have a better idea, how about we still have the sexual harassment but you don't complain."

"And your wife?" she grinned.

"Ouch!" he responded. "You Roedean girls know how to dampen a boy's ardour don't you?"

The waiter arrived with the drinks, and as they both raised their glasses the man smiled and glanced up past his P.A. to the houses above the harbour and then looked back at her. He spoke to the woman whilst still smiling, but his tone did not match his grin.

"And Lucy old girl, while you are talking to mother in London I'm popping up to the village. You see for the last fifteen minutes or so somebody has been watching me." He then looked straight up to where, some minutes before, he had seen the small glint of reflected sunlight on glass.

The boy looking through the telescope got the shock of his life as the man looked straight down the lens at him. He grabbed at his crutches, which were leaning against the wall, and turned away from the telescope, bumping into his father who had just walked out onto the terrace. The big man looked at the telescope pointing down to the harbour, then at his son and made a gesture with his hand, simulating masturbation. Then he let out a great guttural laugh and waved a finger at the boy, tut-tutting and shaking his head. The boy smiled, and as he did, his father produced an envelope from his pocket, marked Omega Bank, and grinned.

At Gatwick, McAllister had eaten a light lunch and was downing his third scotch. He looked at his watch as the waitress cleared his table. "Excuse me, Miss, but I still have a fair bit of time to kill before my flight, is there wireless internet here?"

The Vietnamese girl looked up. "Yeah but up here in restaurant is not very good." She pointed past him. "Down the stairs is better. The hot spot's by the money change."

Having paid and tipped, he made his way down the stairs to the central concourse and sat down opposite the money exchange. He took the small computer screen and keyboard out of his bag and turned it on. As it booted up, he thought to himself: "This is a really long shot, but as I've plenty of time on my hands it's worth a punt."

The girl had been right; it was a good connection. He began his search. He very quickly got nowhere. None of the criteria he put into his totally illicit copy of the Interpol data base seemed to get him what he wanted. He muttered to himself. "Come on Gary, it was an outside chance anyway." He was about to switch off when he had one last thought. "Small island, like a small town, sometimes in small places shops do more than one thing. Like on some of the Scottish islands, the general store might be the post office and, in one case he knew of, the undertakers as well. He typed in the words 'Hardware shop Symi.'

Bingo, there it was. 'Dinos Zafaridis'. Everything was in Greek, but he could make out the phone number. He picked up the Blackberry and called. A man's voice answered in Greek.

McAllister found himself doing what most UK citizens do when faced with foreigners who don't understand them; he began talking too loudly.

"Hello! Do you speak English?" He noticed people were suddenly watching him. The voice on the other end said, "English? No. You wait one moment please."

McAllister answered, this time more quietly, "Right, OK." Then as he waited, he wondered why the person had said they couldn't speak English, in perfect English, and had then, in equally good English, asked him to wait. He waited, and waited. After a while, he wondered if he had been cut off. "Hello?" he tried again, a little louder, "Hello?" He looked at the screen to see if he was still connected. He was. "Hello?" He was about to end the call when a young girl's voice spoke. "Can I help you?"

"Ah yes," responded the surprised McAllister. "Is that Dino's Hardware Shop?"

"Sorry?" said the girl. "This is Dinos. What is hard wares?"

Slightly taken aback the Scot continued. "Well you know, tools and pots and pans and…"

The girl's voice interrupted him. "You want pots and pans?"

"Good Lord, no," he replied, "no."

"We have the no stick ones if you want? Do you want I ask how much?"

"I don't want any pans," said McAllister.

"OK," said the girl, but before he could continue, she beat him to it. "So you want tools? What is it you want, hammer, saw? We have electric drill, Bosch, very strong."

"No," he protested. "I don't want tools."

"Oh, OK," said the voice and the line went dead.

McAllister stared at his phone. That was one of the most bizarre calls he had ever made. He pressed redial and heard the tone. This time the girl answered. "Hello," he said, "I called just now."

"Ah yes," said the girl.

"Yes," he continued, "and I think we were cut off."

"No, I don't think so," said the girl. "I put the phone down."

McAllister was confused. "You put the phone down? Why?"

"You didn't want anything," said the girl. "Have you changed your mind?"

"No," said McAllister, and then very quickly: "But don't hang up... hello?"

"Hello," said the girl.

He was relieved. "Ah, good you are still there."

"Of course," said the girl slightly bemused.

"Right," he continued, "there is something I want." He lowered his voice. "Just hang on a moment." He reached into his bag and pulled out a small empty cardboard box. "Are you still there?"

"Of course." The girl was now intrigued.

McAllister read the label on the box to the girl. He assumed that they would not have them. The girl responded.

"I do not know. One minute, I will ask my father." He heard voices faintly jabbering in Greek. "Hello," said the girl suddenly, making him jump. "No, we do not have those. We have others but not those. My father says they are special."

McAllister sighed. "Yes, they are. I didn't think you would have them, but it was worth a try." He was about to thank her and end the call when the girl interrupted him.

"My father says when do you want them?"

"Oh," said the Scot, very surprised. "Well I will be in Symi tomorrow, in the morning but…" Again, the girl interrupted him. "Wait a moment please." He heard more talking faintly and then the girl came back.

"My father says OK."

"OK?" McAllister was amazed. "You will have them?"

"Yes, of course. He says he will call to Rhodos now and they will be here tonight, or in the morning."

"Great. In the morning, right, well thank your father for me and tell him I am..." He got no further.

"Just a moment," the girl said. He heard more talking. Then the girl spoke again. "How many do you want? He says he thinks they are fifty in one box. He does not know the price."

"Oh that will be fine, one box great. I will see you tomorrow." He was about to end the call again when a thought occurred to him. "Just one thing, where is the shop? I mean how do I find you?"

The girl laughed. "Ask."

"Ask?" he queried.

"Yes." The girl replied. "We are behind the Harani bar next to the baker, but ask anyone, everyone knows Dinos. Goodbye."

The call ended and McAllister looked at his phone and laughed. "Bugger me." He crumpled up the small empty box and let it drop to the floor.

"Well Alex Brown, so much for the blanks."

In a small room, at the back of the house with the terrace high above the harbour in Symi, a young man eased his contorted body into the chair in front of his computer and rested the crutches against the table. His hands were bent and twisted and his shaking head was at an angle to one side, but his fingers glided over the keyboard as he brought up, the programme he wanted.

A small egg timer signal appeared in the centre of the screen over a revolving gold bar.

His father watched and carefully cut up, his soon to expire, bank card which he had taken from his wallet.

The young man reached down and pulled open a drawer just below his computer. He lifted out a small black card reader and, with a shaking hand, connected it to a USB port in the side of his screen. The computer gave a small bell-like tone and the egg timer indicator disappeared, leaving the gold bar, which stopped revolving, in the centre of the screen. In the middle of the bar was a black line which was changing to green running from left to right. When the whole line was green, the boy pressed several keys. He glanced at his father and held out his screwed up hand.

His father, took his new bank card from the envelope marked Omega Bank and handed it to the boy. The boy took it between the knuckles of two bent fingers and in a swift movement ran it through the reader. He handed the card back to his father as the computer suddenly burst onto life with a brief sound bite of ABBA.

"Money money money, must be funny, in the rich man's world."

His father laughed and looked at the screen as five letters appeared impressed in the gold bar. They appeared slowly, one after the other, until they made a word.

'M I D A S.'

The Englishman stopped several times on his way up the main *kalistrata* to the village. In the heat of the day it was a real effort. He passed Taverna Georgio and reached the village square, which at this time of the day was deserted. A stocky middle-aged man was wiping down a table outside his café and he looked up as the Englishman appeared. A broad grin spread over his moustached face. "*Yassas.*"

The Englishman responded. "*Yassas. Mia bira parakalo.*"

"No problem." The man went inside while the Englishman sat down under the canvas canopy that stretched the full width of walkway that edged the square. He listened and was struck by the absolute silence of the village in the hot afternoon. Then he realised there was one constant sound; the continual background clatter of the cicadas. It was so constant that unless he really concentrated, he no longer heard it. The man reappeared with beer in a large frosted glass, and a small bowl containing a mixture of olives and pickled peppers.

"English?" he asked.

"Yes," said the Englishman.

"Thought so," the café owner smiled. "Only the English walk up the steps at this time of day."

He went back inside as the Englishman took a taste of the ice-cold beer and spiked one of the pickled peppers with a tooth-pick that was in the bowl. He put it in his mouth as the café owner emerged with a beer of his own. "These pickles are incredibly good."

"My wife Maria. She is good with that sort of thing." He picked out an olive himself and put it in his mouth as he sat down. He took out the stone and put it on the table.

He continued. "Yes, this she can do. Moussaka? Terrible. Lamb or Goat? You can eat it, but you will remember it for a week, if you understand me, yes?"

The Englishman nodded as he took another mouthful of beer.

"Yes, anything you can keep in vinegar, I think you say preserve, yes? Yes, that she can do. Probably why I have an ulcer. You have a wife?"

The Englishman nodded again. It was something he had noticed here. People had no reticence in directly asking you questions about yourself. He had gone into the small stationary shop in the harbour that morning and found yesterday's Daily Express. By the time he emerged he was sure the little old lady serving him knew his entire family history, the fact that he had been at a private school and his shoe size.

"Can she cook? Your wife?"

"Not bad," conceded the Englishman. He drank more of the beer. It was for some reason, very more-ish.

The cafe owner downed half of his glass in one go. "My father always said 'A good wife is a woman who has lots of different plates, in the kitchen and in the bed.' You see?" He winked.

The Englishman understood and grinned. He was warming to the conversation. "My wife does a good lobster thermidor," he said.

The man laughed. "Fish? You are lucky. I wouldn't trust Maria with fish. I do the fish. They do good fish there." He pointed at the taverna. "You staying in the harbour?" The Englishman nodded. "At the Old Markets." He finished his beer.

The man picked up the glass, and finished his own. "Another beer? On me? Good." He stood and walked back into the café.

The Englishman was beginning to feel relaxed, but he had a strange idea that maybe the beer had something to do with it, that and the alcohol he had earlier.

The man came out with two more large frosted glasses of beer. "You should bring your wife up here. Georgio, best taverna on Symi. You tell them in the morning, they get you lobster for the evening." He put the glasses down and sat.

"My wife's not with me actually," the Englishman found himself revealing as he picked up his beer.

"Ah," said the man, in a way that seemed to invite more information, which for some reason the Englishman felt obliged to give.

"But I do have my personal assistant Lucinda with me and..."

Before he had finished, the man slapped his hand down hard on the table and held up his glass to toast.

"*Yammas,*" he shouted.

"Er *Yammas*," responded the Englishman holding his glass up. They touched glasses and drank.

"I am Lefteris," said the man and held out his hand. "Toby." said the Englishman and shook his hand wondering why he had told him his real name.

"Personal assistant?" asked the man. "So you are here working then?"

"Yes, sort of," the Englishman volunteered and drank again. "Christ," he thought to himself, "if the Americans had a few of these Symi people they wouldn't have needed extraordinary rendition."

"So what work do you do?"

"Oh this and that," he said cautiously.

"I see," smiled the man. "And this girl? This Lucinda?"

Toby nodded.

"She assists you with 'this and that'?" Lefteris gave a broad grin and winked again.

Toby returned the smile. "She certainly does."

"*Yammas*!" shouted Lefteris again and touched his glass to Toby's. "Another thing my father said: 'Sometimes if you can't get a meal at home you may have to eat somewhere else.'" He downed his beer again. "Another?"

The two men talked on for another half an hour and Toby, resisting any more invites to consume more beer, managed to steer the conversation away from him and why he was in Symi, to general chat about the island and what he could see while he was there.

Eventually Lefteris said: "OK, I am going off for nanny nanny."

"Nanny nanny?" enquired Toby.

"A sleep," said the café owner, "before I open up for tonight. You want a last beer?"

The Englishman found himself considering it. The beer had not quenched his thirst at all but it had made him feel good. "Oh what the hell, yes, but a small one."

Lefteris took his glass, along with his own, and went inside. As he did Toby's mobile rang. It was Lucinda. He answered it.

"Hello… What? Oh the Manos fellow. Right, well... I see, nasty little shit, I was right… Has he? Yes, yes, usual thing, but they never hung it on him right?.. I get it… That's OK; we've got someone who can handle him if we need it. I thought he looked like a bastard and I was right. Thanks. Any news on Zoe? OK, I expect she will call when she can. Call that is." He was aware that suddenly he was talking very deliberately, in the way he did when he wasn't exactly drunk, but knew that drink had affected him. "Well I'll be back down in a bit. I've found a place we might eat tonight.... What? I am up in the village actually, outside having a beer with chap called Lefteris...what ? Well only two… What do you mean you see?" At that moment, Lefteris appeared with two large beers. "Two, well ok three if you count the one he just brought me." Lefteris looked at him, winked and mouthed the question, "Lucinda?" Toby nodded. "Hello Lucinda." Lefteris called, which caused Toby to laugh out loud. He returned to the phone.

"Er sorry about that… What? How does he know? Well because I told him… Why? I don't know why, look it's a long story involving fish and lobsters and...no only two beers." He took a sip of the fresh one that had arrived. "And a bit… What? No I haven't yet… Yes I know that's why I came up here… I will Lucinda, as soon as I have finished this beer… Yes, see you in about half an hour." He put the phone down, drank more of the beer and sighed. "Bloody hell, women."

Lefteris laughed. "And she isn't even your wife. Don't worry, they are all the same. It's in the blood. My father always said: 'All you have to do with a woman to keep her happy is accept that you are wrong.'"

"But I haven't done anything wrong," the Englishman protested.

Lefteris smiled. "You are a man. That is enough. You walked up from the harbour in the middle of the afternoon in about forty degrees and you had some beer. Obviously wrong. You should have died of thirst in front of my café. Tell her you are sorry, she will be happy. *Yammas."* He held up his glass and Toby followed suit "*Yammas*."

They both drank.

"Your mistake," continued the Greek, "was telling her about the beer. You see I will go home now and say to Maria that I met a very nice English man, who does this and that, and he wanted me to stay and talk and have a beer but I said, 'no I have been working all morning so I must go home and see my Maria.' And I will kiss her and she will say: 'You silly man Lefteris, you could have stayed and had a beer. Next time you stay and talk. You work hard enough, you deserve a beer.' Easy." He drank again. Toby laughed and followed suit.

"Lefteris, my new-found friend, you are a wise man. And as a wise man, tell me, if I go that way what will I find?" He pointed straight in front of him to the flat-stoned street that bordered the right-hand side of the square and disappeared between two rows of houses.

"That way," replied Lefteris, "goes below and in front of the castle and eventually round to the old steps. It is a flat walk and further on you can see down over the houses to the harbour."

"Thank you my friend," said Toby. He drank the rest of his beer and began to stand. As he did so the full effect of the beer became apparent. "Whoops," he said, a little uneasy on his feet. He knocked the table in front of him with his knee as he stood. "I am not drunk, just what we in England call a little tipsy. What do I owe you?"

“Nothing,” said the man. “As I think you say: ‘The pleasure was mine.’ Yes?”

Toby swayed very slightly. “Thank you Lefteris, doubtless we shall meet again.”

“I wouldn’t be at all surprised,” the smiling man replied. “You take care, and I hope you find what you’re looking for.”

“Right,” said the Englishman turning. He took a few paces, stopped and turned back. “What I am looking for. Why do you think I am looking for anything?”

“Well,” said the Greek, “I don’t think you came all the way up from the harbour, at this time of the day, just for a beer.”

“Good point,” considered Toby. “Good point. You Lefteris are a man of much wisdom. I am looking for something. Yes, and I am going that way.” He pointed ahead of him in the direction he had enquired about and set off.

Lefteris watched as the Englishman set off with a purposeful stride, swaying ever so slightly from side to side muttering. “I am looking for something, yes I am looking for something.”

“And,” said the Greek quietly to himself, “if you go that way Englishman, I think you will probably find it.”

Alan and Konstantina had spent the afternoon looking over the spectacular ruins and around the new museum behind the Parthenon.

“It is fantastic,” Alan said, “and air-conditioned.” Then he pointed to a display on the wall. “Ah, I recognise those, they are the Elgin marbles.”

“Actually, we call them the Parthenon marbles,” responded Konstantina. “Stolen by the British, and we want them back. Look at that display.” It was a reconstruction of what the upper exterior of the Parthenon would look like with the magnificent carvings of the Elgin marbles in place. “That is where they should be, not in London.”

“You feel quite strongly about that, don’t you?” he asked.

“Well actually, yes,” she replied. “Part of my heritage is being held by a bunch of thieves. The British." She was goading him, but he rose to the bait.

"Now come on, just because of a few old stones, to call us all thieves is a bit much."

"Old stones?" she reacted. "Old stones? They are part of one of the most important archaeological sites in the ancient world. If we took some lumps of Stonehenge and put them in the middle of Athens, you would soon kick up a fuss."

"Fair enough," he conceded.

She continued. "The marbles should be returned to their home and they haven't been. That makes you thieves."

"I object to that," he said. "We aren't all thieves. I'm not a thief, to start with."

She had him. She smiled, sidled up to him and whispered in his ear. "Midas?" She giggled and walked off towards the exit.

"Cow," he shouted after her, and several people looked around. As he passed the attendant on the door, a small, dark-haired elderly lady in a trim dark blue uniform, he apologised. "Sorry. Got a bit carried away. It's a superb museum; in fact the whole site is amazing, thank you."

The woman smiled back. "Thank you, sir. It will be even better when we get the marbles back."

He returned the smile. "This is a big thing with the Greeks, isn't it?"

"Oh yes." She took his arm. "I ask anyone who I meet from England to write to their government person."

"My MP?" he asked.

"Yes, that's it. We have tried for many years but we think that it needs the English people to try now."

"My word." He was genuinely impressed by the feeling in the woman's voice. "I'll see what I can do when I get back to England." he said.

"Thank you," said the woman, holding out a badge with the Acropolis on it. "This is for you Mr...?"

"Marks," he responded. "Thanks."

"Do not mention it," she said, pinning the badge on him.

"Alan?" called Konstantina looking back. "Come on, we need to get down to the docks now."

"Thanks," he said, once again to the woman. "Got to go now, got a boat to catch."

"Going anywhere nice?" said the woman, patting the badge.

"Rhodes," he said, "then somewhere called Symi?"

"Ah, beautiful."

"Is it?" he asked.

"Oh yes," said the woman. "Have a safe journey."

Alan walked off quickly and caught up with Konstantina.

"Nice woman," he said.

"Most Greek women are," she replied with a knowing look. "Come on, we need another cab."

As they disappeared around the front of the Parthenon, heading for the exit, the woman watched them go, and as they disappeared out of sight, she nodded to another woman in uniform who was stood across from her. The second lady, of similar age, walked across and took her place as she exited through the doors and walked in the direction the couple had gone. As she got to the front of the Parthenon, she stopped and watched Alan and Konstantina descend the main steps down and out of the site. She took a small green matchbox-sized box from her pocket and pressed a switch on the side. Next to the switch, a green LED light came on and then alternated between red and blue. The woman turned the small device off and took her mobile phone from her pocket, flipped it open and began to text rapidly.

CHAPTER ELEVEN

The Englishman swayed along the path below the ruined walls of the castle in Symi, humming gently to himself. The combination of the heat and the beer was making him feel quite tired, and so he hummed between yawns. There was a steep drop to the first row of houses below the concrete pathway, which made it higher than the roofs of the houses. He stopped and leaned against a small cypress tree growing just below the path and looked down over the harbour. It was a spectacular view. It almost looked like a model harbour from this height.

It was quiet down below, but he could see a yacht slowly turning to back into the harbour side and the white uniformed figure of the harbour master waving at the skipper. He saw the official put something up to his mouth and then take it away, and seconds after he heard a very faint whistle. Then he saw Lucinda walking back to the table where he had been sitting with Nikos. Well, he thought it was Lucinda; it looked like her, yes it was. He raised his hand and waved, and then realised that of course she wouldn't see him. He saw her order a drink and then suddenly delve into her bag and pull something out. It was something small and she was looking at it. "Wish I had binoculars," he muttered to himself, and then remembered why he had come up here in the first place. He looked down along the row of houses below him from right to left. As his gaze moved over to his left, he saw, through a small clump of trees, the edge of stone terrace with a wall around it. He leaned to one side and there it was, on top of the wall. A telescope.

"Bugger me," he yawned. "Right let's find out who has been

spying." He began to walk along the path looking for a way down. He saw a small, rough track which lead down off the main concrete pathway towards the house with the terrace. He was just about to descend when his mobile phone rang, making him jump, and he had to regain his footing as he almost slithered down the rough stony track. He fished his phone from his trouser pocket and looked at the screen. He put the phone up to his ear. "Lucinda? What is it? A text from Zoe? Ah that's what you were doing, looking at your phone... When? Just now, after you ordered a drink. Ah that is because I see everything my dear... No, I am not drunk, just happy." He walked back up the path as he spoke, and along to where he could look down and see Lucinda. "Now you are looking around trying to see me. Look up... No not there, up here. Up towards the church above the castle and then along a bit. I am waving, that's me."

As he did this, he was totally unaware of the old shepherd with his donkey who had been approaching from the other direction. He stopped just before he reached the Englishman and looked down over the harbour and waved as well, although he knew not why. His donkey however continued and stopped between the two of them.

"What donkey?" said Toby into his phone as he turned to his left. "What are you talking about, Lucinda? Ah!" He got the shock of his life as he came face to face with the beast, which promptly began to bellow in that strangulated way that only donkeys can, sounding as though they are being pumped up. Its breath was foul and Toby reeled back as he got it full in the face. The old man laughed, slapped his animal and walked on past chuckling and waving sporadically, making himself laugh again as if recounting some enormously humorous event.

"What?" said Toby recovering. "Oh right, Zoe's text...They will be here when? Tomorrow? Probably in the morning... They are going by ferry to Rhodes first. Good... OK, I'll be back down after I've finished up here. Enjoy your g and t." He waved again, put his phone in his pocket and set off down the rough track. The descent was steep and a couple of times he almost lost his footing. "Toby you idiot, shouldn't have had the beer," he admonished himself. "Mind you it was bloody good." Suddenly, he found himself at the house with the terrace. He could just see the telescope on the wall to his right behind the main house wall. There were steps up to a smaller raised patio that lead to the front door which was open, but it had a thin outer framed door in front of it with a thin mesh over it.

He knocked on the door frame but made little noise. He tried harder; still no result.

"Hello?" he shouted. He heard a deep voice inside call something and then heard footsteps. Suddenly in front of him, behind the mesh screen, was a towering bronze figure in swim shorts. A big middle aged man with a large brown belly and thick muscular arms looked out at him.

"*Yassou!*" he thundered.

"Jesus Christ," said the Englishman. "It's you."

The man who had chased Alan Marks down the street sat in the front of the silver Range Rover Evoque outside the airport terminal in Athens and rubbed his knee again. He turned to his colleague and spoke in Greek. "This really hurts. How did that little twat get away, Louka?"

"That, Gabrielli," said the other man, "is what Mrs Manidaki wanted to know." He folded his phone and put it in his pocket. "She isn't pleased." He turned on the sat-nav screen on the Range Rover's dashboard and a map appeared. "Fortunately for you, me putting everyone on watch has paid off."

"Well I hope she didn't think it was all my fault," responded Gabrielli, still rubbing is knee.

"You heard what I told her," his partner replied. "I told her, he came up the stairs and surprised us and that you chased him down the street but couldn't get him. She said perhaps you were getting too old."

“Too old?” Gabrielli was outraged. “Too old? I might not be as young as you and your poncy brother, but I could still give you a good run for your money.”

Loukas played with the left-hand knob next to the screen and the map zoomed in displaying the street names for a wide area around them. “This piece of kit is amazing, Wasted on my brother. How come she gives him this car? How come? I’ll tell you, ‘cause he is an arse licker. Always was. Hello, now look at that.” He indicated a small red dot which was flashing slowly and moving along a road at the top of the screen. “There they are. Mrs Manidaki says they will be heading for the port so if I’m not mistaken they will turn left in just about,” he paused looking at the screen, “...now. Yes. Right let’s go. Not far away at all.” He started the car and revved it. “Wasted on Manos. Totally wasted. Let’s go get the little English bastard, then maybe I’ll get a present.”

As they sat in the back of the taxi heading for Piraeus, Konstantina turned to Alan. “Now this driver isn’t too bad, is he?”

“True,” said Alan. “But to be fair he has been in heavy traffic so far, I mean once he gets to those narrow streets he could go ballistic like the other guys.” They pulled up behind several cars at yet another set of traffic lights.

“Rush hour,” she commented.

“We will make this ferry, won’t we?” asked Alan.

“I should think so,” responded Konstantina. “I could always ask our man to go faster?” She winked at him.

“Very funny,” he said. “You said this ferry will have a shop?”

“Shop, restaurants, bars, internet. You haven’t been on a Greek ferry, have you?”

Before he could reply, she continued, “Hey, you are alright on boats, I mean you don’t get seasick?”

The outraged look on his face made her smile.

“Seasick? Seasick? I will have you know I have been sailing since I was a little kid. Up until last year, when the company started to need more money, I had a yacht down on the Hamble. I've got my PADI qualification in scuba diving as well, and…" Before he could say more there was a loud bang and the sound of breaking glass as they were both flung forward into the back of the front seats.

"Shit!" yelled Alan clutching his nose, which was bleeding.

"What the hell?" said Konstantina, who had managed to fling her hands up in front of her face, but still felt the whiplash effect on the back of her neck.

The driver, who had seen in his mirror what was about to happen at the last minute and braced himself, got out of the car and walked to the back. He looked down at the shattered rear lights and crumbled bumper. He turned and yelled at the driver of the vehicle that had ploughed into him. The driver of the silver Range Rover Evoque, which seemed to have suffered virtually no ill effects, was unmoved. Still shouting, the taxi driver turned back to his car and pointed at the damage. As he did so, he felt a sharp pain at the back of his head and he crumpled to the floor.

At the same time, having turned in his seat to look behind at what was happening, Alan Marks heard the door behind him open and felt something dig into the back of his neck.

"Get out very slowly, Mr Marks," said a voice with a strong Greek accent. "Unless you want to die in the back of this taxi."

Konstantina, who had been watching the driver of the taxi fall, whipped around to see Alan slowly backing out of the cab. Suddenly the door next to her opened and a hand grabbed her arm, wrenching her from the seat and out onto the ground. She looked up and came face to face with the barrel of a gun. "Get up," said the owner of the gun.

She stood very slowly, her bag over her shoulder, and backed up towards the Range Rover. As she did, a young man got out of a car behind the Range Rover and started to come towards them. "Hey," he called. "What the hell is going on, I've got a ferry to..." He got no further as the man pointing the gun at Konstantina moved his aim slightly to the left, fired once, and returned his aim to the Greek girl. The young man reeled back with a look of bewildered amazement on his face as the blood poured down from his forehead and he fell to the ground, dead. People in other cars who saw what had happened screamed and yelled, several tried to back up, bumping into the cars behind them. By now, Alan was being bundled into the back of the Range Rover and Loukas flicked his gun to indicate to Konstantina to keep going backwards. Soon she and Alan were in the back seat of the silver four-by-four with Gabrielli next to them, pointing his gun at Alan's head. As Loukas got into the front driving seat and revved the car, he said; "One move from either of you and my friend will kill Mr Marks." There was a squeal of tyres and a cloud of white smoke as he rammed the taxi cab forward, reversed and pushed the car behind him back into the one behind that. Then he spun the steering wheel and accelerated out of the gap, going over the head of the taxi driver who was lying on the ground. He steered around the abandoned cab, across the lights, causing a bus to avoid him and career into an oncoming van head-on. Loukas avoided the van and set off down the road at speed as a police car, lights flashing and siren blaring, headed past them going the other way. Ahead of them was another set of traffic lights at red. Beside the lights was a sign-post showing Piraeus ahead and Korinthos to the right. They reached them in a matter of seconds. He suddenly flipped the wheel and turned sharp right, almost going onto two wheels and causing a large articulated lorry, which was coming through the lights, to suddenly veer right and plough into the traffic light post which exploded in a hail of sparks. The silver Range Rover Evoque sped up the hill.

"The magnification on this thing is incredible," said the Englishman looking down into the harbour through the telescope. "I can almost read the bloody paper Lucinda has on the table. And you reckon what I spotted was your boy looking at the tourist girls, eh?"

"Yes," said the Greek. "He might be bent and broken in a lot of ways, but he is still a boy, and his mother still has to get the marks off his sheets, if you understand me?"

At this point, the Englishman had moved along the harbour with his telescopic gaze and alighted on the very girl the boy had seen earlier. "I bloody do understand. Christ. Drakou, you should see this. If your boy sees this sort of thing every day, he'll wank himself into an early grave." He kept looking at the girl, who was stretching her neck back, a movement which accentuated her breasts, in what he found to be a quite alarming manner. "Jesus, I wish I'd had one of these at his age. Where is he anyway?"

"Sleeping," said the big man. "He gets tired in the afternoons. He has another operation in Athens next month, for his legs this time. Thanks to you, I can pay for it."

"Good," said Toby, still glued to the telescope. "I know he can't do much on the computers, but it was a real gift getting him on Nikos so-called scheme. Bloody hell she is bending down, I can't take much more of this, it's not good for the old ticker."

Toby left the telescope and turned to the big Greek man who was carrying two bottles of beer. "Oh Christ no, I can't have any more beer."

"More?" said the Greek. "Ah, don't tell me, at this time of day, let me see, you went past Lefteris café?" The Englishman nodded. "Only you didn't go past, you stopped. Lefteris had finished for the afternoon and you ended up talking, and drinking too much, yes?"

"Yes," said the Englishman, slightly surprised. "How do you know this?"

"Lefteris and I are old friends." The big Greek looked around and lowered his voice. "I had Maria when we were still at school, and if they ever have a row she always tells him." His voice came back to normal as a short, rather plump woman in a flowered apron, with a large beaming smile, came out onto the terrace. She was carrying a plate of small, round batter-like cakes covered in chopped nuts and honey.

"You have had too much beer already my friend, the damage is done, one more won't hurt." He thrust the beer bottle into Toby's hand. The woman held out the cakes to him.

"You must be Mrs Drakou?" said the Englishman, taking a cake. "Thank you."

"My wife Anna," said the Greek. "She doesn't speak English." He returned to the woman and said something in Greek and she replied. He turned to Toby.

"She says she hopes you like them, she made them this morning. They are *loukoumathes*, traditional Greek honey cakes. Her grandmother's recipe."

"They are wonderful," said the Englishman, his lips covered in crumbs and nuts. He looked at the woman and said, rather too loudly, "Thank you, Anna."

The woman smiled, an embarrassed smile. The big Greek said something to her and she nodded at the Englishman and left.

"I told her you were the Englishman who was paying me for a bit of work. She doesn't know what sort of work and she would not ask. I said you had come to talk about business, which I am assuming you have." He indicated a chair for the man.

"Well actually," said Toby whilst eating his cake. "I came up, because I spotted the telescope. I didn't know it was your place."

The big man looked at him with a searching gaze. "You didn't know I lived here?"

"We've only ever met at the taverna in the village, or that first time in Rhodes. Of course I know where your place is by GPS on the system, but addresses mean nothing here, do they? I mean your street hardly has a name."

"I see," said the Greek. "GPS eh? So you have been spying on me then, rather than my boy spying on you?"

"I have not been spying on you Drakou…" The Englishman, suddenly realised the Greek was winding him up. "Ah, very funny. Look, you were recommended by Antoniadis in Athens, and that's good enough for me. He showed me some examples of your work. Very impressive, even if it was some time ago."

The Greek laughed. "Some things you never forget." He cracked his knuckles very loudly.

The Englishman believed him. "Well, those particular skills you have may come in handy shortly. There is a young man called Manos minding Stavroulis."

"I have seen him," the Greek interrupted. "Nasty little bastard, thinks he is a big man. You want I should get rid of him?"

"Not yet," said Toby. "But it may be necessary later."

The Greek took a swig of his beer. "So when does this other Englishman get here with his new Greek lady?"

"Ah yes," smiled Toby. "His new Greek lady. According to Zoe, they will be on a ferry to Rhodes tonight."

"The *Diagoras*," said the Greek man. "That means they will be here by the first ferry from Rhodes in the morning, the *Dodecanese Pride*. The *Diagoras* will get into Rhodes about seven thirty. We will know if it is on time because I will see it anyway."

"See it?" asked Toby. "How?"

"I am fishing tonight at the other end of the island. I go once or twice a week in my boat at this time of year. I have a freezer full of *octopathi* for the winter. Sometimes I take Anna and the boy, but now you have told me this I will go alone. When I see the ship go past on its way to Rhodes I will head back."

"It will go past Symi?" said Toby with incredulity in his voice. "Why doesn't it stop here?"

"Ask the Mayor," said the big man. "It's a long story. Anyway, it will take them to Rhodes, they will get the high speed catamaran and they will end up here about ten. Shall I call you when the *Diagoras* goes past about six in the morning?"

"I can do without that," said Toby. "Look, I'll leave it to you. Get back here in time though because I need you to get Marks and bring him to Tolis when I call you. It will be about lunchtime. I don't want him meeting Nikos before I've had a chance to talk to him. Oh and if the Scotsman turns up, keep him away from him, too."

"Right, but how will I know this Scottish man?" asked the Greek.

The Englishman picked up his phone and dialled. "Lucinda? Send Savvas that shot of McAllister at Gatwick, will you? Thanks." He turned to Drakou. "You should have it shortly and when..."

He was interrupted by the sound of a mobile phone playing the song 'Never On a Sunday.'

"Ah, Melina," said Drakou, retrieving the phone from just inside the door which leads into the house. "Now, there was a woman for a boy to wank over." He returned and winked at Toby. "And I did." He pressed a button and looked at the phone. He held the phone up to Toby. "This is him?"

"That is the Scotsman. And I don't want him hurt."

The big Greek looked back at the picture on the tiny screen and studied it. "The little shit Manos is no problem. But this man, he is different. I am glad you don't want I should hurt him."

"Oh," said Toby. "Why?"

"Because," said the Greek gazing at the screen. "I'm not sure I could."

Alan Marks stood looking at the end of Gabrielli's gun and told the truth. "I don't have Midas."

"Hand over the box," said Gabrielli, and held out his hand. "Now!"

Loukas had pulled the silver four by four off the road at the top of the hill on the road to Korinthos, just up from where the traffic lights were now a scene of chaos. People milled around, trying to free the lorry driver from his crumpled cab. He took the Range Rover down a rough track and parked it at the edge of a huge landfill site, which was a sprawling landscape of household refuse, abandoned cars and the broken hulls of long disused rowing boats. Seagulls flocked in the skies above and swooped down with piercing cries to scavenge amongst the rotting piles of rubbish. The combination of their wailing and the swarms of flies that surrounded stinking mounds of refuse was deafening. The smell was overpowering. Loukas had ordered them out of the car and stepped out himself, leaving the engine running. As he had raised his gun his mobile phone had rung. He answered it. "Yes, Mrs Manidaki. Sorry I can't hear you." He was having to raise his voice almost to a shout over the din of the gulls and flies. "Yes we have them… Do what? Right. Then what do I...sorry..... Anywhere? I can't hear. Just a minute I'll get in the car...I said I'll....hang on." He turned to Gabrielli, who was pointing his gun at the couple. "Marks has a small black box. Get it. Now." He started to get back into the car. "I'll be a minute. Sorry Mrs Manidaki but what do I do then?" He shut the door as he shouted into the phone.

And so Alan and Konstantina had found themselves face to face with Gabrielli's gun.

Alan protested once more. "Honestly, I don't have Midas."

"I don't care what you call it, just give me the box. Now." The tubby man stepped forward and put both hands on the handle of the gun and steadied himself.

Suddenly Konstantina spoke. "I have it." She stepped forwards, taking her bag from her shoulder. "It's in here." She opened the bag and rummaged inside. "What the hell? No, it was here. It was I swear." She looked up at Alan. "Shit Alan, it's gone. Did you take it?"

Alan couldn't believe what he was hearing. He felt the blood draining from his head and his legs beginning to weaken. He shouted in panic as he tried to wave the flies away from his face. "Take it? Of course I didn't take it. You had it. You kept it in your bag. Jesus, Tina."

She screamed at him, mimicking his accusing tone. "Well it's not bloody well here. Look."

She held out the open bag towards Gabrielli who looked in, and as he did, she swung her foot, giving him a sharp blow on the shin just below his already sore knee. The overweight Greek cried out, reeling back and dropping his gun. As he went to clutch at his leg, Konstantina yelled: "Run Alan, run!"

Alan, almost as a reflex, turned and ran towards the mounds of rubbish as Gabrielli, looking up, realised what had happened. He bent to pick up his gun as Konstantina swung her leg again kicking the stooping Greek under the chin, sending him careering backwards with a scream. As she grabbed the gun and swung around, she saw Loukas stepping from the four by four and aiming his weapon. More in instinct than anything else, she raised the gun in her shaking hand and pulled the trigger. Loukas ducked as glass from the front side window of the Range Rover showered down around him. As he recovered and looked up, he saw Konstantina disappearing over a mound of refuse, clutching her bag.

Loukas ran towards the mountain of refuse and shouted at his colleague. "Get up you twat, they are getting away." He clambered over the piles of plastic bags as Gabrielli got up and limped after him. Loukas reached the top of the first heap and surveyed the scene in front of him. Mound upon mound of plastic bags, old fridges and cookers, smashed televisions, wrecked and burnt-out cars, the detritus of human existence.

Gabrielli, breathing heavily and holding his chin, joined him. "Christ, where are they?"

"Somewhere out there, thanks to you." Loukas glowered at the panting Gabrielli. "Well don't just stand there, go flush them out."

"What about you?" his rotund partner responded.

"I," said Loukas, "am going to stand here and, once you have got them to show themselves," he tapped the barrel of his gun to his nose, "I will pick them off. Now go get them."

Gabrielli looked down on the wretched landscape. "But it's stinking."

"Why do you think I am staying up here?" replied the man with the gun. "Go!"

Gabrielli began to clamber down the steep slope of the mound, slipping and slithering over black plastic bags, as flies swarmed around him. "Shit," he exclaimed as he caught his leg on a protruding iron bar.

Alan Marks crouched down beside a battered and open chest freezer, and made the mistake of putting out his hand to steady himself. "Shit!" He recoiled as the heat from the scratched metal burnt his palm where it had been scraped before.

As he climbed up the next mound of rubbish, Gabrielli heard a man's voice swearing. He upped his pace and scrambled towards the top of the next hill of bags, slipping and sliding as he did so.

Alan Marks blew on his hand to try and cool the pain, unaware of the person creeping up behind him.

"Alan." Konstantina's voice made him jump.

"Christ Tina, you scared the crap out of me."

"Shhh." the girl responded putting her finger up to her lips and whispering. "They'll be coming after us."

"They will," said a voice up above them. It was Gabrielli looking down on the couple. He turned and shouted back to Loukas. "Here, they are here!"

"Shut up!" shouted Konstantina. Gabrielli turned to see the gun in her hand pointing at him. "Come down here," she ordered.

"What the hell are you doing?" asked Alan. "We don't want him down here."

"I've got an idea," she whispered.

Gabrielli got halfway down the slope, caught his foot in a protruding bicycle handlebar and tumbled down the rest of the rubbish, landing face down in front of the rusting freezer.

"Get up," said Konstantina. The man moaned and slowly turned over. "Get up now!" she shouted. He rose to his feet and made the mistake of trying to steady himself with his hand on the metal casing. "Fuck!" He pulled back his hand.

"Hot isn't it?" said Alan.

"Konstantina waved the gun at Gabrielli, indicating as she spoke. "Get in."

Gabrielli looked at the chest freezer. "In there? I'll suffocate."

"Tough," she responded, and then shouted, "get in!"

As he began to clamber in, Alan spoke. "He'll boil alive in there."

"Alan," she said, still pointing the gun at the tubby man. "They are trying to kill us. Put the lid down."

Alan gingerly lifted the lid of the freezer, which was also incredibly hot. He did it by alternating one hand with the other until it reached its apex and slammed down, closing the container.

Konstantina was now at the front and had picked up a broken coat hanger. She flipped the metal catch over and slotted the wire into the hole that was meant for a padlock. Gabrielli started banging on the inside of the freezer and they could hear his muffled cries. "That should do it for a while," she said.

"Do what?" shouted a voice up above them on top of the mound. It was Loukas and he was pointing his gun at Konstantina. She spun around and, in a reflex action, pulled the trigger. Nothing happened. She tried again.

"Shoot!" shouted Alan.

"I'm trying to." She was pulling at the trigger.

Loukas slowly began to descend the pile of rubbish, carefully picking his way. "It is jammed. Cheap Chinese crap, unlike this Russian work of art." He fired his gun in the air and a host of seagulls flew up off the tip, squealing and crying, their calls mixing with Gabrielli's increasingly desperate yells.

Konstantina tried to fire once more and still the gun was stuck. She threw it to one side. "Sorry Alan."

Loukas laughed as he reached the bottom of the heap.

"Not your fault," Alan replied turning to face the Greek man.

"Nobody's fault," smiled Loukas. "Just bad luck. Never mind."

As he walked towards them, Alan and Konstantina backed away. Behind them, covered in seagull droppings, was the burnt-out shell of an old Volkswagen Beetle.

Alan was shaking but managed to speak. "Look," he said, trembling, "we haven't got the Midas thing and..." He got no further as Loukas swiftly stepped forward and, with the side of the gun, dealt a swift and painful blow to the side of his face. Alan went down instantly and lay motionless on the ground. Loukas laughed again and turned towards Konstantina, who was backing towards the old car.

"Where is it?" Loukas looked straight at her and walked forwards, leaving Alan's body behind him.

"I told your fat friend in there," she glanced towards the freezer. "We have lost it."

Loukas suddenly spoke to her in Greek. "I don't believe you." He said and then, seeing the slight surprise on her face. "Oh yes, I know you are Greek. One last time. Where is it?" Konstantina stared at him and backed further away. "Very well," he continued. "I count to three and if you don't tell me where the small black box is, I will kill you. Then I will get the truth out of your friend back there." He walked forward as he counted. *Ena, thio, tria*. You had your chance."

Konstantina backed up against the door of the rusting car. She slowly found herself sinking to the floor as the hot metal began to scorch her back through her blouse and she closed her eyes.

Loukas raised his gun until the centre of her head was in line with the small metal sight at the end of the barrel. "Silly girl." He said and slowly began to squeeze the trigger. The bang he heard confused him for an instant and he briefly felt a searing pain in his head just before he lost consciousness. Gabrielli's gun, thrown by Alan Marks, hit him on the back of his neck just below his skull. He gave a brief cry and, as she opened her eyes, Konstantina saw Loukas fall forwards like a felled tree and crash face-first into the mangle of wire and wood at her feet.

"How did you do that?" she stuttered as Alan held out his hand to help her up.

"Cricket when I was a kid." He smiled. "I was a crap batsman and a crap bowler but a mean fielder." He looked at her confused expression. "Cricket, the English game with a bat and ball, never mind. Christ," he said, rubbing the side of his head, "that bastard didn't half hit me. I bloody saw stars. What now?"

As Konstantina stood, she looked at her watch. "We've got half an hour to get to the ferry."

"Half an hour? Jesus Tina, we won't make it," he said.

"We might in their car," she responded with a smile.

"The Range Rover Evoque?" he grinned.

"Is it?" she said.

"Oh yes," Alan replied. "Always wanted to try one. Come on." He started to climb over the refuse, slipped and fell, coming face to face with a split black refuse bag and the maggot ridden, half-eaten carcass of rotting chicken. "Oh crap." He got to his feet quickly and started off again, brushing off maggots that had clung to his shirt from the bag.

"Nice," said Konstantina. "You will smell lovely. Hang on." She halted him, turning back and running over to the wrecked car. She pulled open the door, which creaked and groaned, and pulled out her bag. "Can't go without this."

"Ah yes," he said, "we need the tickets."

"And this," she said, pulling out the small black card reader.

Alan Marks struggled to speak. "But you said it had gone, you even accused me of..." He didn't finish the sentence.

She grinned. "I did, didn't I? Good job I didn't mean it. Come on. Hang on." She bent down and picked up the gun Loukas had dropped. "Might need this too, the way things have been going." She passed him and climbed up the mound.

"Tina," he yelled after her as he clambered over the stinking mound. "You said Midas had gone. You are a lying...I'm not even going to say it. We could have been shot."

"Come on," she said glancing back. "We need to get out of here before the fat thug gets out of the freezer and that one," she pointed at Loukas, "wakes up."

They got to the Range Rover Evoque. The engine was still running.

"On second thoughts," said Alan, "perhaps you had better drive. It's on the wrong side of the road for me and we are in a hurry."

"True," Konstantina agreed getting into the driving seat. "The problem is we need to get to the port in less than thirty minutes and we need to go back down the hill to the traffic lights and turn right. It will be swarming with police by now I would think."

"Yes but," said Alan, fiddling with the knobs on the sat-nav in the dash-board, "this shows where we are. Look, we must be that red dot. The blue there is the sea so that's where we were heading, you can see the port on this map. If I can zoom in a bit more we will get the names of roads." He fiddled some more and the map became more detailed. "That's it. You drive, I'll navigate," he pointed at the cross roads a short distance away. "I'll get us around that cross roads where the traffic lights are. Come on, and turn left when you get to the main road."

"Yes sir," said Konstantina with a smile, as she reversed the Silver four-by-four to turn it around and then headed back to the main road in a cloud of dust.

In Thessalonika Marina Manidaki laughed out loud as Anne Robinson insulted yet another contestant on 'The Weakest Link'. She held up her glass to the television screen "*Yammas,* Mrs Robinson, a woman after my own heart." Still chuckling, she picked up the phone next to her when it rang.

"Hello. Oh, it's you. Well you don't need to worry, we should have Midas back round about now. I haven't heard from my boys, but I am sure everything will be fine. I don't know why you are so concerned; as long as one of us gets it back. We are partners after all... Yes, I know you have an interest and I will not forget that you gave us the codes that made it all possible. Look, I would have thought after all this time you would have trusted Marina. I told you not to send anyone yourself, there was no need. Just a minute, I will check something." She picked up the television remote and pressed a button. The screen changed instantly to a map of the area around Piraeus. A small red dot was moving along a road approaching the harbour. Her expression changed to instant anger. "Idiots." She returned to the phone conversation. "Hello. I am afraid we don't seem to have it just yet, but don't worry, I will sort it out… No, I think it is on its way to Symi but we will have it before it gets there. I will call you back." She slammed the phone down. "Jones?" she screamed. "Jones?" The butler appeared in the doorway. "Look at that." She pointed at the screen. "Look. Why are men such fools?"

The butler responded in the politest way he could. "I am not entirely sure ma'am."

"Well they are," she replied. "Mindless fools. Get me Spiros in Kos. Quickly".

Jones picked up the phone and began to dial.

"Then get me an ouzo and get me Loukas. I have something rather unpleasant to do, in fact, get me Loukas first." Jones dutifully put the phone down and picked it up again, waited a few seconds to see if Mrs Manidaki was about to change her mind again, and then began dialling once more.

They were only a short distance from the harbour when Konstantina suddenly stopped the Range Rover.

"What are you doing?" asked Alan. "I've got us dead on track to get there, it's only around that corner." He pointed forward. "We are practically on the dockside and we've still got ten minutes."

"Which is why I have stopped," she replied. "The police will be looking for this car, we are lucky we haven't been spotted already. We certainly would be seen be in the harbour."

"I am so glad you came," said Alan, getting out of the car.

"In a funny way, so am I," she answered as they set off down the street at a fast walking pace. "You know, despite being shot at and everything." They rounded the corner and the port of Piraeus was in front of them, with the main entrance just across the road and the big 'E' sign above the gate. Directly behind the gates was a big ferry with its huge back door down on the dockside and several large lorries entering into the gaping black hole which was the hull.

"That's ours, the *Diagoras*," said Konstantina. "We are going to make it, just."

"We're going to make it," said Alan, breathing heavily as they jogged the last few yards to the ship. "But I wonder if our fat friend did, or if he boiled alive."

"He'll be cool," she said as they walked up the long gangway onto the ferry.

"Cool?" said Alan, beads of sweat dripping from his face.

She smiled. "Well he was in a freezer."

Alan moaned as they boarded the escalator that took them up to the reception area on the ship. "Bad joke, really bad joke," he said as they reached the reception area. Then he felt the air-conditioning. "But this is cool, really cool."

Loukas was looking at Gabrielli's gun and pulling the action back and forth. "Cheap crap." He muttered and looked at his bedraggled colleague. "Why do you have cheap crap?" His mobile phone rang very loudly and he grabbed it from his pocket and answered it. "Bloody noise." His head felt like a needle had been put through it. "Yes, Mrs Manidaki. Sorry Mrs Manidaki… What? Yes I know they are… You can see it on your screen? Right, on the ferry.... I would think so by now yes… Why didn't we?" Before he could explain the old lady stopped him. He listened and replied. "Yes Mrs Manidaki, yes that is the reason… Will I what? Sorry did I hear that correctly?.. Very well, Mrs Manidaki... Yes. You would like to talk to Gabrielli? I'm sure he can explain." He handed the phone to his red faced partner, who was standing in the open freezer bathed in sweat.

"Hello? Mrs Manidaki? What happened? Well it's a bit complicated, but basically they got away while I was... No I didn't but... my fault? Well I suppose you could say that yes… Yes I understand. You are very understanding. You allow everyone a mistake, and that is very generous because we all make mistakes… Sorry, my mistake was making two mistakes in one day? Well I don't know about... sorry, too old for this game? I don't think so… What retire? Well I wasn't thinking of... " The suggestion that he should retire was the last thing he heard, and his response was the last thing he said, as the bullet from his own gun entered the side of his head just above his right eye and exited on the other side in a spurt of blood, at the same height just above his left eye. He crumpled back down into the freezer and Loukas dropped the lid on his head. He looked at the gun. "Well well, it seems to be working now."

CHAPTER TWELVE

Spiros Mavrilis took a bundle of money from the open till behind the counter of Gucci Gold, a jewellery shop on the harbour side in the main port of Kos. He stuffed the money into his jacket pocket and bent over the shop owner, who was cowering on the floor. He stooped and picked the man up by his lapels.

Spiros was a big man in his mid-thirties. The sort of man whose jacket just stretched over his well-developed muscles. His face bore the scars of a violent past. "Next time," he said to the trembling thin little Turk with broken glasses, "when Mrs Manidaki says she wants the money now, she means NOW!" He head-butted the man and, as a spout of blood shot from the man's head, Spiros dodged sideways, letting go of the jacket and allowing the quivering body to drop to the floor.

He glowered at the whimpering blood-covered shop keeper and, reaching inside his own shirt, pulled out a gold chain from around his neck, which bore a cross, and kissed it. "May God bless you," he said and made the sign of the cross over the Turk, then stamped hard on his head. The man squealed and fell silent.

Spiros fumbled in his pocket as his mobile phone rang. "Hello, yes Mrs Manidaki I have the money." He looked down at the Turk. "He is as well as can be expected... Another job? The *Diagoras*? About four tomorrow morning I think, on the way to Rhodos… Yes I can... a small black box? You will email a picture of the man? OK. And when I have the box? Of course it will be a pleasure. Consider it done, Mrs Manidaki... naturally, there will be no trace."

On the *Diagoras*, Alan put down the carrier bags as he took the key card for the cabin door from his pocket.

"I told you there would a shop on the ship," said Konstantina, picking up the bags.

"I know," said Alan. "But I didn't expect designer gear, and that restaurant we passed looked a bit good. I think we will have a meal there."

"After we have showered," said Konstantina. "Judging by the way that woman in the shop tried not to get too close to us, I think we might smell of rubbish." She followed Alan into the cabin.

"Wow!" Alan exclaimed as he looked at the room. "This is like a mini stateroom. I know you said deluxe," he smiled, as he looked into the shower room which was in mock marble with a shower cubicle, toilet and wash hand basin, "but this is better than most hotels I've been in. This is like a cruise ship."

"We do ships in Greece," laughed Konstantina, putting the carrier bags on the small table and sitting down on the long sofa that nestled just under the wide window which looked out over the bow of the ship.

Alan turned back and scanned the accommodation. "There's a television, a fridge, even a bowl of fruit. And look at the size of that double bed." He stopped and blushed slightly, realising what he had said.

"It's all they had left," Konstantina smiled.

"That's OK," he said, trying to cover his embarrassment. "I could sleep on the sofa."

"True," said Konstantina, standing up again and walking past him to the bathroom. She turned and smiled at him. Then kissed her forefinger and tapped him on the nose with it. "You could." She closed the door.

Outside the café where Lefteris had plied Toby with beer, Drakou parted company with the Englishman.

"Goodbye my friend, and don't worry I will not call you at six in the morning, unless the *Diagoras* has sunk."

"Thank you," Toby called back as he headed down the main steps towards the harbour, "I will think of you fishing while I eat at that fine taverna." He pointed at the sign for Taverna Georgio.

"You could do worse," called back the Greek as he set off through the village.

The square and the streets surrounding it were now busy with people. The thin figure of Manos stepped out of the small alleyway that ran beside Lefteris' café and he looked down the steps seeing the Englishman disappearing downwards. He glanced up towards the lane that ran upwards between the houses and saw that Drakou had gone. He turned back to the alleyway and beckoned Nikos Stavroulis out of the shadows.

"They have gone. So which way is the big man's house?"

Nikos was reluctant to reply, but had no real choice. "That way." He pointed towards the road that ran towards the castle. "But is this a good idea?"

Manos stepped forward until he was face to face with Nikos. "Not your problem. I want to see the little crippled shit. If the other two twats you used didn't shaft you with the kit, then that only leaves the freak boy. Unless of course it was you trying to screw with Mrs Manidaki?"

Nikos was trembling. "No, no it wasn't."

Manos grinned. "Pity, cause then I could just kill you." He turned. "Come on, show me where the cripple lives."

In the house Dimitri clicked the mouse and the cursor on his computer screen opened a folder labelled 'Midas Plus Phase Two'. He scrolled down the table of contents until he reached the file labelled 'Airport Athens'. He clicked the mouse again and the camera view of an ATM appeared on one side of his screen and a copy of the ATM screen filled the other half. Dimitri watched as a young man put his card into the machine and the menu appeared on his half of the screen. He saw the young man type in his pin number and then Dimitri typed in Greek 'Pin Number Correct.

You have qualified for today's special prize do you wish t[obscured]
For YES press one for NO press two.'

He looked at the confused face of the young man as he thou[obscured] for a moment then pressed the one button.

Dimitri typed again 'Congratulations, you have won ONE MILLION EUROS. Collect from your local branch tomorrow.' He laughed out loud as the young man punched the air, walked away from the machine, came back, jumped up and down and did a small dance. Dimitri was wishing he could see the scene that would ensue the following morning in a bank somewhere in Athens. A message appeared in the corner of his screen 'Security Time Out'. He clicked the mouse again and connection to the ATM disappeared. The screen saver appeared, a tumbling, random series of numbers flying around the screen.

The boy descended into deep thought. Now he had perfected Midas Plus and established the live links to ATMs, how was he to develop it, and keep it secure?

Suddenly he heard a knocking at the front door, then raised voices as his mother answered it. He was about to haul himself out of his chair when a tall, lean figure appeared in his doorway.

"So you are Dimitri the idiot, are you?" Manos glowered at the boy. "Well, speak up boy, or are you dumb as well?"

Dimitri waved his right arm from side to side and made an effort to speak. What came out was a mixture of mumble and parts of words as he dribbled spittle down his chin.

"Very good cripple," said Manos. "Unless you're play acting."

"Leave him alone." It was Dimitri's mother, Anna, pulling Manos back.

Manos lashed out with his left arm and the woman stumbled back against the kitchen door with a yell.

"Hang on," Nikos tried to intervene but Manos turned on him.

"Shut up! If this boy really is a drooling vegetable, then he has nothing to hide." He turned back and looked at Dimitri. "If on the other hand it turns out he has a brain, I might have to make sure g vegetable anyway. Get up, boy.”

he room and lifted Dimitri up by his arms onto boy.” He let go and Dimitri’s legs buckled. He rashing down, his arms striking the desk in front crack and spinning him sideways as he collapsed nd sprawled underneath the desk. His mother wailed again.

“Get off my boy,” she screamed. “You bastard.”

Manos turned and looked straight at her. “Shut the fuck up or I will kill the little shit anyway. Now let’s see what he has been doing on this computer of his, shall we.” He turned back and kicked Dimitri’s legs out of the way. As he did, he knocked the desk and the screen saver on the computer screen vanished leaving the windows screen with a list of files on it.

“Now,” said Manos bending over the keyboard and looking at the screen. “What have we here?” He surveyed the file names. “Nothing obvious. Games? What’s this?” He clicked the mouse and the screen filled with other file names. He clicked on one and the computer burst into life with a cacophony of loud electronic music as Super Mario invaded the screen. “Jesus, what crap.” Manos clicked again. He scoured file after file and then went back to the main screen. “Bollocks. This is all little kids’ stuff. Maybe you are a thick little twat.” Suddenly his eyes alighted on a shortcut to Explorer. “Right let’s see what we do on the net cripple boy.” Internet explorer opened and Manos immediately went to the browsing history. “What the fuck?” He clicked on the only entry that showed for the last week. “You dirty little shit,” Manos laughed, as he clicked an option that had appeared on the ‘Red Tube’ site that was now in front of him. “Into anal, are we?” He turned and looked at Anna. “Your boy might be crippled, but if he carries on looking at this stuff he’ll be blind soon, look at that.”

Anna saw the threesome writhing on the bed and the woman sucking a man’s penis as his partner entered her anus with rapid thrusting movements.

Dimitri's mother spoke through her sobs. "He is still a boy, even though he cannot speak or do anything else much. He has the same feelings as you."

Manos smiled and looked down under the desk at Dimitri. "Dirty little fucker. I could put him down for you if you want." He kicked Dimitri hard on the legs, then stood up. "Come on Nikos, let's get out of this shithole." The two men left and, as Dimitri crawled back out from under the desk, he pressed, once more, a small switch on a unit behind the main computer box which he had pressed when he fell under the desk. Immediately the screen on the top of the desk went back to the old screen-saver, with the numbers flashing across in rapid succession. His Mother helped him up.

"Are you alright?" She kissed him several times on the top of his head.

"I'm fine mother," replied the boy, with near-perfect speech, trying to fend her off.

"You are a damn sight cleverer than that idiot," said his mother, smiling and pinching his cheeks as he sat back in his chair. "Now then, my beautiful son I will make you some lemonade."

"Thank you mother," he replied.

Her smile faded slightly as she reached the doorway and turned back. "And then you can explain to me why you are looking at filth on the computer."

Alan Marks stood in the shower, poured the small bottle of shower gel on the tray in the shower cubicle over his head and just let the warm water cascade over him. All the tension and fear and adrenaline of the last two days began to drain away. How had he ended up here? It was like an extraordinary fantasy. The card that gave him endless money, the car chase, the Greek thugs who tried to kill him, the strange Scotsman, Nikos; it was all becoming a bizarre dream. And then there was Konstantina.

Alan stepped out of the shower, dried himself and put a towel around his waist. Konstantina? What was he to do about her? Did he have to do anything? She was out there in the cabin. There was one large double bed. It had been embarrassing when they had entered the cabin, but she didn't seem put out. He began to get that fear that all men get in situations where there is obvious attraction but they are unsure if it is reciprocated. What if he made a move and had read it all wrong? What if he didn't make a move and he'd got it all wrong? What if he was imagining the whole thing and she wasn't attracted to him at all and would think he was some sort of lecherous pervert? He needn't have worried. As he stepped through the door back into the cabin, she was sitting on the end of the bed, drying her hair with a towel and leaning over slightly to her right. The other towel that had been around her had dropped to her waist and Alan could see, in the mirror opposite the bed, her beautiful olive breasts and erect nipples. The effect on him was instant and he wasn't sure whether to retreat into the shower room or stay as he blurted out. "Oh, I'm sorry."

She stopped drying her hair and smiled at him in the mirror. Glancing down at the towel below his waist she replied "Well you don't look sorry, Mr Marks."

Alan blushed and was about to back away when Konstantina turned and put one hand out to his waist, and slowly and gently pulled the towel apart until it fell to the floor. Her other hand began to gently stroke his penis as he tried to speak, but only got as far as "I" when she stopped him with a gentle "Sh." And then slowly she began to kiss his shaft, working her way up with tiny kisses until she took the tip of his penis into her mouth and caressed it with her tongue. Alan gasped as she removed it and rose, slowly kissing him all the way up his body, gently biting at his nipples and finally kissing him deeply and passionately as they slowly descended onto the bed. Alan pulled her towel aside and almost before he knew it he was inside her, moving with a soft gentle rhythm. She was warm and moist and inviting and he was instantly completely lost in a wave of sex and passion. It was warm and slow and calm, with gentle stroking and kisses and feelings of incredible power and trembling. He caressed her breasts and moved down her body withdrawing and turning. He began to gently lick her clitoris and she turned to take his penis once more into her mouth. They turned and kissed and stroked and gently enjoyed each other in a way neither had enjoyed a sexual encounter before, his penis travelling the length of her olive tanned body and her fingers massaging every part of his torso and groin. It culminated with him suddenly entering her from behind with a powerful series of thrusts, which brought gentle whimpers and eventually a tremendous mutual orgasm which had them both crying out loud, she with a scream and him with a huge groan. They collapsed side by side on the bed and for a moment there was silence until she slowly began to giggle and he started to laugh.

"Mm," said Konstantina. "Your wife's friend was right, on the phone yesterday. You are a sex maniac."

"Me?" laughed Alan. "That's rich." He turned and kissed her. "That was wonderful."

She quietly agreed. "Yes, it was, wasn't it? I was going to ask if you wanted me to wear the wig, but I didn't really get the chance."

"Next time," he said laying back down. "Next time."

"Oh," she responded. "Next time? Well Mr Marks, we are taking a lot for granted aren't we?"

He smiled. "Too right we are. Don't know about you but I'm starving. How about we try that restaurant?"

"Alan Marks!" she exclaimed, and picked up a pillow and hit him hard across the face with it.

"What?" asked Alan, pulling the pillow off. "What's up?"

"Men!" she sighed. "We make incredible love, and all you can say is let's go eat."

"Aren't you hungry?" he asked.

"Well yes," she replied.

"So what's the problem?" he said getting to his feet.

"The problem," said Konstantina looking at the clock radio by the bed, "is, that apart from spoiling a very romantic moment, the restaurant doesn't open for another hour."

Alan shrugged his shoulders and dropped back down onto the bed. He smiled and began to run a finger up her naked thigh.

"What are you doing?" she asked, in a put-on stern voice.

"I," said Alan, moving his hand over to her belly and slowly down between her legs, "I am taking a lot for granted."

Konstantina gave a short intake of breath. "So you are Mr Marks, oh yes, so you are."

CHAPTER THIRTEEN

Gary McAllister had not had a good flight. It started badly when the flight was called and several people pushed past him at the gate because they had something called 'speedy boarding.' As he boarded, along with all the others who had not had the foresight to book the legalised queue jumping scheme, he let it be known to the steward exactly what he thought. Of course, the several Scotches he had imbibed pre-flight made him slightly louder anyway as he launched into, "Why would any prat be that keen to get on this shite aircraft, anyway?"

Things had gone from bad to worse when he was seated next to an elderly woman who insisted on telling him her entire life story and that of her wonderful daughter who had married a good, hard-working Greek but she didn't see why they had to call the first child after his father and not her own. The woman became more and more maudlin as she downed Bombay Sapphire after Bombay Sapphire with diminishing amounts of tonic and thankfully, eventually fell asleep. The problem then was, she snored.

McAllister was relieved when the announcement of landing finally came and smiled when the steward announced the temperature at twenty four degrees and set to rise during the day to the high thirties. Getting light trousers and a shirt at Gatwick had been a good idea, even though it meant dumping his leathers in left luggage at an exorbitant rate. As he refastened his safety belt, he ran over the situation in his mind. Apart from his boss and his possible relationship with organised crime, something else troubled him. Why had he not seen anything of Marks or the girl? They must be on their way to Symi, but why weren't they at Gatwick? "I suppose," he muttered to himself, "at least with any luck I will find the answer to this Midas thing in Symi."

"Symi?" The woman next to him turned suddenly. "Did you say Symi?" Before he could respond she continued. "Wonderful place. Very beautiful, in a Greeky sort of way you know? Now then if my Alicia lived there I could understand it, but no, they have to be in Rhodes because of Yiannis' work. Mind you, he works hard don't get me wrong..." The woman continued but McAllister had switched off and gone back into his own thoughts. Suddenly the woman pulled him back with. "I said are you going there alone?"

McAllister was jolted back. "What? Oh no, I'm meeting some people there."

"Meeting them there?" queried the woman. "Where are they now then?"

"Good point," responded McAllister. "Good point."

Alan Marks woke suddenly in the early hours of the morning, and for a moment couldn't work out where he was. Then, seeing the silhouette of Konstantina looking out of the cabin window, backed by the moonlit sea, it came back to him.

"Sorry," she said quietly, "I was just looking out at the sea. We left Kos about half an hour ago, around four, and the sound of the anchor woke me."

"It didn't wake me," muttered Alan.

She smiled. "I don't think an earthquake would have woken you. You were sound asleep. Mind you, you have been through a lot in the last few days."

"Yes," Alan replied, getting out of the bed and joining her on the sofa under the window. He put his arms around her. "It has been a test of endurance, particularly the last few hours."

She elbowed him in the ribs. "Endurance? I'll show you endurance, Mr Marks." She turned and stood in front of him, her naked body glistening in the moonlight. "After I have been to the loo." She headed for the shower room door.

"God and you say I'm unromantic," laughed Alan.

The door closed and he looked out at the shimmering sea. It was beautiful, but something was bothering him. He looked behind. The darkened cabin was not completely dark. There was an intermittent, faint green glow. He looked across the room. It was coming from the other side of the bed. Alan slid on his stomach across the bed and saw, on the floor below him, Konstantina's bag. The flashing glow was emanating from inside. He leaned down and pulled the top of the bag apart. Under the Midas box he found the source of the faint flashing light. "A mobile phone?" he found himself saying out loud.

"What?" came the question from inside the shower room.

Alan pulled the Blackberry 8320 from the bag. The screen was displaying a symbol of an envelope with a star on it. He found himself unable to resist the urge to thumb the curser along and press the pad over the symbol. The message was displayed:

'Well done... Expect merchandise in the morning.'

Alan was stunned. He scrolled up the text message to see what had been sent to prompt this response, and there it was in a separate line above.

'Have Midas and Marks on ship. Will deliver merchandise by morning with any luck.'

Suddenly, the shower room door opened and Konstantina stood watching Alan lying on the bed. "Alan, why are you looking in my bag?"

"Why?" he said standing up. "Why? You have a mobile phone?" He held out the phone with the screen facing her."

"Yes," she responded, "so what's so..." she got no further as he carried on.

"And I am 'merchandise'? Merchandise?"

"I can explain," she began.

"No need." He was pulling on his trousers. "I'm going to be

'delivered' by morning with any luck apparently." He grabbed at his shirt.

"Look," said Konstantina, walking towards him.

"Stop," Alan shouted putting his hands out. Then he pulled the shirt over his head. "Bugger!" He pulled it down and ripped the Acropolis badge off. "That is bloody sharp." There was blood on the back of his left hand. He threw the badge across the room and it hit the far wall with a loud metallic ting and fell to the floor with a clatter, as it split in two. Konstantina shot a glance across at the debris in the gloom on the floor.

Alan picked up the Midas box and waved it in front of her. "Here, some merchandise for you to deliver to your gangster boss, whoever he is." He tossed it on the bed. He pulled his bank card from his back pocket and held it up. "I will hang on to this if you don't mind. Because right now this piece of merchandise, namely me, is pissing off." He opened the cabin door, stepped out and slammed it shut.

Konstantina stood in the dark of the cabin and yelled, "Shit!" She hit the light switch by the bedside table and rolled over the bed, leaned down and picked up the two pieces of the badge. The outer casing was the Acropolis badge, but the other part was a small silver disc with a pin stuck to the back of it. It was slightly warm and, as she put out her tongue to touch it, she felt a very slight tingle. "Damn!" She spun around and shouted at the door. "Alan, Alan come back."

Alan Marks was halfway down the corridor towards the stairwell by then. Stepping over several bodies clustered by the walls in sleeping bags, he reached the stairs and brushed past a large muscular man in a suit, nudging the man's shoulder as he did so. "Sorry," said Alan and continued left towards the double doors that led out onto the upper deck. Had Alan looked around he would have seen the man he had nudged, Spiros Mavrilis, walk a few paces, pause and turn to watch him exit through the doors. The big muscular Greek smiled, put his hand inside his jacket and removed his gun. Then, with his other hand he raised the gold chain from his chest and kissed the crucifix.

"May God bless you Mr Marks."

Outside, Alan felt the warm wind on his face as he turned and walked towards the front of the boat. To his left, had he looked, was a large outcrop of land sloping up from the sea in the dawning light, a tiny island called Sesklia, just off the farthest end of the island of Symi. Ahead, the sky was red and growing brighter into green and yellow as the sun came up over the Turkish coast. None of this registered with Alan as his mind was a turmoil of anger and fury.

"How bloody stupid," he shouted. "What a prat. I've been played all along. But why? She could have just taken the bloody box in England and given it to whoever the pissing gangsters are." He looked down at the dark water far below him and the wash spreading out from the bow of the ship. It was moving rapidly away from the boat in a continuous stream and was strangely beautiful and threatening, both at the same time.

"Sod it." He stood up straight. "I'm going to find out what this is all about." He turned and immediately backed up against the guard rail in shock as a wave of adrenaline shot though his body. Spiros was stood in front of him a short distance away, pointing his gun directly at Alan's head.

"Mr Marks, I believe?"

Alan found he was too terrified to lie. "Yes." He was trembling.

"I thought so. I want you to give me the small black box. Now." Spiros had a slight smile on his face which sat uneasily with the scars, pock-marks and broken nose, and gave him a very menacing expression.

"Black box?" Alan knew what the man meant, but he felt confused. "You mean the Midas thing? Actually I don't have it anymore, and..."

Spiros stopped him by moving forward and coming very close to his face. Alan felt the gun dig into his ribs.

"But you know where it is?"

The man's breath was heavy with garlic and smoke and Alan struggled not to retch.

Suddenly this made no sense. If Konstantina was working for the bad guys then who the hell was this? Was he the Greek version of the Scotsman, and if so why did he want Midas? Much against his first instinct, he suddenly had an inclination not to tell the man where Midas was. He stuttered, "I, er that is I'm not exactly sure. You see, I don't quite understand..." he got no further.

In what seemed like one swift movement, Spiros removed the gun from Alan's ribs and stuffed it in his belt. He grabbed Alan's shirt collar with one hand and his belt with the other. He lifted him off the floor and tipped him backwards until his head was out over the guard rail. He let go of Alan's collar and was holding him, simply by his belt buckle. Alan Marks was balanced on the guard rail out over the sea, which was about thirty feet below. It all happened so quickly that Alan had no time to protest at the pain he felt as the seam of his trousers dug into his crotch.

"Understand any better now?" said the Greek.

Alan looked to one side and down at the water rushing past way down beneath him. All at once, the sound of the wash seemed incredibly loud. He was about to speak when he heard a woman's voice shouting in Greek. Spiros turned suddenly and went to grab his gun, letting go of the belt buckle as he did so. For a fraction of a second, which seemed like forever, Alan remained balanced on the guard rail. He tried to raise himself, but it was too late as he toppled back over the rail and tumbled over and over towards the sea. The last thing Alan Marks felt was the hard stinging smack of the water on his back as he hit the surface of the moving sea. Then the cold salt water rushed into his mouth and lungs and ears, as he began to sink, and the world went black.

On deck, Spiros Mavrilis never got to grab his gun. By the time his hand touched the handle, he was already falling towards the deck as one bullet pierced his heart and then another entered the top of his head as he fell forwards.

Konstantina lowered her gun and ran to the side of the ship. She looked down into the black water. She ran along the guard rail heading towards the back of the ship, still looking down. She gazed out briefly from the stern, with tears filling her eyes. She let out a long shrill cry. "No!" She stood for a moment in silence.

Then she wiped her hand across her cheek, turned and headed back to where the large Greek was slumped on the floor. She knelt down by the body and rolled it over towards the guard rail. He was a big man and the effort required would, in normal circumstances, have been too much for her. However, with tears uncontrollably streaming down her face and feelings of intense anger welling up inside her, she pushed Spiros Mavrilis through the bottom gap in the guard rail. The body of the large Greek dropped down into the sea with a huge splash and sank almost immediately. Konstantina didn't watch him go. She simply tossed her gun over the rail, sat on the deck in the pool of blood he had left behind and sobbed.

In the villa on a hillside near Thessalonica, Marina Manidaki awoke abruptly in her chair and stared at the television screen in front of her. It took a while for the old lady's eyes to focus. Why had she woken? She stared at the screen which displayed a large map of the Aegean and several small, ship-shaped icons showing the shipping routes and the tracks of certain boats. She fumbled with the remote next to her and pressed a button. The picture magnified and zoomed in on one particular icon. It was a small yellow boat shape. She rolled a ball in the centre of the remote with her wiry index finger on her frail right hand and an arrow passed across the screen from the right-hand side and hovered over the shape which was moving very slowly towards the island of Rhodes. The word 'Diagoras' appeared in small letters beside it.

"Jones!" she attempted to call loudly but only a croaky thin voice emanated from her mouth. She tried again, with not much more success. "Jones!"

The butler shuffled into the room in a brown checked dressing gown and leather slippers, yawning. Even Mrs Manidaki was surprised to see him.

"You almost called, Madam?"

"You're not funny," she rasped. "You're English, remember? Now why is the *Diagoras* not flashing? And there is no sound. Look." She pressed the volume button on the remote again and again.

Jones took a pair of thin wiry spectacles from his dressing gown pocket, put them on and peered at the screen.

"Well?" she asked.

The butler pondered for a moment then spoke. "I would venture to suggest, ma'am, that the tracking device is no longer operational."

Marina Manidaki slammed the remote down on the small table next to her and mimicked her lackey. "The tracking device is no longer operational." Her voice was returning and getting louder. "Of course it's not operational you buffoon or we would hear it. Why isn't it working? Why?"

Jones, suitably chastised but none the wiser took his life in his hands and suggested a possible reason.

"Could it be, ma'am, that Mr Mavrilis has carried out ma'am's wishes?"

Marina had picked up the remote and was pressing the volume button again. "Don't be so ridic..." She paused. "Yes, yes of course. He's disposed of the Marks man. You're right."

Jones attempted a smile. "Thank you ma'am."

Marina's mind was beginning to turn. "But has he got Midas? And why hasn't he called me? Phone him Jones, phone him."

Jones picked up the telephone on the table next to his mistress and dialled. He listened for the ringing tone, then handed the handset to the old lady.

On the deck of the *Diagoras*, Konstantina was getting up, still sobbing quietly and holding on to the guard rail, when she heard a faint buzzing sound. She wiped the tears from her eyes with her sleeve and looked around the floor of the deck. She shifted slightly sideways and suddenly looked down as she felt a strange vibration on the outside of her left foot. It was a mobile phone vibrating against her foot and the guard rail. She picked it up and looked at the small screen which displayed a name flashing slowly. Suddenly her sobbing stopped. She recognised the name. She looked at the phone for a moment, then pressed the receive button and put the mobile to her ear. She listened until the voice at the other end finished speaking and then she spoke. Her voice was calm but hard. She spoke in Greek very slowly and very quietly getting softer and softer until she had almost finished, when she paused for an instant and shouted into the phone: "You fucking geriatric cock-sucking bitch." She pressed the button to end the call and threw the mobile phone high into the air and out into the sea.

In her villa near Thessalonika, Marina Manidaki screamed and threw her own telephone at the television set, shattering the screen and causing the whole appliance to explode with a loud bang, with a shower of sparks and a cloud of acrid grey smoke.

"Geriatric?" she screeched. "Geriatric? Cow, bitch, whore, daughter of a pox-ridden whore and a donkey." Trembling, the old lady stood up.

"I gather we have a problem, ma'am?" enquired Jones.

Marina turned on him. "Yes we have a problem, and don't be smart with me. Yes Spiros is dead and that, that...." She found she had run out of expletives, "Girl, that girl, says Marks is dead too and she has no idea about anything called Midas. Did you hear what she called me? Get the jet, I am going to get dressed and then I am going to Rhodos. Get Tassos to meet me there with the helicopter. He can take me to Symi. I am going to sort this out for myself. If I do nothing else, I am going to kill my godson and that girl."

She began to leave the room, stooped and faltering but getting faster as she went. As she reached the doorway, she turned back and pointed at the television. "And fix that." She left the room.

Jones looked at the smoking wreckage that had been the forty two inch Panasonic high definition LCD television and muttered quietly. "Certainly ma'am, of course ma'am, I'll get my screwdriver and some fucking sticky tape."

Just before six o'clock, in the bay of Sesklia at the western tip of the Island of Symi, Savvas Drakou broke the surface of the water with a large octopus on his spear gun. He trod water as his huge left hand ripped the wriggling creature from the three prongs and stuffed it into the net pouch around his ample waist. He looked into the distance, watching the *Diagoras* as it continued on to Rhodes. The wash just reached him and he bobbed up and down in the waves, looking back at his blue and white wooden fishing boat. It moved slowly up one side of the wash and down the other. He smiled, spat the salt water from his mouth and pushed the mask up onto his forehead. He looked at his watch. "Time to go." As he blew his nose clear and wiped the sweat from his eyes, some way off, maybe forty metres, maybe more, in the still calm waters of the azure blue bay, he thought he saw something large floating, just under the water. "Was it a shark? A dolphin? Or, no it couldn't be. A person? A body."

His great arms began to power him through the water. Those great muscular arms which had, in their time, squeezed the life from more than one poor sole in the Athens jails, in the days of the Junta, had him near the object in no time. As he approached, he could see it was a body, a fully clothed body.

Some pissed tourist no doubt. "Had too many ouzos and fallen off a boat most likely." He grabbed the shirt and, as he did, the body rolled over in the water.

"Help me. Help me."

"*Panormitis!*" Drakou gulped in a mouthful of water and coughed it out again. "You're alive?"

Fully clothed out here at six in the morning, with no sign of a boat, and this man was alive. The man began to sink as he turned.

Drakou grabbed the shirt again and pulled the man above the surface. “English?”

The man grunted. “Yeah.”

Drakou rolled him onto his back again.

“You are one lucky bastard.”

He started for his boat, on his back holding the man’s head above the water.

“If I save your life you owe me one big beer, OK?”

The great sonorous voice rumbled in the man’s ear.

Alan Marks spluttered, coughing phlegm and salt water out into the sea.

“No problem. I’m the richest man in the world.”

Drakou gave a deep guttural laugh. “In that case, two beers.”

CHAPTER FOURTEEN

Gary McAllister turned sideways and opened his eyes just in time to stop himself rolling off the bench he had been lying on for the last three hours. After he landed, he had rescued his baggage from the carrousel, taken it to the toilets and removed the gun, putting it in his holdall. He left the bag in the gents loo and then he had taken a taxi from Rhodes Airport, asking the driver to take him to where the boat went to Symi. The driver duly obliged and dropped him off in Kolona harbour right opposite the *Dodecanese Pride*. This was a high-speed orange catamaran ferry which was stern-first against the harbour with a large sign hanging from its top deck which proudly announced 'Symi and Kos departure 8.00.'

Terrific; he had nearly four hours to wait. The back of the ferry was a wide boarding gangway which was wide enough to take small cars and vans but was raised just enough to discourage early would-be passengers, like McAllister, from boarding. Tired from his flight and the constant wittering of his unwelcome flying companion, he had sat down on the nearest bench overlooking the harbour. The harbour was filled with a multitude of craft, from the small sailing boats to, across the other side from where he sat, large cruise ships. He could make the shapes out silhouetted against the moonlit sky. The air was warm with a gentle breeze and he sat, pondering why he had not seen Marks or Konstantina. He had looked all over the airport and at the arrivals boards. No more flights were due in from London and none from Athens until much later in the morning. Perhaps they had gone that way, but there had been an urgency to get here so it didn't make sense. Unless they had done it all yesterday, somehow. His tired brain was confused. As he thought, he gradually moved to lying on the bench and eventually he closed his eyes and drifted off. Now he had woken suddenly and, as he opened his eyes and prevented his fall off the bench, he was almost blinded for an instant by the morning sun. It was light. Christ, he hadn't missed the ferry? He looked to his left. No, it was still there, thank God. Then there was the loud blast of a ship's hooter and he realised that it was that noise that had just woken him, it had sounded just now. He looked across to the entrance to the harbour and a large ship was slowly manoeuvring into the side of the harbour wall opposite where he sat. There was much churning of water and smoke bursts from its funnels as the forward thrusters chewed up the water and moved the huge vessel into the side of the dock. In the bright morning sun he could clearly read the lettering on the side of the ship. *Diagoras* and underneath the word *Athena*.

There was a loud bang as the broad gangway of the *Dodecanese Pride* next to him dropped and hit the stone of the harbour. He jumped and a dark-skinned moustachioed man in dirty blue overalls shouted at him from the back of the ferry in Greek. When McAllister looked confused the man shouted in English. 'Sorry, I make you jump up. Hey, you going to Symi or Kos?"

"Symi." McAllister shouted back.

"OK," called the man. "You get ticket over there." He pointed to a little ticket booth directly opposite the ferry about twenty meters away. McAllister hadn't noticed it when he arrived, but it was now open and there was already a small queue of travellers purchasing tickets. He stood, stretched, and began to walk towards the booth. As he did, the man from the ferry disembarked and began to lift some boxes that were obviously waiting to be boarded. McAllister took a slight detour and approached the man.

"Excuse me, but that ship over there, the *Diagoras*?"

"Yes," said the man, "the *Diagoras*, just come from Athens. Some of her passengers will be coming here as it's on time. Sometimes if it's late they miss us but today they are lucky. What do you want to know?"

"Exactly what you just told me," responded McAllister. "Exactly."

Toby, the Englishman, turned over as he awoke in the large double bed in his room in the Old Markets Hotel. He slowly moved towards Lucinda's back, pulled back her hair from her left ear and whispered into it. "Miss Frobisher, this is your early morning call."

Lucinda stirred and felt the hard penis slowly slipping down into the crack of her cheeks.

She murmured softly, without opening her eyes or turning, but gently moving her hand down to caress the swollen member and guide him further between her cheeks. "Oh, sir we are up early aren't we?"

"Rather," responded Toby manoeuvring himself to begin to gently thrust his penis, deeper.

"Mm." Lucinda gave an inviting soft moan, feeling the moisture begin to trickle over her hand. "And am I right in thinking sir would like to come up the back way this morning?"

"Oh God," said Toby rising up on one elbow, "you are a dirty bitch, let me have you."

Suddenly there was a loud ringing as the mobile phone on the bedside cabinet burst into life.

"No, no," shouted the Englishman as he was suddenly thrown into a wild orgasmic shudder.

Lucinda felt the flood of wetness filling her crotch and beginning to run down her inner thighs.

"I'll get the phone then, shall I?" she sighed, reaching over to pick it up. "Hello, Lucinda Frobisher can I help you? Oh yes, he is here alright, hang on a moment." She looked at Toby pointedly. "He's just coming." She held out the phone. "It's for you. A woman."

Toby went to take the phone and then whispered loudly. "Christ, it isn't..."

"Don't worry, sir," smiled Lucinda. "It isn't the wife from hell. It's Zoe."

"At this time of the morning?" He grabbed the phone. "Hello, Zoe? What? How? Shit. But...are you sure? Thank God for that... Yes I understand, don't worry it's been less than thirty seconds, I'll read the encrypted text."

He pressed a button on the iPhone and then looked at the screen. "She said the postman's gone."

Lucinda sat up in bed. "What? Jesus Toby!"

Toby was pressing buttons madly. "Ah, here we are." He was reading from the screen. "Yes, it's OK, the parcel is intact apparently."

Lucinda sat back against the headboard. "Well thank God. Are you sure?"

"We will find out for sure later today but according to this," he showed her the screen. "Midas is safe with our courier but Marks is dead."

"That's all very well, Toby," she responded, "but wasn't he a bit crucial, I mean how do we deal with the Scotsman now?"

"Good point." Toby frowned. "I'll have to think about that one."

"While you are thinking," said Lucinda, taking the phone from his hand and putting it back on the bedside cabinet, "you might have had your morning constitutional but your P.A. hasn't." She bent down and pulled out the bottom drawer of the cabinet. She took out a large vibrator and handed it to him. "Rabbit please, Mr Fox." She pushed down the bed clothes to reveal her naked body. "Tiggywinkle wants to be shagged."

Toby looked at the gleaming beast. "This is all very well, old thing, but it's liable to make a chap feel a bit inadequate."

Lucinda smiled sarcastically. "If the cap fits. And I am not your old thing." She licked a finger and began to rub it between her thighs, whilst feigning a little girl voice. "Please Foxy, Tiggy wants her rumpies."

Toby turned on the vibrator and as he did so the mobile phone gave a loud but brief single tone. He stopped the sex toy and picked up the phone. He looked at the screen and pressed some buttons. Then he began to laugh. "Jesus Christ. I don't believe it."

Lucinda sighed. "Neither do I. What now for Christ's sake?"

Toby was still chortling. "It's Marks. He is still alive. Fuck me."

"No, Toby," said Lucinda, grabbing the vibrator and turning it on. "Fuck me."

Toby put down the phone and took the dildo back with a smile. "Leave it to Foxy, Tiggy." He began to slowly move the vibrator up her inner thighs and she began to whimper slightly and widen her legs.

Suddenly the mobile phone burst into life again.

Lucinda sat up and screamed. "I don't believe this. Who the hell is it now?" She picked up the phone and shouted into it. "Who the hell are you? This had better be bloody important, because it's interrupted my fucking shag."

In Thessalonika, Jones the butler remained calm on the phone. "Ah, Miss Frobisher I believe? Sorry to interrupt you, Miss. Seven five one three here, code word? Aegean. Is it possible to talk with your boss, please?" There was a pause. "Sorry to disturb you sir, but I have reason to believe Mr Marks may be dead, sir… Oh is that so sir? That is good news. Also, I thought you should know that the Old Bird has flown south sir… Yes I believe she will be, yes, later today I would imagine. I think my work here is finally done sir? So, if it is alright with you I will make my final exit…That's very kind of you, sir. I would like to say it's been a pleasure but quite frankly in these last few years it's been one hell of a bloody nightmare… That is very generous as bonuses go sir, and if I may say so I think I deserve it, but please thank mother in London will you. Look I'll be off now, I wouldn't want to deprive Miss Frobisher of her, erm 'fucking shag' I think she called it, sir?... No of course, as the grave sir, you know me. Naturally I will tidy up here, no loose ends. Some things you don't forget with age...Yes, thank you sir, my regards to your good lady wife."

The first thing Alan Marks became aware of was the sound. A low droning hum, somewhere above him, and in the background, a dog barking somewhere far off. In the distance, the faint straining bellow, of what sounded like a donkey. Then chickens, he could hear chickens. Next it was the incredible warmth, all-encompassing and aromatic, a warm bath of aromatic fragrance all around him. And then a gentle intermittent breeze on his cheek. The dog had stopped, but a cockerel had taken over, stridently asserting his presence, albeit a long way off. There was a bell, now, far, far, away. A dull clang of a ring, slow and monotonous. Then, nearer, a ship's hooter, long and low. Where was he? He felt stiff and ached all over. He opened his eyes and took time to focus as the bright light of a Mediterranean day flooded in. Blue, powder blue, was all he could see. He turned his aching neck slowly and up to the right he saw what looked like bunches of grapes, suspended from a vine, hanging below dark, flaking wood. The hum, that's what it was. He focused on two huge yellow and brown hornets clambering over the grapes.

"Bastards. Every year the same." The sonorous voice stirred a memory. Why did he know that voice? He licked his lips and felt the sharp tang of salt. The sea, of course, that was the voice of the man who grabbed him in the sea.

"The bastards, I put out stuff for them but no they have to have the grapes. Bastards. How you doing, Alan Marks from England?"

Alan turned and saw a great brown weathered face beaming at him. It was a face of a man who had seen his share of life. It had creases and lines and grey stubble and a broad wrinkled brow leading up to a shining brown head. Then there was the smile, a broad, full-bodied smile with gleaming white teeth and one golden sparkle of a crown. The man was naked to the waist with a great mass of greying hair over his mahogany brown chest and down onto his huge belly which bulged over his black, loose-fitting swim shorts. Who was this man? And how did he know him? He tried to lift himself up to look around, but it was an almighty effort. The man helped.

"Careful, you almost drowned. If you came off the *Diagoras* you had a great fall too. I am surprised you are alive." He eased him up with a strong, firm, grip. Alan sat back, realising he had been lying flat, dressed only in his boxer shorts, on hard nylon canvas on a metal tubular sun-bed, the head of which the man had now raised. He was on some sort of terrace or patio with a low wall to the left of him that he could not see over and a house to the right, fronted by an old wooden pergola covered in a grape vine, festooned with bunches of dull green grapes and several hornets. "So Alan Marks, what are you doing in Symi?"

The directness of the man threw Alan. "Symi? I am in Symi?"

"You are now," responded the Greek. "You were in the Aegean on your way to hell or heaven or whatever you believe in, until some stupid Greek pulled you out. As far as I can see you came off the *Diagoras*. It passes the end of the island on its way to Rhodos. Until some idiot in the government persuades the ferry company, or somebody's brother bribes somebody's cousin to make it stop here, you have to go to Rhodos first and get another ferry here. That way two sets of bastards make money. They're all crooks, anyway. Beer?"

He bent down and picked up a large bottle of beer, took the top off with his hand and offered it to Alan. "This is Mythos. Greek beer, not your German shit."

Alan took the beer. "Thanks, but it's a bit early."

The man raised another and touched it to Alan's. "*Yammas!*" he shouted, making Alan visibly jump. The Greek gave a loud guttural laugh which made his enormous belly ripple. "Here's to the English, er what do you say in your country, mer woman? Mer girl?"

"Mermaid?" Alan stuttered.

"That's it, but you are not a woman. Mer man, yes?" He touched the bottle again. "Here is to the English mer man of Symi. Alan Marks." He raised his bottle and gulped down almost half the contents, wiped his dark ebony arm across his lips and belched loudly. "*Yammas*."

Alan was about to ask how come he knew his name when a woman appeared from the house with a small bowl. "*Savvas, psarasoupa*?"

"Good," said the man, getting up. "This is my wife, Anna. She has some soup for you, Symi fish soup, very special." He turned to the plump smiling woman and said something in Greek very quickly and they both laughed. The woman handed the bowl of soup to Alan and then spoke to him in what appeared to be an apology and dashed back into the house.

"She has forgotten the spoon," said the man. "I was telling her, that as we have discovered you are a mer man and as this was fish soup, you might not want to eat your cousins."

The woman returned with the spoon, and the man indicated to her to leave, in a gentle but firm way.

"Right eat up, you need something." The man stood and walked towards the doorway into the house. As he reached the door, he turned back and smiled at Alan. "Then I think we have some things to talk about Alan. It is Alan isn't it? That is how you say it, yes?"

In the Villa in Thessalonika, Maria, the large middle-aged Greek cook didn't hear the butler enter the kitchen as she rolled out the pastry and listened to Anna Vissi, the Greek singer, on her iPod. She jumped as he tapped her on the shoulder. She pulled out one earpiece and turned on him. "Mr Jones, you are a wicked man. Frightening a woman of my age, I could have a heart attack, you could have killed me."

"True," smiled the butler. "So what is the music today my roley poley Greek pudding?" He tickled her waist and she slapped his hands.

"Stop it, you naughty Englishman." She offered him the earpieces. "This iPod is the best present I ever get. Even though you are a bad man. Thank you. Listen, this is Anna Vissi singing '*Af ti Ti Fora*,' she is wonderful."

He put the small white plugs into his ears and listened. Then he spoke loudly, as people do who are wearing earphones. "It's very good. What is she saying?"

Maria began to shout back. "It's about..." She realised as he shook his head that he couldn't hear her so she pressed the iPod at her waist. "Can you hear me now?"

He nodded.

She smiled at him. "It is about a woman who has made mistakes with a man in the past and is saying this time she won't make the same mistakes with a man again. I think you will understand that, Harold." Her smile had faded and become a knowing grin.

Harold Jones removed the earpieces and smiled back. "That was a long time ago Maria, and we all make mistakes."

"True," she responded. "It was a long time ago, and I am over it. Why do I bring it up now?" She was about to turn back to her pastry when he stopped her and took her arm and turned her back to face him. He smiled again. "Why do you bring it up now? Because you are a woman, and women never forget."

She gave a small laugh. "True, you wise old man. What do you want anyway? I am busy."

The butler sighed and suddenly looked very serious. "Listen, Maria. I am leaving and I won't be coming back." He raised his voice to stop her interrupting him. "Do not ask why. I have very little time. I do not have time for a discussion. So you can come with me and live happily into old age in England, or you can stay here and... well, you can stay here."

It struck him immediately that she seemed less than surprised. It was almost as if she had been expecting this moment and had in some way prepared for it. There were tears in her eyes as she said, "I cannot go Harold, not now, it is too late. I did love you, but now we are friends."

"Ah," Harold Jones sighed. "Friends. Oh dear, the unkindest cut of all."

He took her right hand, raised it in front of him and kissed it. He then turned, left the kitchen and walked down the long hallway of the villa. He reached the front door and opened it. Outside was Mrs Manidaki's maroon and grey Rolls Royce Silver Shadow. Harold Jones, real name Barnaby Wilde, got into the car and drove out of the villa, crashing through the electric gates and setting off all the alarms in the property.

Maria the cook watched from the open front door as the car sped away, picked up the hallway phone and dialled.

Alan Marks could not believe his eyes. He stood in the doorway, watching a boy with twisted hands and arms type rapidly on the keyboard of a computer. Numbers were flashing across his screen. But this wasn't the thing that stunned Alan the most. What amazed him was the object lying on the floor at the boy's feet.

"It is Midas," said the deep guttural voice in his ear.

Alan jumped, as did the boy at the computer. He stuttered something in Greek and the big man replied and then turned to Alan. "He is worried that he has let you see the small box."

"Well yes," said Alan. "Forgive me. I was just looking around, I didn't mean to..."

"It is alright. He is my son and he made your Midas box too. Where is it?"

Alan looked at the big man and realised he was not smiling. "I don't have it."

The man raised one eyebrow.

Alan felt obliged to continue. "It is with a girl who was travelling with me. Look, I don't want to be funny, but how do you know my name?"

The man smiled again, took Alan by the arm and led him back outside to the terrace. "You will find out why I know who you are in a while, what is important now is the box. Who has it?"

Alan suddenly found himself getting angry. He shrugged off the man's hand and backed away, towards the wall by the telescope. "For Christ's sake I have been chased by gangsters, shot at, dumped off a bloody ferry by some thug and lied to by some bitch who said she was helping me. Then you fish me out of the sea, and don't get me wrong I am grateful, but now I find out your boy in there is the whole reason I am in this soddin' mess."

The man sat down on the sun-bed that Alan had been lying on. He sighed. "So as I said, the Midas box. This girl, who is she?"

Alan was about to explode again and then realised it would be pointless. "Oh, God knows. She's Greek, Christ I should have seen it coming, of course she is Greek, sorry no offence. Konstantina. Er Zouroudi or something."

The man looked surprised. "Konstantina Zouroudi? You are sure?"

Alan was exasperated. "Sure? No of course I'm not sure. I'm not sure of anything. I'm not sure about you. I mean how do I know I can trust you? I mean you saved my life, fine, but..."

The man stopped him by raising his hand. "I must make a quick call." He picked up a mobile which was lying on the floor under the sun bed and began to dial. "And yes, you can trust Savvas Drakou, if for no other reason than you have, how do you say in your words, something on me, yes?" Alan looked puzzled.

Drakou smiled. "Midas? My boy in there? We have a Midas?"

Alan realised what he meant, but still felt uncomfortable. He had more questions but didn't get a chance to ask them as the big Greek spoke into his mobile. "The Englishman says a girl called Konstantina has the box...oh, I see." He began to laugh. "Right, I will. I'll wait in Pedi bay? OK." He finished the call and looked at Alan and gave a huge grin. "Konstantina? Of course my friend. Of course this Konstantina has the box." He stood and walked towards Alan. "Before you ask anything else, I cannot tell you anything but everything will be clear soon. In the meantime welcome to Symi." He turned Alan, who looked down over the wall and saw below him the most amazing sight. It was the harbour of Symi far below, surrounded by a myriad of houses tumbling down three hillsides. The harbour was a long u-shape which stretched out on its far side where he could see a tall clock tower and then beyond to the turquoise blue sea of the Mediterranean and the distant hills of Turkey.

Alan was amazed. "It's stunning. I mean, it's just stunning."

"You want to see close?" said Drakou, indicating the telescope.

Alan walked over to the telescope and looked in. "Jesus, that's incredible. Bloody hell, all the yachts, and people, Christ it's like you are down there."

Drakou chuckled. "Yes, my boy likes to look at the girls. That is the harbour, Yialos. Nice to go to, but better to live up here."

"I can see that," said Alan, scanning the harbour side. "You can even see the names on the boats. Panormit… hang on what's that Panormi…"

"*Panormitis*," said the big man. "A big name here. That boat is named after the Saint Archangel Michali Panormitis. He has the biggest monastery on Symi. You have a problem? You go to Panormitis. He will tell you what to do. You have heard of him yes?"

"Afraid not," said Alan, still looking.

The Greek shrugged and crossed himself. "Sometimes I think you English know a lot about a lot of things and nothing about what is important."

"Now that," said Alan not really listening, "that is a beautiful boat. *Wind of Change*. Now that is a yacht."

"And," laughed the Greek, "if you have a lot of money it can be yours. It is for sale. At the moment it is the property of the customs but if you have about a hundred thousand euro I can get it for you. The owner was taken by the port police for smuggling Afghanistan people from over there in Turkey. He was part English and part Iranian or something, anyway, a bastard. He had fifty people on that boat, children, women, anyway they catch him and now they have his boat. It will not sell here, and by the winter it will end up round in the boat yard and be stripped down for bits."

Suddenly there was a loud blast from a ship's hooter.

"Now you will see something," laughed Drakou. "Look."

Alan looked up from the telescope and saw the bright orange *Dodecanese Pride* catamaran ferry approaching the entrance to the harbour. The ferry slowed as it approached the harbour entrance and then, without stopping, turned in its own length and backed towards the side of the harbour, a short distance from the clock tower.

"You want to see some fun?" said the big Greek. "Look into the telescope now."

Alan obeyed and focused on the rear of the catamaran as the back slowly lowered to the harbour side. As it did, and almost before it had touched the ground people were disembarking, carrying bags and parcels. Small motorbikes and mopeds darted between the people and a large green Land Rover followed, miraculously avoiding killing anyone. Almost at the same time, those waiting on the land began to surge forward, weaving between those disembarking to get onto the boat.

"Unbelievable." Alan found he was laughing. "I've never seen anything like that. People must get injured or killed."

Drakou was chuckling. "Never been known."

Alan gasped. "Hellfire!"

"What is it?" asked the Greek.

"It's her," Alan responded. "Konstantina. Shit, and the Scotsman. Christ, are they together?"

Drakou pushed him aside and looked into the telescope. He saw Konstantina stepping onto the land from the boat, and, in the crowd behind her, Gary McAllister.

"So that is the Scottish man?" Drakou watched as Konstantina walked slowly through the crowd followed by the Scotsman.

"You know him?" asked Alan.

"No, but he was expected." Drakou didn't look up from the telescope. He turned it slowly to his left and saw, further along the harbour Manos sitting with Nikos and looking toward the approaching line of people. "As I thought. Right." Drakou left the telescope and picked up his phone again. "I need to stop this." He dialled and began to talk in Greek rapidly as Alan looked back into the eyepiece of the telescope. Konstantina had now walked quite a way along the harbour front and McAllister was some ten yards behind her, obviously watching her and following. She seemed unaware of him. She slipped on her left shoe and stopped to put it back on. McAllister immediately stopped and made as if to look in a shop across the road which had rows of leather belts hanging on a rail outside. He kept one eye on the Greek girl and as she moved away he followed.

Alan heard Drakou in the background. "That should do it. Kyriako is down there."

As he spoke, Alan saw a white motorboat pull into the harbour wall just below Konstantina. The young bearded boy at the wheel waved at her and she stopped. They had a brief conversation and Konstantina stepped down onto the front of the boat and sat in the bow. Immediately, the boy swung the wheel and, in a turmoil of churning water, the boat was heading out from the harbour towards the open sea. Having followed the boat, Alan swung the telescope back to where McAllister had been standing, but he had gone.

Alan felt a slap on his back.

"Come on Alan Marks, your dry clothes are inside. You need to get dressed, we are going to Pedi."

"Pedi?" asked Alan, looking up. "What is Pedi? And why are we going there?"

"It is a bay away from the harbour and has a very nice taverna." Drakou glanced towards the house door and lowered his voice. "With a very nice waitress, with what you say, a nice arse. Come on."

Alan began to follow and then stopped. "But what about Konstantina?"

"No problem," laughed the Greek. "Konstantina doesn't exist. Come on."

High above them Marina Manidaki slammed the phone down into the arm of her seat on the private Lear jet.

"English shit." She pressed a button above her head and a young man immediately appeared from the front galley and was by her side.

"Now then young man, I want you to tell Captain Yiannis to call Thessaloniki and instruct the boys at the airport that a Mr Harold Jones is not to reach England. I do not know his flight but he must be stopped. By stopped I mean killed, understand?"

The young boy nodded almost in a bow and turned to go. He was stopped by the old lady's voice.

"Oh and if they cannot find a Harold Jones, kill somebody called Wilde, Barnaby Wilde."

CHAPTER FIFTEEN

McAllister, frustrated at having lost the girl, decided that he would at least stick to part of his original plan, and be prepared. He had found that what the girl on the phone had said was true. He had asked one person when he reached the small bridge at the end of the harbour and had been directed straight to Dinos' Hardware Shop. Actually, not so much directed as taken. The small old lady, dressed completely in black had insisted on taking him. It had taken less than five minutes, but he realised as he waved her goodbye that in that five minutes, she had determined he was not English but from somewhere called Scotland, single without children , but with a good job at a bank, had a brother and two sisters and was giving up smoking. All he knew of her was that she had a middle-aged daughter who had lost her husband at sea and left her with two children and that if he was free any evening while he was there he was welcome to dinner.

"My Nicoletta makes a very good *stifado*," called the old lady as she headed off down the narrow street. "Ask Dino where we are, Maria the baker's wife, he will know."

"Fine." McAllister waved back. He muttered under his breath. "What the hell is a *stifado*?"

"A rabbit stew," said a voice in a Birmingham accent. "And her daughter makes the best on Symi."

McAllister swung around and found himself looking at a slim middle-aged blonde woman who was astride a small moped and just pushing it off its stand. "Mind you, if you do go you might end up with more than a *stifado*. Nicoletta's OK, but the mother? There are those who say the husband threw himself off the boat in that storm. You see Mr, er...sorry?"

McAllister felt obliged to reply. "McAllister, Gary McAllister."

"Well Gary, when you marry a Greek girl you also marry her mother. Be warned." She kicked the moped into action.

"I have no intention of marrying a Greek girl," said McAllister.

"Yes, I know love," she smiled, a broad smile. "But you're only a man, so you're always at risk dear." She held out her hand. "Jean, Jean Hennessy. I run a bar up in the village."

"The Jean and Tonic?" enquired the Scotsman.

The woman looked surprised. "You've heard of it?"

"You could say that," he replied.

The smiling blonde continued as if he hadn't spoken. "Of course you have, it's in 'The Rough Guide to Greece'. Mind you, you don't look like a 'Rough Guide' reader to me. Have we met before? No, I never forget a face. I know you from somewhere, though. It will come to me. Anyway if you're staying, pop in tonight. I've got single malt."

Before he could ask 'how did you know?' She had beaten him to it. "How did I know? You're a Scot. I've got some Balvenie."

McAllister was amazed. "You have Balvenie? Here?"

"And why not?" was the instant response. "And before you ask, yes it's the old style bottle. I don't stock any crap."

"This place is something else." McAllister found he was chuckling.

"This place is Symi," smiled the blonde and headed off down the narrow street.

He watched her go, then turned to enter the shop and found he wasn't surprised to be greeted at the door by an elderly Greek man in a tan work coat. "The man on the telephone yes? The man for the bullets? Come in, they are here. I am Dinos. You would like coffee, yes?"

"I would like coffee please," said Barnaby Wilde as he relaxed into his seat in business class on Olympic Airways flight 7689 to London Heathrow from Thessalonika. The stewardess brought him a cup and poured in the brown steaming liquid. Wilde sipped the coffee. "Mm," he said to the large Greek man sat next to him. "This is good coffee."

"Good," said the man with a smile. "I hope you enjoy it Mr...?"

"Wilde," said Barnaby. "Barnaby Wilde."

The man smiled again. "Really? Barnaby Wilde. Yes Miss, I will have coffee also. He took a cup and the girl poured him a coffee. "Well Mr Wilde, being Greek I am a great believer in making the most of the moment." He raised his cup in salute. "So live every day as if it is your last, love every woman as if she will be your last, and in this case enjoy your coffee as if it will be your last."

Barnaby Wilde smiled and raised his cup to return the salute.

He did enjoy his coffee. And it was his last.

For Alan, the ride down the long straight road from the village to the bay of Pedi, past ruined houses, half built houses and olive groves, on the back of Drakou's small motor bike, avoiding several goats, had been hair-raising. So as they sat down on thin wooden chairs at a small green table on a small concrete jetty that pushed out into one side of the bay in front of the small Taverna Aposotolis, Alan took a deep breath and sighed. "Christ Savvas, my bloody legs are still shaking."

"I have the something for that," laughed the big man, who then shouted, "Lemonia."

A slim young Greek girl with olive skin and shoulder-length dark hair, wearing denim shorts and a white lacy blouse, appeared in the doorway and giggled. "Savvas?"

The big Greek grinned back. "*Theo ouzaki! Agape mou*."

The girl blew him a kiss and went back inside.

Drakou sighed. "Now that would make your legs shake."

Alan looked across to the small shingle beach which was next to the tavern. There was a row of half a dozen umbrellas held in concrete blocks and several white plastic sunbeds. The sun beds were beginning to be occupied by sun worshippers, one or two of whom had stepped across the hot stones and into the water to cool down.

"Whales," whispered Drakou. "Beached whales. The white ones are the English whales."

Alan found himself sniggering. He looked down into the water which lapped gently against the jetty. He stood and walked out to the end of the jetty, still looking down. "Christ, you can see right down to the bottom, even out here. There are fish and things and bloody hell it's clear." He looked back at the taverna and to the other side where there was a large Greek fishing boat lying slightly to one side on a slipway which ran down the other side of the jetty. It was newly painted in bright blue, with a white and red line running around it, almost at the top where the sides met the deck.

Alan returned to the table. "That's a great boat."

"They built it here," said Drakou. "In the yard at the back."

He indicated a cluster of ramshackle sheds behind the taverna surrounded by broken hulls of long dead boats and parts of old engines.

Alan was astounded. "That was built here?"

The Greek gave him a puzzled look. "Yes. Why?"

Alan felt slightly uncomfortable but voiced his surprise. "Look, I don't want to be rude but I find that a bit hard to believe, I mean it's just sheds and mess and, well you probably have electrics but what else I mean..."

"Nikitas," said Drakou. "We have Nikitas. He builds boats." He indicated a small wiry middle-aged man who was wearing dark paint stained shorts and nothing else. He was gathering bundles of wood together by one of the sheds. He was bare foot and had skin that was almost black.

"He built that?" said Alan looking at the fishing boat, with a note of pure disbelief in his voice.

"And," said Drakou, pointing at a small blue and white wooden boat tied to the jetty by a long rope, "he built that. My boat, in which I catch fish and occasionally Englishmen."

"So let me get this right, Mr Drakou," said Alan, "you have a house on a hill on this island. I mean it's a nice house with a great view, but it's… anyway you ride a battered motorbike and own a small wooden boat built by that bloke over there, in a shed out the back."

Drakou smiled. "That is me, yes."

Alan looked around and lowered his voice so that he wouldn't be overheard. "But your boy? He is some kind of computer genius. Midas? I don't get it." Drakou looked at him quizzically. Alan continued, feeling the need to explain. "You have access to incredible wealth. I don't mean to be rude but you could be living in luxury, you could have so much more."

Drakou smiled, and sighed "Ah." It was the sort of 'Ah' that said 'Oh I see.'

Just then, Lemonia came to the table with a tray and put down two small glasses, a carafe of ouzo, a jug of water and a large plate of watermelon slices.

"Oh, we didn't order melon, did we?" said Alan, looking at Drakou.

Lemonia smiled at him as she poured the ouzo. "No, it is how you say in English 'on the home' yes?"

Drakou laughed. "House, on the house."

Lemonia giggled and slapped him playfully on the arm. As she turned he returned the slap, but on her small but firm buttocks. She turned as she backed away towards the taverna door, waving her finger at him and smiling.

Drakou turned back to Alan and lifted his glass. "*Yammas.*" Alan returned the compliment.

"More, eh?" said Drakou. "More?" He opened his arms gesturing to present the bay. The sea was still and the distant Turkish hills were beginning to disappear in the gathering heat haze. "More? Look. The sea, like a passionate woman, now she is quiet, inviting, by this afternoon when the meltemi wind blows she will boil with fury. Beautiful. You see my boat there?" He pointed. "Two hundred and twenty horses power, Evinrude diesel. Get me out of any trouble in bad weather. More?" He took a swig of the ouzo. Alan felt obliged to copy and gasped as the fiery clear liquid hit the back of his throat. Drakou laughed and poured water into Alan's glass, which immediately turned the remaining ouzo a milky white. "Try with water 'til you get used to it." Alan sipped the watered-down version and found it surprisingly pleasant. He nodded approval and found, despite what he had been through, he was beginning to feel more relaxed.

"You see," said Drakou, pouring himself another ouzo, "tomorrow I may come down here, look at the beautiful Lemonia, have a little dream, slap her bottom, have a glass of ouzo and then do a little fishing. Then maybe I come back and have another ouzo, then perhaps catch a few octopus. If the night is hot then maybe I take my boat and my nice big wife Anna to St George's Bay. We have barbeque, drink some wine and then put down a blanket and perhaps I fuck my Anna under the stars. She will say 'No, no, Drakou not here' and afterwards she will kiss me hard and say 'You are a bad man Drakou, but I love you.' In the morning we swim in the sea and come home. She will sing all the way back on the boat. Maybe in the afternoon I come down here and have an ouzo, flirt with Lemonia, then perhaps I catch a little fish." He indicated the sun beds. "I see the whales come here for holidays. They work all year to come here for two weeks. They have this for two weeks." He put both arms out in front of him indicating the bay again. "They have Symi, for two weeks. And the one thing they all share is; they all go home because they want more. If you go back to your country Mr Marks, and your busy life, and your emails and your expensive car, next time you think 'I would like more.' Think about Drakou, sitting here drinking ouzo, looking at Lemonia and her beautiful firm arse, perhaps thinking about taking Anna on my boat to St George's Bay for a fuck under the stars to make her sing.

Maybe just catching a little fish. Think about me, Alan Marks and see if you still want more. I have enough my friend. It may be less than you Mr Marks, but perhaps sometimes less is more."

Alan was amazed. "Less is more? Christ Drakou, now you're a bloody philosopher?"

Drakou smiled and looked him straight in the eyes. "Bullshit!" He raised his glass again and drank down the rest of the ouzo in one. "*Yammas!*" he shouted and banged the glass on the table. "Lemonia!" he shouted. "More Ouzo! Mr Marks might need to get drunk."

"Why might I need to get drunk?" enquired Alan.

"Because," said Drakou, looking out beyond the end of the jetty at a white speedboat that was approaching, "you are about to meet an old friend."

Manos picked up the mobile from the café table when it rang. "Yes Mrs Manidaki…Well I am not sure, there was one girl but...yes Mrs Manidaki I'm sure she will try to find Nikos…Yes we will…You will be here when? Very well Mrs Manidaki… The Scottish man? I think so yes. He went to the back of the harbour I think but... yes of course I will...Yes we will expect you then." He put the phone down and turned to Nikos. "Drink that beer, we have work to do."

Nikos gulped his beer down. "She is coming here?"

"Yes, and you had better hope that girl gives you the box thing that she has or you are a dead man. Now your English friend is dead that girl is your only hope." Manos stood. "Come on."

Nikos emptied the glass and put it down. "We have to find the girl, yes?"

"No," responded Manos. "Mrs Manidaki says the girl will find you. No, we have another job. That man who was following the girl? We have to find him."

"Find him?" asked Nikos.

"Yes," said Manos, "and by find him, I mean kill him." He turned and walked away.

"Oh right." said Nikos, standing up. "What?"

He followed Manos. Had he looked behind him, he would have seen the tall Englishman called Toby emerge from the cafe and flip open his mobile phone.

In Pedi, Konstantina jumped off the front of the white speedboat as Kyriakos guided it into the jetty.

"Alan!" She ran to the table. "Thank God you're alive." She went towards him but he stayed seated.

"I am alive, no thanks to you. You tried to have me killed Konstantina."

Before he could continue, Drakou stood and interrupted. "Alan, relax. Look I think we need to clear up something. This is not Konstantina, this is Zoe Tsavari."

Alan looked at the Greek man and then at Konstantina. "Zoe? What the hell?"

The girl sat down in the chair opposite. As she began to speak, Drakou's mobile phone rang. He answered it. "Yes? I see… Kyriako is here. I will tell him." He walked towards the boy, who was tying a rope from the speedboat to the jetty. As he went he glanced back at the couple. "Don't kill each other until I have spoken to Kyriako."

"Look," said the girl, looking straight at Alan. "I couldn't tell you who I was, I wasn't allowed to."

Alan was confused. "Not allowed to?"

She continued. "And I didn't try to kill you Alan. My job was to keep you alive, and I'm so glad you are." She put her hand out to his but he withdrew.

"Your job? Your job? Who the hell are you?"

She smiled at him. He was surprised at the effect it had as he felt his anger fading.

"I can't tell you yet," she responded. "But you are very important to the people I work for."

Alan sighed. "Well I'm glad I am important to someone, even if they are gangsters."

“They are not gangsters.” She looked around to where Drakou was talking to the young boy who was untying the boat, and lowered her voice. “Look, I can’t tell you too much at the moment, but just remember when you meet my boss, they need you, that’s all. They really need you.” She stopped as Drakou came back to the table.

“Where is he going?” She watched as Kyriako backed the speedboat away from the jetty.

“He has work to do in the harbour.” He sat down and glanced up as Lemonia approached with another carafe of ouzo. Just then, the big man’s mobile phone rang again. He picked it up. “*Ya?* OK.” He put it down. “Lemonia forget it we have to go. Come on you two.” He put ten Euros on the table and stood. “You will have to get drunk later, Alan Marks. Right now you have an important meeting in Tolis.”

“Just a minute,” said Alan. “ I’m fed up of just being told what to do. Important meeting. Meeting with who, and what makes it so important? I might not want to go.”

Drakou smiled at him. “I think giving you ouzo was a mistake.” He bent down and looked straight at Alan. “I also think you will want to go, because it is what you say in your language, a matter of life and death.”

In the harbour, McAllister emerged from the cool darkness of Dinos’ shop into the bright sunlight and searing heat that was building up to midday. He hadn’t realised just how long he had been inside. Once the old man had realised this man knew guns, guns had to be produced and discussed. More thick sweet coffee was consumed and then stories of exploits with guns had to be relayed. All this in broken English. Then after more coffee there was the in depth discussions about the English police not having guns but Greek police having them. After more coffee and many goodbyes, but with his bullets, McAllister eventually extricated himself. He stood in the street and pondered what to do next. He needed to find some shade and time to sit and work out a strategy. He walked past several shops selling trinkets, holiday clothes and cheap jewellery, a bakery that smelled wonderful and then through a narrow alleyway lined with bars and vegetable stalls to emerge once more on the harbour front. He spotted a large café bar which had a canopy under which were arranged some small polished rattan and glass tables surrounded by large red cushioned chairs. That looked like just the spot. The harbour was busy with tourists and he could see that since he had been to the shop, two larger ferries had arrived. The café bar was relatively quiet and he dropped his holdall and sat down on one of the chairs facing out towards the harbour.

A young man with a tray approached him. "What can I get you, beer?"

"Why not, yes one beer." He reasoned with himself it might be a bit early for scotch in this heat.

"Big beer or small beer?" asked the young Greek waiter.

"Oh what the hell, big beer." He replied, and as the young man turned and left McAllister pondered. "How come they always know you're not native?" As he looked out at the lines of people following tour guides along the harbour front, he settled into the very comfy chair. Now then, why had Marks not been on the ferry? How was he to find him and the girl who had shot off in a boat? How was he to get the Midas box? Then there was the business with the Greek connection, the whole reason he had come here. To get the bigger picture. And there was his boss. What was the old duffer's role in all this? The trouble was the old 'Psychic Mac' thing was kicking in and he didn't like the thoughts he was getting. He felt the reassuring discomfort of his gun in the small of his back, tucked into his belt under his shirt. That was something else. He had automatically felt the need for a gun so obviously he felt under threat. But from whom? Not Marks; the more he thought about Marks, the more he thought he was somehow a victim. The girl? Unlikely, but then why was she here? The boy arrived with the beer and put a small curl of paper in a small glass in the centre of the table. The Scott looked at him quizzically. The boy responded. "*To Logariazmo*. The bill."

McAllister went to put his hand in his pocket and the boy raised his hand. "*Meta, meta...*later." and walked away.

The Scot took a gulp of the ice cold beer and sat back. This was good, he was beginning to get all the thoughts out. This was what he had always done in big cases in his days in the Met. It's what he always told young detectives. 'When everything is kicking off and you've got an information overload, stop. Take half an hour to just sit and let it all run over in your mind like a film. Then you will know what to do next.' So he took another sip of the beer, put his head back on the soft red cushion that was on the back of the chair and let the events of the past two days begin to run over in his mind.

He needn't have concerned himself about what to do next, however, as the decision was about to be taken away from him.

He suddenly felt a sharp prod in his upper back through the soft upholstery of the chair. His instinct told him immediately it was the barrel of a gun, and he wasn't wrong. He opened his eyes and sat up. He was about to turn when a young man's voice, with a strong Greek accent, very softly spoke to him from the seat behind.

"Stay just where you are, Scottish man, unless you want to die in that chair."

McAllister replied in a low quiet voice. "I don't know who you are but I don't think you are about to shoot me in front of all these people."

The voice replied. "That is because you don't know who I am. I don't want to kill you here, it would be messy. But if I have to I will."

There was something in the young man's voice that told McAllister this was true.

The voice continued. "In a moment you will leave here and walk across the road to the edge of the harbour. There is a boat there, a yellow Bay Liner speedboat. You will get into it and wait. I will be watching you. If you try to run, I will gun you down."

McAllister began to rise.

"Slowly," said the voice, with increased volume and venom.

McAllister had barely got to his feet when suddenly a young man on a bicycle veered off the road in front of him, narrowly missed him and crashed into the table behind, falling onto the glass and shattering it. Immediately, everyone in the café stood and there was instant commotion. There were glasses and chairs everywhere and, as he spun around, McAllister saw the man who had been sitting behind him groping on his hands and knees for a gun which had spun away under another table. The boy from the bike was instantly up on his feet and heading for McAllister, treading on the grovelling man and flattening him as he went.

"Run!" he yelled at the Scotsman, who turned to his right but was immediately pulled around by his left arm as the boy guided him across the road and down the harbour side.

Suddenly he stopped and jumped sideways into the front of a white speedboat which was moored at the harbour wall.

"Jump!" he called to McAllister, who without thinking obeyed and landed on his knees in the front of the boat.

"Fuck, that hurt," he shouted clutching his left knee. The boy gunned the engine into life, climbed over McAllister and let the rope off the front, swung back over the Scot and was standing at the wheel, backing the boat away from the harbour side as McAllister began to stand. The boy spun the wheel and the Scotsman tottered sideways.

"Get to the back," called the boy.

McAllister duly obeyed and turned as he reached the back, only to be thrown backwards into a seat at the back of the boat as the boy opened it up and raised the boat up onto its plane. McAllister looked back over his shoulder at the wash as they sped out past the moored ferries at high speed and saw the chaos that was the cafe, with people standing and waving arms and screaming at each other.

Then he saw a figure emerge from the crowd, dragging another man with him. The man looked out towards them and pointed, then hit the other man around the head and began to drag him across the road to what looked like a bright yellow boat. Just as they were getting down onto it, they were lost from view as the boy swung the speedboat sharply past the clock tower at the harbour entrance and out towards what looked like a long promontory stretching out into the open sea. It had a cluster of small white buildings at its base and rose to two high peaks of rock. McAllister clutched the side of the boat as they bumped over small waves and it looked to him as if the boy was heading at high speed straight for a line of cliffs. Just as he was about to shout out in alarm, he saw the gap between what he thought was a headland and the main island. It was in fact a small island on its own. As they shot through the gap the boy shouted back and pointed to the smaller island. "That is Nimos."

"Great," shouted McAllister. "But where the hell are we going?"

"Not a clue," shouted the boy.

As they came out of the small straight into open sea, the nature of the surface changed and now they were bouncing over much higher waves and spray was showering over them.

"I think," shouted McAllister, spitting the salt water from his mouth, "they are coming after us."

"Really?" called the boy. "Right." He suddenly swung the boat hard right and hit an oncoming wave which splashed water high into the air and crashed down into the boat, soaking both of, them.

"Woooo!" yelled the boy in delight, and pushed hard on the throttle. He was looking to his right at the small island and they were now on the other side of it. He suddenly dropped the speed and McAllister lurched forward. The boy had seen what he was looking for. He slowly manoeuvred the craft back into a tiny inlet which doglegged to the left behind a low outlet of rock. He cut the engine and threw several blue fenders over the side to protect the plastic craft from the rocks. Then quickly moving to the front of the boat, he lifted a hatch and dropped a small anchor on a chain over the front and secured it to a cleat on the bow. He looked over the rocks and out to sea. All was quiet apart from the gentle lapping of the water. Anyone going past would not see them.

McAllister was about to speak when he got a terrible shock as a loud bleating above him made his heart jump. The boy laughed and hissed at a large black goat which was perched on a narrow ledge just above them. It scrambled upwards and away showering the small boat with tiny stones and pebbles.

"Good move," said McAllister stroking pieces of grit from his hair.

"Yeah," said the boy, turning his attention back to the open sea. "Don't want that bastard drawing attention to us if they do follow us.'

"Look," said the Scot. "Have you any idea who they are?"

"Sort of," said the boy, still looking out to sea. "One of them is Nik Stavroulis, slimy git, but wouldn't hurt a fly. Don't know who the nasty shit with him is, but apparently he wants to kill you. So I was told. But I blew that for him. Probably wants to kill me now, as I stood on him."

McAllister was still trying to process all that had happened. "Hang on. You were told? So you crashed that bike on purpose?"

"You're quite bright for an ex-copper." The boy smiled but kept looking out to sea.

Now the Scotsman was really taken aback. "How do you know that?"

The boy's concentration didn't waver. "They told me."

Before McAllister could ask the obvious question, the boy raised his hand and whispered. "Keep it down. Listen."

There was a low droning of a boat engine growing louder.

"Yeah, I thought so." The boy was still whispering. "Once they got through the straight and saw the open sea, they would know we weren't ahead of them. I thought they might double back around here. Let's hope they just go on by."

"Let's hope so," said McAllister, taking his gun from the back of his belt.

The boy glanced back. "My God. He said you were hard but Jesus, a gun."

Before the Scot could respond, the boy waved his hand again as the sound of the approaching power boat grew. When the bright yellow craft passed the inlet, the sound was deafening as it echoed back from the rocks.

"Hang on," shouted the boy.

Before he could ask, Gary McAllister realised why, as the wash from the passing boat hit the rocks and crashed back into the inlet rocking their boat wildly. The boy fended the boat off the rocks as the Scotsman hung on to the side. Eventually, the waves subsided and the sound of the passing engine faded. They sat in silence for a while until McAllister spoke. "What now?"

"We wait," said the boy taking a mobile phone from his pocket. "Until I get a message saying...oh shit." He held up the phone. "No signal back here, bollocks."

"You seem to have a very good grasp of English?" McAllister enquired.

The boy was walking to the front of the boat holding the phone out. "English mother, Greek father, not sure who. Damn, now we have a problem."

"You are waiting for a message? Who from?"

The boy put his phone back into his pocket. "Can't tell you that, and there is no point shooting me for the information, unless you know how to drive a Larson four point five litre powerboat."

"Not a fucking clue," said McAllister putting the gun back in the belt at the back of his trousers. "So looks as if we're stuck here for a bit."

"Well," said Kyriakos, "I'm not going out there for a while." He lifted a hatch in the floor of the boat. "Beer?" he said producing a can.

"Thanks." McAllister took it and looked at the can. "Mythos?"

"Greek," said the boy. "None of your German or Belgian shit."

McAllister flipped the tab and foam shot out all over his chest. Kyriakos laughed. "Must have been the ride." He held his own can over the side and opened it carefully, letting as little go as possible. "Grab another," he said, indicating the hatch.

As McAllister bent down, he asked: "You were that boy who took the girl this morning from the harbour?"

The boy turned slowly. "Could be. And?"

"I was following her." McAllister looked up.

The boy smiled.

"I didn't know that."

"I think you did." The Scot opened his beer over the side carefully. "Don't kid a kidder son. Where did you take her? Hang on, I bet you can't tell me that either."

"Look," Kyriakos sighed, "I don't do this." McAllister looked puzzled, so the boy continued. "You know this, whatever it is, racing around being chased by criminals."

McAllister took a swig from the can. "Mm, not bad. What do you do then?"

The boy sat down. "Well a bit of everything, you know, take people around in this boat. Carry a bit of luggage up to the village, a bit of water-skiing. You name it."

"Mm," said the Scotsman, "but you seem a bright lad, doesn't seem like much of a career."

The boy laughed as he bent down and picked up a small pink thong from where the beer was stored. "It has its perks. Better leave that here or my girlfriend will kill me. Look, I'm twenty five, done the university thing, now I spend my days in the sun, meet loads of girls and its great. One day I'll get a proper job but right now this suits me fine. I expect I'll end up snagged by some girl one day. You married?"

The directness of the question set McAllister on the defensive. "Was, yes, but it all went tits up. My fault."

The boy was attempting to hang the thong on a rock above the boat. "Ah, another woman eh?"

"You could say that. A mistress called the Metropolitan Police." McAllister finished the can of beer and found himself reaching for another. "Why in God's name am I telling you all this?"

"Don't know," said the boy, having finally managed to hang up the thong. "Perhaps I'm just..." He stopped mid-sentence and suddenly looked out over the rock. "Listen."

They both froze. There was the dull sound of an engine in the distance growing louder. "Oh shit no," said the boy as the sound got louder and then dropped to a gently ticking over. He looked tentatively over the rock. "Shit they are out there. Nikos may know about this place, he used to live on Symi when he was a kid. I bet he's trying to remember it." He saw the man at the front of the yellow speedboat pointing. The boy looked behind him and saw, above, hanging on the rock the pink thong. "Shit, and I thought the worst that could happen was Lemonia would find it."

"Have they seen us?" asked McAllister.

"No," replied the boy, "but they've seen that." He pointed at the thong then peered back over the rock. "Hell they are coming this way." The boy was beginning to panic.

McAllister heard the engine of the yellow boat pick up slightly as he took his gun out once more. The engine was getting louder and McAllister had just made his mind up to stand and fire over the rock when there was another noise. It was the sound of a mobile phone. Kyriakos grabbed his phone from his pocket and then realised it wasn't his that was ringing. He shot a glance at McAllister, who shook his head. "Mine's on stun."

Kyriakos looked back over the rock to see the man at the front of the yellow boat on his phone. "How come he gets a signal?" he whispered, ducking back down. "Bastard's probably on Turkcell." Then there was another noise. It was another engine sound getting louder, but more rapidly. All at once it was deafening. Suddenly, as they both looked up, a small black helicopter passed overhead.

McAllister stood up immediately, looking over the rock, gun pointing forward ready to fire, only to see the back of the yellow speedboat moving away at great speed around the rocks and out of sight.

"Jesus that was close." The boy sat down. "Shit I feel quite sick." Suddenly the boat rocked again with the wash but this time he just let it happen.

"You OK?" asked McAllister.

The boy took a deep breath. "Yeah I think so."

"Delayed shock," responded McAllister.

"I suppose so," said the boy. "Wow. My stomach feels like its full of eels and my head's really, I don't know."

"Right," said the Scot, pushing the boy's head down. "Head between your legs, get the blood back."

The boy stayed in that position for a few moments, then slowly rose up. "Thanks mate." He held out his hand and McAllister took it. "Nice to nearly die with you Mr...?"

"McAllister, Gary McAllister," he replied. "And you?"

"Oh, Kyriakos," said the boy.

"Well Kyriakos," McAllister smiled, "it was nice to survive with you, and thanks for the rescue in the harbour. What do we do now? I don't think we should go back there."

"No," said the boy. "Those guys were in a hurry, but I bet that's where they've gone. We'll give it five then head out until I get a signal and with any luck somebody will tell me where to go next."

McAllister was about to say 'But I might not want to go with you' when something stopped him. "Maybe, just maybe," he thought, 'for once I'll go with the flow."

He finished off his second beer and sat back, watching the boy pulling in the fenders. Whoever had sent this lad wanted to keep him alive, whereas whoever sent the yellow boat definitely didn't. Then there was the mobile phone call as the helicopter passed over. Coincidence? Maybe, maybe not. So why did he feel so relaxed? No sooner had he asked himself this than he had his own answer.

It was probably because the picture of what was going on suddenly became a lot clearer in his mind. “Hey Kyriakos, let’s go.” he said.

The boy turned. “I don’t know, I mean it might not be clear out there.”

“Oh, it will,” said McAllister. “Trust me, it will.”

CHAPTER SIXTEEN

As Alan got up onto the back of the battered Suzuki pickup truck which had arrived outside the taverna in Pedi, he found he was getting more confused. Sitting in the back was a rather smart man in tan linen trousers, a cream cotton shirt and a straw Panama hat. He looked like a caricature of an ex-English public school boy.

"This is my boss," said the girl he now knew as Zoe. "Alan Marks, this is Toby."

The man smiled at Alan as he sat down opposite him. "Pleased to meet you, Mr Marks. I understand you have had an interesting journey." He put out his hand to shake Alan's and Alan, almost as a reflex action, took it.

Zoe jumped down from the back of the pickup and climbed onto the back of Drakou's small motorbike. The smart English man slapped the top of the cab and the pickup took off.

The man shouted over the noise of the very loud diesel engine. "Hang on Alan Marks, we are off over the top of the island to a quiet little bay called Tolis. We can have a good chat there, but it may be a bumpy ride."

As the truck climbed higher and higher up the hill through the village, the road began to wind as they left the bay far below them. Alan felt it wasn't such a bumpy ride, but then as they looked down over the village and he saw a spectacular view of the island stretched out before him and across the water to the distant hills of Turkey, the tarmac suddenly ran out and they were bouncing over a rough rock-strewn track. They passed small ruined farms and deserted terraces and olive groves as well as the occasional well-tended field with beehives nestling under old olive trees. Crossing over the spine of the island, they headed down towards the sea on the other side as Drakou and Zoe passed them to avoid being engulfed in dust and disappeared down the rough track ahead of them.

All Alan could see as he hung on was the sea far below him and the coast of Turkey in the distance. The road became suddenly steeper with sharp curves as it snaked down to sea level. As they rounded a sharp bend cut into the rock of the hillside, it dipped violently and Alan saw the most beautiful rocky bay stretched out in front of them. At one end, where the road finished, was a small terracotta tiled roof taverna with a large patio complete with a shaded raffia canopy overlooking the sea. As the truck came to a stop in a cloud of dust Alan found he was mesmerised by the sight in front of him. A broad open space surrounded the small rustic building in the middle. He jumped down, following the neat Englishman, who said. "Find us a table while I talk to Kostas." As Alan walked away, the man began to get into the cab and talk to the driver of the truck. Alan felt the burning heat of the sun which he hadn't noticed whilst bumping along in the back of the truck. He walked around the side of the taverna and was glad to get under the shade as he saw Drakou and Zoe seated at a table overlooking the sea under the broad wooden and raffia canopy. There were about a dozen such tables, all with chairs and all were deserted. As he looked down the rough stone steps to the long thin shingle beach, he saw a line of eight large upturned cable drums all with folded sun umbrellas sticking out of them and all with two white plastic sunbeds either side. All were deserted.

As he approached the table, Drakou could see what he was thinking. "It's the wind. The meltemi begins again. Look out there, I think you call it white horses."

Alan Marks looked out to sea and saw that it was indeed quite choppy with large waves breaking in white crests.

The big Greek smiled. "Most people come here by boat, and having come by road you will know why. Today it's too rough out there, so nobody comes. Maybe later some Greeks will come for a swim, if they have a truck or a car they don't give a shit about." He looked up. "But only the English," he indicated Toby who was still deep in conversation with the driver of the truck, "and their mad Greek friends," he pointed to himself, "come over land in the middle of the day."

As he finished speaking, a slim petite girl, who Alan thought bore more than a passing resemblance to the waitress in Pedi, came out of the taverna and ran over to the table, leant over the back of the chair and kissed Drakou on the cheek, then immediately slapped him in the face. "You bad man, you go to see my sister in Pedi this morning before you come to see me. I may never speak to you again. But..." she looked at Alan Marks, "you bring a handsome man too so perhaps I will forgive you."

Drakou laughed and looked at Alan. "This is Helleni, she is Lemonia's sister and they are both in love with me of course. But as I tell Anna, why not? They are only human." The girl smacked him on the back of the head and turned to Zoe. "Why do you have anything to do with this man Zoe? He is a pig."

"True," said Zoe, putting her arm through Drakou's, "but a lovable one. This is Alan Marks from England."

Alan, who was about to sit, stood back up again and held out his hand, The girl ignored it and planted a kiss on his cheek. "Hello Alan Marks from England. Are you rich and are you married?"

Alan found he was blushing and looked at Drakou who was grinning.

"Well, I may or may not be rich, I'm not sure anymore, and I am married but won't be for very long. How's that?"

The girl looked at him with mock coyness. "But are you free, Alan Marks from England?"

Alan looked at Zoe, who held his gaze.

"Well?" said the girl.

Alan stayed looking at Zoe. "I'll get back to you on that."

"Helleni, you beautiful creature." It was Toby. "Drinks all around. Beers for every one?"

"Water for me," said Zoe.

"Fine," said Toby. "That's beer for these two and water for Zoe, and for me?"

"I know what you want," said the girl with a smile, and set off into the taverna. Alan looked beyond her and saw the truck they had come in climbing slowly up the hill in a cloud of dust, heading back the way they had come.

"Right, sit down Marks," said Toby, taking off his hat. Alan sat opposite the man who looked straight at him. "We haven't much time; Nikos Stavroulis will be here with his thug soon."

"Nikos will be here?" said Alan, completely surprised.

"How do you know that?" asked Zoe.

"Ah well," said Toby, "I told Kostas I was here to meet an old friend from England called Alan Marks who arrived this morning but didn't want anyone to know. And just to make sure I tipped him five euros."

Drakou laughed. "He wouldn't like that."

"Exactly," responded Toby. "He will tell Stavroulis as soon as he gets back."

Zoe looked worried. "He might call him before that."

"I doubt it," said Toby, producing a mobile phone from his pocket and smiling. "Not without this. People really shouldn't leave these things on the front seat, should they? Now Alan Marks, to business. Zoe, you have Midas?"

Zoe produced the small black box from her bag.

"Good," said Alan. "Glad to see you have the rest of the merchandise."

"Alan, it wasn't like that," Zoe protested.

"Whatever," said Alan and was about to continue when Toby stopped him.

"Children, children we do not have time for a lover's tiff. Now the thing is Mr Marks, we need the Greeks to think they have got this little toy back, and your Scottish friend Mr McAllister to get it too. You see, we have a pretty good idea who the Greek running this is, and who the connection is in Britain. It is somebody very high up in the financial world, so we need the trail to go straight to them. Our feeling is that neither will tell the other they have it, at least not before we nab them."

Alan suddenly banged his fist on the table. "I'm sorry, but quite frankly who the hell are you and what the hell has all this got to do with me? I was just trying to save Nikos' life and now you're talking about giving the Greeks their toy back. It's a toy that nearly got me killed."

Just then, Helleni arrived with a tray of drinks and began to put them on the table.

"Well," said the rather plummy man in the linen shirt, as he sipped his Pimms. "What has it to do with you? Technically nothing." He turned to the girl who was putting down a glass of water in front of Zoe, "Helleni, this is one of the best Pimms I have had in a long time. Where did you get the mint?"

The girl pointed to the rough stone wall at the back of the stone terrace, and under a bright red hibiscus tree was a very large mint bush. Then she pointed at Drakou. "He say you like the Pimms with mint, so he bring a bush at Easter."

The man laughed and looked at Drakou, who held up his beer. "*Yammas*, Drakou, you are a real friend." Then he turned back to Alan. "Where were we? Ah yes. Who the hell are we? I am sorry, Mr Marks, I can't tell you that, but I can tell you who the hell we are not. We are not MI5, MI6 or any other M for that matter. There is no M in front of our name and suffice to say you won't find us in the phone book or on the internet and you can't get us with a freedom of information request because there is no record of us. All I can tell you is that we are truly international with offices in London, Geneva and New York. My particular department was set up when the world banking organisations took the developed world to the edge of chaos and meltdown. Now most of that was sheer incompetence and greed, but it became apparent that some of it might be linked to organised crime or even terrorism. Also certain leading bankers in the City of London were identified as being, how can I put this, dodgy."

"Look, this is all very fascinating," said Alan, interrupting him, "and assuming I even believe this James Bond crap you're telling me, how come I'm sitting on a Greek island in the heat of the day having been shot at, chased halfway across Europe and dumped in the sea? Why me?"

"Good question, Mr Marks." Toby took another sip of his Pimms. "God, this is good. The thing is we have known for some time that a Greek crime syndicate was planning Midas and we suspected an English bank connection. We also knew that the boy who developed it had been disposed of. Once we found out Stavroulis' company was making it, we recruited Drakou here who we discovered had a bit of a history with secret squirrel stuff many years ago. The fact that his boy was on the inside was genuinely a stroke of luck and very useful, especially as they think he is stupid. When he alerted us that he thought the Midas box had been sent to you, we got Zoe, Miss Konstantina Zouroudi to you, transferred to the First National Branch in Farnborough from head office in London where we had already placed her."

Zoe suddenly spoke. "Look Alan, at the start we didn't know if it was a mistake or you were part of it." She smiled at him. "I mean, I pretty quickly worked out that you had discovered what Midas was by mistake and you were no gangster."

Alan looked at her. "Oh great. So when I met you at the cash machine you were waiting for me?"

Zoe glanced at Toby, who nodded, then she turned back to Alan. "When our mole in the bank's fraud office told us Midas had been activated I was instructed to tail you and make contact. That morning when you left home and turned right onto the Farnborough Road, I had a pretty good idea where you were heading and…"

Alan stopped her. "So I was conned right from the start?"

Before she could reply Drakou spoke. "Alan, she was only doing her job."

"Yeah," Alan sneered. "And bloody good she is at it too." He turned back to Zoe. "So I was just another job?"

She returned his look. "At the start."

"The thing is, Mr Marks," said Toby, "when it became clear you were not part of it, and not only that, First National had sent their Scottish bloodhound after the Midas box, I'm afraid you became potentially very useful. Once McAllister came on the scene we had the British bank connection confirmed, you see?"

"I don't bloody believe you people," said Alan. "I mean, you are so bloody cold about this. Only doing a job? Connections confirmed? Now I am potentially very useful? I've been nearly killed on four or five separate occasions in the last forty eight hours. Christ, early this morning I nearly fucking drowned."

"Yes, I can see your point," said Toby, finishing his drink and waving at Helleni, indicating he would like another. "I appreciate this might not be the best time to bring this up, but as we are a bit pressed for time, you could do one last thing for us. Deliver the Midas box to the Greeks, and to your Scottish friend."

Alan was astounded, "You are taking the piss, aren't you? You have to be out of your mind. If you think I am going to..."

Toby raised his hand and stopped Alan's tirade.

"Try and stay calm Mr Marks, and before you say 'but there is only one Midas box,' do not concern yourself with small details, more whether or not you are prepared to do this."

"Bloody hell, I thought I was making my feelings pretty clear on that matter," said Alan.

Toby remained remarkably cool, which in itself was disconcerting to Alan. He was seething, but the fact that the man opposite him remained completely composed, almost nonchalant, was very unnerving.

"You see Mr Marks," Toby continued, "we have a problem you and I. The Greeks now know you are alive, so as far as both them and the Scotsman are concerned, you are the probably the one person who can deliver Midas. Now, before you get all worked up as to why you should do it, hear me out." Helleni placed another Pimms in front of him and he smiled at her. "Thank you. Now Alan, I could give you a lot of guff about duty to Queen and country, the greater good, putting something back into society and all that tosh, but as its bloody dangerous you might well tell me to eff off. So let me put it this way." He took a sip of his drink. "Marvellous. Your company, Mr Marks, has gone down the shitter, for whatever reason, owing vast amounts of money. You have partaken in what amounts to a major fraud and been implicated with international organised crime. Let's not even go down the road of causing a near-fatal accident in Farnborough and leaving the scene of that and another on the M3, where the driver was found shot dead incidentally. We could be looking at twenty years, plus."

Alan could hardly believe what he was hearing. It was all true, sort of, but not the way he saw it. "But" was the only word he got out before the man continued.

"But, on the other hand; to the rest of the world, Alan Marks fell off a ferry this morning just west of a Greek island called Symi and was never seen again. Just another drunken Englishman drowning the sorrows of his failed business in ouzo and the Aegean sea. So he has no debts, no worries and no longer exists. He is, however, now born again as?" He indicated to Drakou who produced a passport from his pocket.

Drakou opened it and read out, "Anthony Miller."

The man smiled and downed the rest of his second Pimms. "Alan Marks, Anthony Miller, A and M, so as you find the adjustment easy. On the other hand, you could say no."

Alan wasn't quite sure what to say.

"Take your time," said the posh Englishman, "but not too long. Helleni? More drinks for everyone." He raised his glass and the girl hurried over and took it.

As this was happening, Alan looked at Zoe, who gave a slight nod. He turned to the man. "You need me, don't you?"

The man sighed, smiled and looked at Zoe. "My, my Miss Tsavari, we have got it bad haven't we? You really like this fellow, don't you? I suppose I can think of worse reasons for leaving the service."

"Leaving?" Alan looked at Zoe.

"Ah, she hasn't told you that bit," the man continued. "Yes, apparently you have stolen her heart and, by the way, one of the best Greek operatives we have. Anyway, to your point, do we need you? In a word: yes." At that moment his mobile phone rang. He flipped it open. "Kyriako? Good...Tolis. I know it's pretty rough out there." He stood up. "Just a moment, I need to take this call." He walked a short distance from the table.

"Alan," said Zoe. "You don't have to do anything you don't want to, but just listen to him. I know it doesn't feel like it but you can trust us."

"Really?" Alan had a note of sarcasm in his voice. "Too right, it doesn't feel like it."

Toby flipped the phone closed and turned around. "Right Alan Marks, let's get down to horse trading." He sat down opposite Alan again. "OK, we've got you a fresh identity, but that won't pay the rent. Now we could quibble and haggle, but first of all you cannot keep your bank card I'm afraid." He held his hand out and Alan pulled his bank card from his back pocket and handed it over. "Thank you," said Toby, holding it up. "Oh, and while we're at it, Zoe?" He held out his hand to Zoe while still looking at Alan. She took her card from her bag and handed it over. He smiled. "Thank you my dear. Now Mr Marks, as I was saying, whilst you can't keep the card, I am empowered by my masters to offer you remuneration in kind, as a sort of compensation."

"What, a lump of cash?" asked Alan.

"I'm afraid not, no. I said 'in kind'." The man shook his head. "Since all the expenses rumpus in England and the cutbacks everywhere, every chitty and cheque is the subject of scrutiny. No, we can't do money, but with our connections we can do lots of other things, Aston Martins, Flats in Marbella, a small helicopter, nothing too pricey but..."

Alan interrupted him, "The *Wind Of Change*."

To Alan's astonishment the man laughed and said "The two masted ketch for sale in the harbour? Good choice."

"Very good," echoed Drakou.

"Man after my own heart," said the Englishman. "She's yours Mr Marks." Then his smile dropped. "But only of course if you are ours."

CHAPTER SEVENTEEN

"So," said McAllister to the boy who was just putting his phone down. "You know where we are going?"

"Depends. I am told you want to find a man called Alan Marks?"

McAllister grinned. "Now how the fuck do you know that? I know, I bet you can't tell me. Well quite frankly who gives a shit? You know where he is?"

"Better," laughed Kyriakos, starting up the boat. "I can take you there. I'd put this on though if I were you." He went past McAllister and pulled up the top of one of the seats in the front of the boat, pulling out two bright orange life jackets. Putting one on, he handed the other to McAllister. "It's going to get pretty rough around the other side of the island. This wind is the meltemi."

McAllister put his arms through and fiddled with the black plastic catch around his waist. "And that's bad, is it? That wind."

"Put it this way." said the boy as he pushed the throttle forward and the boat lifted itself up. "None of the taxi boats are running that side today and they are all twice the size of this."

"Is it safe?" asked the Scot.

"Well, let's see." The boy was smiling and looking intently ahead as they rounded the promontory that was at the end of the tiny island of Nimos. Suddenly the sea changed as if someone had turned on the waves and they hit a big one. It felt to McAllister as if they had taken off. No sooner were they in the air, than they smacked down hard on to the surface of the water again.

"Fantastic," yelled the boy. "Let's do it." And he pushed the throttle forward again.

"Oh yeah, let's," said McAllister, less than convinced it was a good idea, as he wiped his sleeve across his wet face. "Can't think of anything I'd rather do."

As Nikos Stavroulis stepped off the speedboat in the harbour, he saw Kostas' truck pulling up outside the café where a group of people were gathered, helping to clear the broken glass and wreckage. As Kostas stepped out of the cab, Nikos whistled to him. He ran across the road and looked back at the wreckage.

"Christ Niko, what happened there?"

"You don't need to know." It was Manos who had stepped up onto the harbour from the boat behind Nikos. "Take us to the football pitch."

"That's in Pedi," said Kostas. "Why do you want to go there?"

Manos stepped forward and grabbed him by the throat. "None of your fucking business but if we don't get there quickly, Mrs Manidaki will be very upset as she is waiting there. And if she gets upset, somebody, and I mean you, will pay." He let go of Kostas, who started coughing and looked at him with distain. "Oh for God's sake just take us there." Manos started to walk over to the truck as Nikos followed, taking Kostas by the arm.

"Oh, by the way Niko," said Kostas, struggling to speak in more than a whisper. "That Marks man you were waiting for is here."

Manos stopped and turned. "What did you say?"

Kostas stuttered. "The man Marks, from England. He is here on Symi, in Tolis."

Manos stepped closer to him. "You are sure it is him?" Kostas, half afraid to speak, nodded. Manos smiled at him with the dead smile that was his speciality. Then he took his mobile phone from his pocket and dialled. Looking at Kostas and Nikos, he walked away and said: "Stay there." He walked across towards the truck and began to talk into the phone. It was a short conversation. He shouted to the two men and beckoned them. "Come. Kostas, take us to the football pitch, now."

As they rounded yet another headland, McAllister, who was by now soaking wet, was beginning to feel sick. "How much bloody further is it?"

Kyriakos was standing at the wheel of the speedboat, looking over the wind visor which was covered in spray. "Almost there my friend, boy this is cool." The boat once more rose high over an oncoming wave and smashed down into the trough. As they headed in towards a bay, the sea calmed and ahead McAllister could see what looked like a small beach with folded umbrellas. Raised above it and behind was a canopied terrace and a small building. As they drew closer, he could see a concrete jetty pushing out into the sea and Kyriakos steered towards it and slowed the boat. As they approached it, the boy cut the engine, threw two fenders over the side and jumped off the front, guiding the boat into the jetty. "Right Mr Mac, you go up to the taverna and I'll keep an eye on the boat. In this wind, I don't want it ending up being matchsticks on this jetty."

McAllister looked up from the jetty, but could see nothing and so he walked over to the steep stone steps that took him up to the terrace high above the beach. As he reached the top, he saw to his left a couple sat at a table with drinks in front of them. They were facing away from him. The other tables were deserted, apart from two men seated at a table near the taverna door and they were deep in conversation with a young girl who was standing with a tray in her hand. He walked towards the couple. As he got nearer, the man of the two turned and saw him. He stood immediately. "Come on Konstantina, time to go." The girl got up quickly.

"I don't think so Mr Marks," said McAllister producing his gun, but keeping it low down so the people at the taverna couldn't see it. "Just sit back down very slowly." Alan Marks and Zoe began to sit when McAllister issued another instruction. "No, on the other side of the table please." They moved around the table and sat opposite McAllister, who could now see the taverna behind them and the girl with the tray coming towards them. "Just act normally," he said, as he sat and put the gun under the table on his lap.

The girl with the tray spoke to him in Greek. McAllister looked at her, bemused.

"She wants to know if you want a drink," said Zoe.

"Oh fine," said McAllister. "Do they have Scotch?"

Zoe spoke to the girl and the girl responded.

"Well?" asked the Scotsman.

Zoe spoke to her again and the girl said, "Johnny Walker."

"I'll have a beer," said McAllister. The girl smiled and walked away.

McAllister smiled at Zoe. "So she speaks some English then." He turned to Alan. "Well well Mr Marks. We have spoken on the phone, and briefly in the street, but I was beginning to think we would never meet. How do you do?" He held out a hand across the table and Alan shook it nervously.

"I've been better," he said.

"And Miss Zouroudi, I believe?" he held out his hand to Zoe. "Looking much lovelier than your photograph on the First National Bank records."

Zoe shook his hand and smiled weakly.

"Now I think you both know why I am here. You have Midas; we want it. By 'we' I mean the First National Bank."

"Just a minute," said Alan. "Do you mean to tell me that my shit awful bank has sent a hit man all the way across Europe to track me down just because of a few quid out of a cash machine?"

McAllister laughed quietly. "Hardly a 'few quid' Mr Marks, and I am not a 'hit man' as you put it, more a sort of debt collector. Anyway, I am sure you would rather I came after you than the police did. Prison can be a nasty place for a man of your social status. We wouldn't want the police involved anyway. Bank losing money to a fraudster? Cash machines not reliable? Think of the publicity.

Not good for business. So for the sake of all concerned I'd like your bank card to start with."

"I don't have it anymore," said Alan.

McAllister sighed. "Oh dear, and I hoped this was going to be easy. Oh well, how about the small black box and while you're at it your Greek connection?"

"Greek connection?" Alan tried hard to look confused.

"Oh please Mr Marks, I am not a fool. Mr Stavroulis I believe, yes? He sent the box to you? Well that was the gist of the phone call you received in the restaurant in Farnborough, wasn't it? You look surprised Mr Marks. Now I am fully prepared to believe you are an innocent in all this. You know, apart from ripping off the bank to the tune of several thousands, so give me the card, the box and the crook who supplied it to you and we'll call it quits. I'll tell my people you fell off a cliff or a boat or some such. As long as you never go back to England, you'll be fine. So how about it?" As McAllister spoke, Helleni came over and put a bottle of beer and a glass in front of McAllister. He thanked her and she said something briefly to Zoe in Greek. She was walking away as the Scotsman spoke to Zoe.

"I would call her back love if I were you."

"Why?" asked Zoe.

"Because," said the Scot, smiling, "that man over there has got it wrong.

Zoe looked confused. "Sorry I don't understand?"

"That's funny," said McAllister, "because you are Greek. Shall I translate it for you? That girl told you not to worry because somebody called Toby said the bullets in my gun were blanks. Wrong."

Zoe stayed looking at him but called out, "Helleni?"

The girl came back. As she reached the table, McAllister said. "Tell her to let Toby know that I replaced the crap bullets his man gave me in England with the real thing."

"Why don't you tell her?" she asked.

"Because," said McAllister, "a nine month secondment to Interpol in Athens eight years ago means I learned to listen and understand a lot. Didn't mean I could say that much."

Zoe turned and spoke to Helleni. The girl was obviously shocked and immediately ran back to the taverna.

"Thank you," said McAllister, and then after a pause. "Zoe."

Zoe smiled. She might not like this man but she found she had a growing professional respect for him.

McAllister turned to Alan. "So Alan Marks, before this young lady's boss comes over to join us, which he will because his curiosity will get the better of him, what about the Midas box?"

As Kostas pulled the pickup off the road down to Pedi, onto a small rough track that led to the football pitch, Nikos saw the small black helicopter, its blades slowly coming to a stop. The pitch was bright green astroturf surrounded by white fencing and a small stand for about a hundred people to one side. The Eurocopter 130 was sitting in the centre circle. Kostas pulled onto the pitch and stopped the truck. Kostas was about to get out when Manos stopped him.

"You stay here. Niko, you come with me."

Manos and Nikos walked from the truck across to the helicopter. As they approached Nikos could see his godmother sitting in the back of the cockpit behind the pilot. There were two other seats and the door was open.

"Nikos." Marina Manidaki held out her arms. "Kiss your godmother."

Nikos leant into the helicopter and kissed his godmother on the cheek.

"Good. You are a bad boy, you know that? The trouble you have caused me. But apparently this man Marks is alive after all so we may have a happy ending. Get in. Manos, why is that idiot in the truck still here? Get rid of him."

Manos walked back to the truck as the pilot fired up the engine on the helicopter. "Kostas my friend." He shouted over the sound of the rotors. He leaned into the cab and put his right hand around Kostas' neck and pulled him to his chest in a hug. He whispered in Kostas' ear, "Mrs Manidaki would like to thank you for all your help."

Kostas didn't even feel the knife enter under his ribs until Manos twisted it, by which time his life was already slipping away. He would be found on Friday when the Symi under fifteen team turned up for their game against Kos.

A few moments later, the small black helicopter was rising up from the football pitch in Pedi bay watched by the driver of a small white Fiat Uno with the logo Glaros Car Hire on the doors. It had stopped halfway down the Pedi Road. Lucinda Frobisher pulled on the handbrake and picked up her mobile phone.

"I'm sorry to break up this little party," said Toby, slipping his phone into his pocket and approaching the table at the taverna in Tolis, "but needs must."

"I told you he wouldn't be able to resist," said McAllister, putting his hand under the table to his lap.

"There really is no reason to shoot anyone, Mr McAllister," said Toby. "And my man over there would make sure you never left alive anyway." McAllister looked over at Drakou who was still seated at the taverna door but raised his hand in greeting. Toby continued. "Believe it or not I would be very happy for you to get your hands on Midas and we fully intended for you to get it, after a little haggling. But..."

"We?" said McAllister, still holding the gun under the table. "What has MI6 got to do with this?"

"I am not MI6," said the Englishman, surprised at the question.

"But you were," said the Scot. "I never forget a face. The Marylebone job when that Russian doctor died after brushing shoulders with a businessman we never traced. Needle puncture to the neck, as I recall. My Chief Inspector was furious when you lot stepped in. I was very young at the time and so were you. We never met properly but you were there. You collected all the files and ended up shagging our Desk Sergeant Julie which pissed me off as it happens 'cause I was shagging her too."

"It would be very nice to take a trip down memory lane with you, Mr McAllister," said Toby, "but right now I have a more pressing concern. We are about to get a visit from royalty."

"Royalty?" Alan was surprised.

Toby smiled a wry smile. "The lady they call here in Greece 'The Queen of crime'."

"Mrs Manidaki?" asked McAllister.

"I am not even going to ask how you know that," said Toby.

As he spoke, they all became aware of a low throbbing sound, distant but getting louder, somewhere out beyond the headland. As they all looked seaward, a small black helicopter appeared, skimming low over the water. It rose gradually as it neared the beach and then rose above up to the level of the terrace and hovered there. The occupants, three men and a woman were staring at them as they stood looking at the helicopter through the swirling dust. McAllister tried to shout, but the force of the wind took his words away and no one heard him yell, "What the fuck are you doing?"

Then the helicopter rose and disappeared back out around the headland and was gone.

For a moment, they all stared out to sea as the cloud of dust settled around them.

Zoe broke the silence. "What the hell was that all about?"

"I don't know," said Toby. "But it wasn't good. I think we should all leave. You and Alan go with Kyriako in the boat and I'll call Lucinda."

"Just a minute," said McAllister, "there is the small matter of Midas." He raised his gun and his voice. "Now I don't know what the fuck you lot are all getting into here, but leave me out of it. Give me the box and I'll take the boat."

In the helicopter Marina Manidaki turned to Nikos. "Well?"

"Well," said Nikos, "his hair is shorter but the man in the middle, behind the table in the cream shirt, was him."

"Alan Marks?" she asked.

"Yes," confirmed Nikos.

"There's a good boy." She gave him a playful slap on the face. "At last your mother can be proud. As your godmother I think my work is now done." She stayed looking at Nikos as she spoke to Manos. "Manos, let's get on, shall we?"

Nikos Stavroulis died the instant he hit the rocks. He then slipped slowly into the sea. His body, or what was left of it after the fish had devoured most of the flesh, washed up and was jammed in a narrow rock crevice on the coast of Turkey, opposite the island of Symi some ten miles distant. It would not be found for some time, and was never identified.

Zoe looked at Toby, who nodded. She reached into her bag.

"Just a minute," said McAllister, pointing the gun at her.

"It's all right," said Toby. "She has the box in her bag. Anyway, you may be a lot of things, Gary McAllister, but I don't think even you would gun down a girl just for reaching into a bag." As he spoke, Zoe removed the Midas box.

"I think this is what you want, is it not?" She handed over the box and McAllister took it.

As he backed towards the steps still holding the gun, he saw, out of the corner of his eye, Drakou stand and begin to walk towards them. He shouted to him. "Stay there or I will shoot your friend here." He pointed the gun at Toby.

"He will," shouted Toby. Drakou stopped.

Suddenly they all became aware of a sound they had heard before. Keeping the gun on the others, McAllister glanced to his left and saw the helicopter approaching at speed. Then he saw the flash below the cockpit and instinctively yelled "Down!" at the others as he dived below the table. The gun mounted on the underside of the helicopter fired rapidly, drawing a trail of small pockets of dust along the jetty as Kyriakos dived out of his boat and into the water. Next the small craft rose and strafed the top of the canopy, splitting the raffia and smashing the glasses and bottles on the tables under which everyone had cowered. Some tables collapsed as the bullets ripped through the tops and into the legs. A group of chairs, at the far end near the steps took the full force of a salvo and splintered into pieces. Then the pilot turned his attention to the wall of the taverna, smashing the windows and shattering the small oil lamps that hung on the rough stone walls. As he reached the door, Drakou dived inside, grabbing Helleni and taking her with him as pots and pans above their heads clattered and banged with bullets ricocheting of them and into the taverna. Then the helicopter twisted around and began to land on the rough piece of barren land right next to the terrace. Red dust rose from the ground like a fog and enveloped the taverna and the tables and chairs. McAllister slowly crept out and, rubbing his eyes, grabbed the Midas box which had dropped at his feet. He stood and began to run towards the steps. He only managed a few paces when suddenly he tripped over a smashed chair and, flying forward, let go of both box and gun. He landed face-down in a pile of broken glass and splintered wood, looking directly at half a broken beer bottle a few inches from his eyes. The sound of the engine died and he could feel shards of glass piercing his clothing all the way up his body. He struggled to his knees and felt broken glass dig into his skin. "Fuck!" he shouted as he got to his feet, feeling blood trickling down his legs. He couldn't see his gun, but he saw the Midas box a little way in front of him, surrounded by bits of splintered wood and raffia. He was about to go towards it when a rather smart pair of blue deck shoes appeared through the dust cloud behind the box.

"Not a good idea, Scottish man." It was Manos. McAllister looked up and saw him.

They eyed each other almost like gun fighters in the old west. Manos smiled and suddenly pulled a gun from behind his back. "Bang!" McAllister jumped and Manos laughed. "Oh dear, I made the old man jump. I was told you were very good. Maybe you were, once." He suddenly swooped to scoop up the black box and immediately a boot crushed his wrist and there was a single blow to the back of the neck. To say he felt nothing would have been untrue, he certainly did, but in an instant, as the crumbling bone of his fifth vertebrae punctured his spinal cord, twenty five years of fun, hate, laughter, resentment, revenge, violence and charm was gone.

"Shouldn't have called me old," said McAllister, picking up the gun and the box. "Always a mistake." He stood, turned and felt a searing pain in his hand as a bullet hit the gun and sent it flying across the floor and down the steps. He dropped the Midas box as he grabbed his other hand and yelled with pain.

"I agree with you," said the rather cracked voice of an elderly and very smart Greek woman who was facing him, some distance away, and holding an automatic in one hand and a walking stick in the other. The dust was settling around this bizarre image in a long red evening dress. She had short white blonde hair and a bright gold necklace with matching earrings. Her face was over made-up and lined, but her eyes were sparkling. She spoke with a strong Greek accent. "That is the trouble with the young, they no longer respect age. We do, don't we Mr McAllister? Because we know with age comes wisdom. You see a younger woman would have killed you for what you just did to that sweet boy. I on the other hand have the wisdom that comes with age. The wisdom that tells me you are far more use to me alive." She beckoned him closer and lowered her voice almost to a whisper. "You see you can go back to England and tell your boss, silly old bastard, that he doesn't need to worry anymore because I have got Midas back. OK? Good. Do you know I was rather pleased with that shot. Still got an eye, haven't I? How is your hand?"

"Fucking painful," said McAllister clutching his hand and sitting on one of the few undamaged chairs.

She grinned. "Good." She stayed looking at McAllister but

raised her voice. "It is all right, the rest of you can come out, just do not come too close." She glanced over at the taverna and saw Drakou looking out. "Especially you Mr Drakou, or Tassos my pilot will shoot all of you, won't you Tassos?"

Tassos, who was stood by the helicopter holding another automatic, held up his hand, indicating that he would. Alan stood up slowly, dusting himself off, as did Toby and Zoe, who was clutching her bag.

"Ah, you must be the young lady who called me a bitch on the telephone?" said the old woman, looking at Zoe. "Do you know who I am?"

"I do," said Zoe, slinging her bag over her shoulder.

"You see, Mr McAllister," she turned back to the Scot. "The folly of youth. She knows I am Marina Manidaki and yet she calls me a bitch. Kids, they have no respect. Would any kid in the old days have called Capone, or the Krays bastards? No." She looked over at Zoe again. "Tassos, kill her."

Tassos raised his gun as Alan stepped in front of Zoe. "No!"

Mrs Manidaki raised her stick and Tassos lowered his gun. "Well, well it's Mr Marks, the stupid Englishman. If you had let my boys have Midas in Athens, none of this would have been necessary."

"Then kill me instead," Alan replied.

"Alan!" exclaimed Zoe in alarm.

"Oh dear, Mr Marks," said the old lady. "Fallen in love, have you? Are you really prepared to die for her?"

Alan stuttered and found he was shaking. "If I have to, y...yes."

The old lady laughed out loud. "No dear, you don't have to. Never let it be said Marina Manidaki stood in the way of true love, or at least a good screw. I am getting bored. Give me that box." She waved her gun at Alan and indicated the Midas box on the floor.

Zoe suddenly pushed in front of him. "It's all right Alan, I'll get it. After all, it's my fault you're here." Before he could reply, she was walking over to the Midas box.

"How touching," said Mrs Manidaki. "Take it over to the helicopter, dear, and give it to Tassos." She turned back to McAllister and Zoe bent down and picked up the box.

As Zoe went to stand, she tripped on her bag which was dangling in front of her. She scrabbled forward, raising a small cloud of dust and grabbed the box. She stood again holding the box, turning around and trying to rearrange her bag.

"Bloody thing," she said, taking the bag off and throwing it to Alan, who only just managed to catch it. She turned to Mrs Manidaki. "Sorry," she said, and walked over to Tassos.

Marina Manidaki looked at Alan. "Clumsy girl, I hope for your sake she is better in bed. Tasso, start the engine." Tassos jumped into the cockpit and started up the engine. The rotors began to turn as the old lady backed very slowly towards the helicopter. She shouted over the sound of the blades and the engine. "Oh, Mr Anstis?"

"Yes?" Toby shouted back, amazed to be suddenly addressed in this way. Through the cloud of dust that was rising, he faintly heard the old woman's voice.

"Say hello to your father for me. Ask him about the Isle of Wight festival, sixty nine."

The helicopter rose into the air and turned pointing out sea. It headed out over the jetty and then suddenly tilted to the left and began to go in a wide arc over the bay.

"What the hell are they doing?" said Toby.

McAllister looked up. "I think I know, quick, inside." He headed for the taverna as he saw the helicopter once more heading for them. Down on the jetty, Kyriakos, who had just got out of the water, dived back in.

"Shit!" shouted Alan, as they all ran for cover. The bullets rained down on the terrace and suddenly before he could reach the door of the tavern, Toby fell, yelling and clutching his arm. He dragged himself into the doorway using his other arm. There was the sound of more gunfire and then a loud bang as Drakou's motorbike exploded, showering pieces of metal onto the terrace. Then there was silence.

Zoe rushed over to Toby. "Are you all right?"

"Just nicked my arm, the bastard."

They waited for a moment. Eventually McAllister looked outside. "It's OK, they've gone."

Slowly everyone emerged. Kyriakos appeared at the top of the steps, dripping, and much to his surprise, everyone clapped. He took a bow. A few minutes later as they sat around in the wreckage that had been the canopied terrace, Helleni bathed Toby's arm and wrapped a bandage around it. Drakou appeared from inside with a tray of beers.

"Good man," said Toby as his mobile phone rang.

"Take that will you, Zoe?" he said.

Zoe picked it up and answered. "Toby's phone. Hi, Lucinda. No, it's Zoe. No, he's OK, just a slight scratch on his arm. We're patching him up now."

"Tell her to get the Chief of Police to get rid of Manos' body." Toby said. "Tell him he fell down the steps. Tell him I said so."

"Did you get that?" said Zoe into the phone. "Good. Yes, all went according to plan. Are they? Good, I'll tell him." She ended the call. "Lucinda says from what she could see on top of the hill, the helicopter is heading for Kos, so they should be over open sea now."

"Right," said Toby.

"Just a minute," said McAllister. "What's all this 'all went according to plan' crap? The fucking bad guys have ended up with Midas."

"Not yet they haven't," said Toby. "And true, it wasn't all according to plan, well not the original plan but it worked out bloody well, considering."

"Bollocks!" exclaimed the Scotsman, pointing at Zoe. "She gave them the box."

"No, she gave them 'a' box," said Toby.

"But not 'the' box," said Zoe, producing a small black identical Midas box from her bag.

"Bugger me," said McAllister. "So you had given me a fake."

"Er, no. You had the right one. This one," said Zoe holding up the box. "I just switched it when I picked it up off the floor."

"That's why you didn't want me to do it," said Alan. "And all that fumbling about."

"Sometimes for a stupid Englishman you are quite bright," she laughed as he poked her.

"Yes, thanks to Mr Drakou's son," said Toby, "we had more than one box."

Alan smiled at Drakou. "Why doesn't that surprise me?" Drakou gave him a knowing look.

"Yes, but hang on," said McAllister. "What happens when the Queen of crime finds out she's got a fake?"

"Good point," said Toby, grinning. "But she won't. Drakou, if you would be so kind?"

Drakou took a mobile phone from his pocket. "Of course." He tapped at the keyboard three times and put the phone back in his pocket.

"Good," said Toby. "That's that." Far off in the distance, there was a dull thud. "That's the trouble with these small helicopters, so unreliable. Give me a proper plane anytime."

"So just a minute," said McAllister, looking at the small black box. "That is the real Midas?"

"It is," said Zoe.

"And it's yours," said Toby.

Zoe handed the small black box to McAllister.

"Just like that? It's mine?" queried the Scotsman.

"On one condition," said Toby. "That you guarantee it goes to the right place."

McAllister smiled. "Oh yes that's definitely where it's going."

"I thought I could trust you," said Toby, looking at his watch.

“That’s a shame, it’s too late to get a ferry to Rhodes now. I suggest we all eat at that taverna up in the village. What is it Drakou?”

“Georgios,” said the big man.

“That’s it,” said Toby. “And it’s on the firm.”

“Well if we are going up to the village,” said McAllister, “I know a bar where they do a cracking single malt, so I’m told. This could be quite a night.”

CHAPTER EIGHTEEN

The following lunchtime, an unshaven and slightly dishevelled McAllister was settled in the soft red comfy chair outside the harbour bar, having paid yesterday's bill and retrieved the holdall he had left there. He had smiled as he looked at the contents including his palmtop computer which were all still there. He'd muttered to himself: "Wouldn't happen in King's Cross." His smile had gone as he had looked through the copy of yesterday's Daily Mail which was lying on the table. He looked up, dialled a number on his mobile and watched as the *Dodecanese Express* catamaran ferry backed in to the quayside in front of him. He took another gulp of the ice cold beer he'd ordered. "Hair of the proverbial canine." Then he listened to Sir Charles Bower's exaggerated Etonian tones on his voice mail. When the message was finished he sighed as he glanced again at page five of yesterday's Daily Mail. "A small headline." He thought. "Bank Worker Found Dead In Lift." How was he going to play this? He put the glass down, steeled himself and then dialled. The call was answered almost immediately and McAllister attempted to field the barrage of questions.

"Yes Sir Charles… I have been a bit tied up, sir. I mean, I'm on a Greek island and the signal….Yes of course I have it… Am I sure? Absolutely certain. It's sitting on the table in front of me... No, no it's in a bag sir, not on display." This was a lie and it made him smile. He was beginning to work out exactly how he was going to play this.

"Well it must be a relief sir, I'm sure the board will be very... they don't? Oh I see sir, I just assumed you would have…Right, well I'm sure you had good reason… Of course sir, the fewer people who knew…the Greeks? Yes, I had worked that bit out Sir Charles. I must admit it threw me at first." There was a short silence. McAllister waited, an old trick he had learned when questioning villains in the Met. Most people hate silence in a conversation and very often feel they have to fill it, particularly if they are in any way embarrassed about the subject matter. He didn't have to wait long.

"Why did it throw me? Well, I mean, they are organised crime sir and at first I wondered how they knew about certain things and then of course I realised that … Of course Sir Charles… I'm sure there are very good reasons… The global financial climate? I see, I think sir…Yes well if all the banks got into problems there wouldn't be another bail out, I can see that… No well I wouldn't, not being a finance wizard myself… A sort of insurance policy? Right yes. I get it… Am I right in thinking Midas wasn't meant to happen to our bank though?" He waited again, and wasn't disappointed with the response. "Unfortunate? Yes you're right sir, a stroke of bad luck... How did it come about? No I never really got to the bottom of that sir, just a mix up with software I think and that bloke Stavroulis' company cocking up an order… Marks? No, no worries, sir. Well put it this way he won't be bothering any of us again." As he said this he saw the sleek blue ketch on the other side of the harbour raise a small Greek flag and a Red Ensign. "Yes, well sometimes you just have to do what you have to do sir. Yes I'm getting the next ferry out." As Sir Charles waffled on about what a splendid job he had done and about giving him John Foley's job as head of security now he had retired and a bonus and maybe boosting his department if he wanted with more time off. McAllister couldn't help but smile. However, his smile was short lived as Sir Charles offered him a new P.A. …"Yes, I will sir… No, that's OK, if you want HR to select someone that's fine… Yes sir, very difficult to replace… Yes, these things do happen... A silver lining sir? I don't quite follow… Ah yes, Sophie knew about Midas. Did she? Even so I don't think she would have….no I don't… Too trusting?" He paused. "Maybe I am sir. Yes, maybe I am… I'm sure you're right sir…Yes, better safe than…Look sir I must go or I'll miss this ferry." This was a lie; the ferry was not due to go for another half an hour. "Yes, nine tomorrow, Gatwick, squeezy jet, only one I could get…Yes sir I look forward to it." He finished the call, took a deep breath and found himself consumed with rage. "Shit, shit, shit."

"Language Mr McAllister, language." It was Jean. She pulled the moped back onto its stand, dismounted and sat down next to him. "Off on the ferry then, having got rid of all my Balvenie last night? Is this goodbye, Mr Mac?"

McAllister was still seething and not ready for cheery banter. "What? Yes, yes. Sorry I've just had some really bad news."

"Oh I'm sorry." She signalled to the waiter who was chatting to three young English tourist girls at a table inside. "Bad news? Are we talking Glasgow Rangers lost or you got the sack? How bad are we talking?"

McAllister sighed.

By his reaction she could see the man was very upset. The waiter came to the table. "Get this man a large Scotch, not that Bells crap you give tourists, the single malt you boys keep at the back." The waiter nodded and went inside.

"Thank you," mumbled the Scot.

"I've been running a bar for twenty years, you get an instinct for this kind of stuff. So don't tell me if you don't want to. If you do I'm all ears and no gob."

"A very good friend of mine died just before I came here," he began.

"I'm sorry love." She seemed genuinely sympathetic.

"Yeah," he continued, "but I only just found out the reason."

As he spoke, the waiter put a very large glass of light gold liquid in front of McAlister. He drank it down in one and exhaled with a slight shudder. "Jesus that's bloody Islay, or Skye. Bring me another."

Jean gave a gentle smile. "Christ Mr Mac you can drink can't you? Must have been a very good friend."

As McAllister put the glass down and looked at her a notion began to stir. "Have you got a pen and paper?"

She chuckled. "I'm a woman with a handbag, I've got every bloody thing." She took her bag from the pannier on the front of the moped and opened it up. "What for?"

"I wonder if you could post this for me?" He held up the small card reader. "Will ten euros cover it?"

She handed him the pen and took a napkin from the next table. "No problem, put the address on that."

McAllister scribbled away. "That's the address. It's very important. You won't forget?"

She acted affronted. "Just because I am blonde Mr McAllister doesn't mean I'm thick. Like, just because you're Scots doesn't mean you're mean. Although I've been here for five minutes and you haven't bought me a drink."

As the waiter delivered the second Scotch, McAllister instructed him to bring the lady whatever she desired.

"Small beer," she requested. "So this is going to a police station?" She read the napkin.

"It certainly is. And here is the ten euros." He handed her a note. "Oh, one thing before you take this." He pulled out his bank card from his wallet and ran it through the card reader. "There, my insurance policy, Sir Charles fucking Bower." He could see she was getting worried about him. "I'm fine, a little the better for the Scotch thank you, but fine." He handed her the box and kissed his card.

"Hey, I hope you haven't buggered it up." She looked at the card.

"Buggered it up?" he laughed and swigged down the second scotch. "Oh I've buggered it up all right, but not the card."

"Whatever you say." Her beer arrived and McAllister ordered another Scotch.

"Be careful," she warned, "you'll get drunk very quickly in this heat."

"I sincerely hope so," he laughed.

She stood. "I'm off to the loo, keep my beer cold."

McAllister watched her go then picked up his phon, "Now then, to un-bugger what I have buggered." He dialled. "It's ringing. Bloody police, never there when you want them. Oh great I've got several options, press one if you're being raped, press two if you're being murdered, hang on three." He pressed a button. "Hello, Maida Vale nick? Pansy Probert please… Sorry, DS Roy Probert … Who is calling? Tell him it's Psychic Mac. Psychic, never mind... Gary McAllister... Thank you." There was a long pause. "Oh great bloody Greensleeves." The music played over and over. He was about to give up when suddenly it stopped. "Pansy? McAllister, Psychic… Yes. Listen, I'm in Greece…Yes bloody cushy job, now shut up and listen. I haven't got much time and I am about to make you an Inspector... You'll see. You will be getting a present in the post in about a week I would think. It's a card reader. Now when you get it, run a bank card through it then pop it in an ATM. After that call Sir Charles Bower at First Independent Bank and tell him you know all about Midas…Yes Midas. That's right…Yes well done, that is what my secretary was trying to write in the blood. You're getting quicker Pansy. Trust me son, this will be the biggest case you'll ever get. This is the stuff Superintendents are made of, so don't let the bastards take it off you. Look I will call and tell you more when I get to Rhodes or email if I can find a computer… When am I back? Good question. This week, next week, sometime, who knows? Give me your mobile number Pansy." He took another napkin from the table next to him. He wrote DS Probert's number on it and stuffed it in his pocket. "Got it. Got to go catch a boat now, talk in the next twenty four." Of course he never would.

"OK?" Alan called to Zoe.

"Yes, it's fine." She made sure the anchor was secured and then glanced to her left. "If we are quick we can be out of the way of that ferry."

Alan turned the wheel and pointed the boat out to sea. As they headed out a small power boat passed them slowly on its way into the harbour and Alan waved at the driver, "*Yassou Kyriakos*." Kyriakos waved back. "Plenty of wind out there, *kalo taxithi.*"

"*Kalo taxithi.*" Marks responded.

Zoe came back to the wheel house. "Very good Alan Marks, oh sorry Anthony Miller, getting quite fluent aren't we?" She slipped her arm into his. "What does it mean then?"

"Sorry?" queried Alan.

"*Kalo taxithi*. What does it mean?"

He smiled. "Not a bloody clue."

She laughed. "I thought not. It means have a good trip. *Kalo*; good, *taxithi*; travel."

"Very economic you Greeks, aren't you?" he observed. "We have four words, 'have a good trip,' you have two."

"True." she responded. "Like *s'agapo*."

"Oh, what's that mean?"

She kissed him on the cheek. "One word instead if three…I love you."

Suddenly, the ferry behind them gave one long blast on its hooter

"It's about to leave," Zoe looked behind them.

Alan glanced over his shoulder. "It's OK, we'll motor out until it passes, ride the wash, then, put up the sails when we get out past Pedi Bay."

"Aye aye captain." Zoe saluted and giggled and he smacked her bum.

Gary McAllister looked at the harbour from the top deck at the back of the ferry and waved at the blonde lady standing by her moped, who waved back as the boat pulled away from the dockside. "Bloody place." He felt a strange emotional turmoil, a new feeling for him. "Maybe it's the Scotch," he rationalised. "Maybe it isn't."

He watched the people on the dockside waving to friends on the boat. Some were smiling and some were crying and being comforted by others. Next to him, a slim, middle-aged woman with white blonde hair was staring back at the harbour with tears trickling down her face. McAllister took out a napkin from his pocket, saw Pansy Probert's number on it, paused for a moment then passed it to the woman. "Here."

She took the napkin, dabbed at her eyes and spoke in a strong Scandinavian accent. "Sank you, I always get like this when I am leaving Symi."

"Always?" McAllister responded. "You come here a lot?"

"For over twenty years now, and every time I go it is hurting, you know?"

McAllister looked back at the harbour and up at the tumble of houses spreading up the hillside to the church at the top. "It is certainly very beautiful."

The woman spoke, still gazing fixedly back at the harbour. "Oh ya, beautiful and annoying and irritating and frustrating and wonderful and crazy." She dabbed her eyes again.

"I think I would go along with most of that," said McAllister, "and I've only been here a few days. Tell me if you love it so much, why don't you stay here?"

"Ah, zere you have it." She smiled, her gaze still on the island. "Because I have a life in Stockholm, with a job and children who never leave home and an ex-husband who never leaves and this and that and oh dear. If only we could just do what we want to, you know? If only life vas that simple." She handed him back the napkin and turned to go inside the ferry.

He looked down at the smudged number on the napkin. "If only." He dropped the napkin over the side and watched as it was devoured in the wake of the ferry, which was now picking up speed and moving out beyond the clock tower. He looked up at the island again and as he did a young man turned a small power boat into the wash of the ferry and rode the waves bouncing up and down. He looked up and waved at McAllister, who found himself waving back. "Goodbye, Kyriakos."

As the boy turned the boat in towards the harbour, McAllister watched him and muttered. "If only life was that simple." He turned to look out to sea and saw the sleek blue ketch ahead to his right. He recognised the couple at the helm. He watched them for a moment and then slowly sat down on the seat below the guard rail. He carefully removed his shirt and put it down next to his wallet on the seat. He removed his shoes and set them neatly below the seat next to his holdall. He stood and began to remove his trousers. As he did, a woman shouted on the far left of the ferry: "*Delfini, delfini.*" All the people on the top deck moved over to the left-hand rail, pointing and gabbling in a myriad of languages, straining to see the gunmetal forms of three dolphins jumping through the water and diving over the wash of the ferry.

McAllister seized his moment, climbed over the guard rail, dropped the twenty feet into the sea and disappeared, with hardly a splash. A small boy on the lower deck was the only one to see him go. He waved and turned to his mother. "Man in water mama." He pointed. The woman looked. "No dear that's a boat, not a man, a boat. Boat in water." This would lead to great confusion with the child who insisted for several months afterwards on calling men boats and vice versa.

On the ketch, Alan, eased on the throttle, turned towards the wash of the ferry and rode the double wave. The boat settled down and, becalmed for a while. They watched as the ferry cleared the headland and headed for Rhodes. There was a gentle breeze beginning, coming out from the land with a vague aroma of herbs. High up in the town, a bell tolled and a donkey bellowed.

"Right, that's that," said Alan. "Now we can think about doing some proper sailing as soon as we get a bit further out." He was just about to pick up speed when the boat rocked from side to side. "What the hell?"

Alan and Zoe looked back over their shoulders and saw a wet bedraggled head appear at the top of the ladder on the stern.

"Scotsman coming aboard," coughed McAllister, as he heaved himself onto the back of the boat.

The two sat staring at him in amazement.

McAllister spat overboard. "Jesus that water is salty. Do you have any Scotch on board?"

"I don't know," replied Alan.

Zoe stood. "I'll have a look."

As she turned towards the cabin, McAllister spat overboard again, pulled a dripping bank card from his sodden underpants, held it up and grinned.

"Right then my friends. Where are we going?"